THE VISITORS

MIRANDA RIJKS

INKUBATOR
BOOKS

CONTENTS

PROLOGUE

'*Strip off.*'

What the hell! I eyeball them and try not to let the dismay show on my face.

'*We're talking to you! Take your bleeding clothes off.*'

I have never met two people quite so smug and butt-ugly, but what choice do I have? I remove my trousers and top and drop them onto the plastic chair.

'*Underwear off!*'

I turn away. One of them grabs my clothes and starts rifling through them, checking empty pockets, feeling around elastic waist-bands. What the hell do they think they're going to find?

'*Let's have a good look at you. Turn around. Arms up. Now squat.*'

'*What?*' *I stare at them, eyes narrowed. One of them produces a mirror. The other grins at me, exposing a mouth full of chipped teeth that protrude at jagged angles.*

'*We need to check if you've stowed anything away. Up inside you. Just get on with it.*'

'*No. That's the ultimate humiliation.*'

'*You might have thought of that before you got done for murder.*

Now do as I say, or you'll regret it big time. Oh, and one little warning. No fancy words in here. No I'm-so-clever questions. Keep your head down and your mouth zipped; otherwise you won't last five minutes. You're a nobody now. A number. A murderer.'

I want to yell that I haven't even been tried yet. That in England you're assumed innocent until proven guilty. But instead the word murderer reverberates inside my head. I shut my eyes and grit my teeth. Then I squat and try to ignore the hot breath on the back of my neck, the sound of gum being chewed in my ears, the horror show that has become my life.

'Stand up and put your underwear back on.'

My clothes feel sullied now that they've been handled and examined.

'Sit on the BOSS.'

'The what?' I hear the tremor in my voice, and I hate myself for it.

'The chair over there. Body Orifice Security Scanner. To check you ain't got any illegals stuffed up inside.'

I thought that was what the mirror was for. Or perhaps it was just so they can get their cheap kicks. I suppress a shiver as I shuffle to the chair. I sit down, trying not to think about the people who have sat on this before me, their filthy skin leaving repulsive residue behind.

They talk between themselves, discussing the mundanities of their lives, as if I'm not here. And I shouldn't be here. How the hell is it even possible?

I'm back waiting again, handcuffs around my wrists that chafe and clink whenever I move my hands. I study my fingers, checking for any remnants of blood. Is that a speck under the nail of the middle finger on my left hand? I mustn't think of it. All that blood. The fear. The loss of control. The madness. The black hole in my brain. I peer closer at my hands, but now all I see is blood. Red, viscous blood that seeped through everywhere and stained me.

'What you in for? Murder?'

I've tried not to look at my fellow prisoners in the holding cell. One of them is shaking uncontrollably, a face eaten away by drugs, gaunt and rotting from the inside. It's the other one who is talking to me, black eyes latched onto my face, an expression of superiority that suggests I'm in charge around here.

'Oi. I'm talking to yeh.'

I nod and stare at the ground.

I want to stamp and shout and tell them they've got it all wrong. They don't understand. That I don't belong here, and I never will. That it's a travesty and I'll be off home soon. Terror is gnawing at my empty stomach, destroying any rational thoughts. I am a good person. I would never knowingly take a person's life. Surely, I wouldn't.

1

TWO WEEKS EARLIER

I stand at the front door, squeeze my eyes shut, and then open them again. What would I think if I were arriving here for the first time? Hopefully, I would be impressed and pleased that the property is larger and more welcoming than the online pictures suggest. But then again, how do we know what filters other people view things through?

The barn is long and thin, a single storey constructed from the original materials – bricks, stones and slates. Daniel was adamant about that. If we were going to do it, the renovation needed to be as authentic as possible. No factory-made roof tiles for us. The original slates were carefully removed and replaced, and any that were broken had to be sourced from local reclamation yards. You would have thought that the building was listed, so careful we were to find workmen that could do traditional lime mortar grouting and post and pegs for the reconfigured timber frame. Whilst the renovation of the fabric of the barn was largely Daniel's domain, the interior was, and is, all mine.

I walk with bare feet from the entrance lobby into the open-plan kitchen, gliding silently across the wood laminate floor. It's a country-style kitchen with handmade tiles and easy-to-wipe-down surfaces. Designed specifically to be a holiday cottage, I have made sure that everything is stylish and hard-wearing. I breathe in the scent of the bouquet of pink lilies in the clear glass vase and notice a pollen-coated stamen that I haven't snipped off. I find the kitchen scissors and carefully cut the end, catching it in a sheet of paper towel. I don't want any stains on the new eggshell blue cotton tablecloth. Turning around, I double-check the things on the wooden kitchen trolley behind me. An apple has slipped to one side of the white china fruit bowl, so I adjust the bananas, apples, lemon and oranges piled up high. Inside a wicker basket is a bottle of white wine, a carton of eggs and a loaf of freshly baked bread. Next to it is a retro-styled tin with a homemade Victoria sponge inside. I hope it tastes as good as it looks. Baking doesn't come naturally to me, so the kids have been treated to many cakes over the past couple of months, helping me perfect my skills.

Padding through to the living room, I run my finger over the dresser to double-check there is no dust. Of course, there isn't. Nevertheless, I plump up the cushions on the brown leather sofa for the third time. I poke my head around the doors of the two bedrooms. The linen is all freshly ironed and wrinkle-free, the pillows smelling of lavender. I have put another vase of freshly picked sweet peas in the master bedroom. Towels hang on the heated towel rails in the en-suite and the separate shower room and new, especially commissioned soaps printed with the barn's name, Best View Barn, lie on the sink, next to the bath and the walk-in shower. I allow myself a little smile. The place smells fresh and new, not of paint, but of delicately scented flowers and furniture polish and a hint of that wonderful aroma you get when you stand outside after a torrential downpour. It's as ready as it's ever going to be.

'Mummy! Mummy! Joel hit me!'

I sigh and hurry to the door. Rosa is standing outside, her

hands on her hips, her dark brows knitted together. She's wearing a pair of dungarees without a T-shirt underneath. No pretty summer dresses for my eight-year-old daughter. I don't see any evidence of her brother hitting her, and there are no tears. I suspect it's a ruse for having a sneak inside the barn.

'Can I come in if I take my sandals off?'

'No, Rosa. You've already been inside, and everything is perfect. Let's go and get a drink and see what your brother is up to.'

Rosa trots next to me as we cross the drive and climb up the wide stone steps towards our house. Joel is playing with Peanut, or rather tormenting our long-suffering black Labrador, and I don't see any evidence of a fight between him and his sister.

'I hope they're going to be nicer than the last lot,' Rosa says.

'They weren't so bad.' I think of the older couple, the wife with straight, lanky grey hair and thin lips that curled downwards and the husband who never spoke. They were perfectly civil; kept themselves to themselves. The place was clean and tidy when they left, the beds stripped. I sent them an email thanking them for staying at Best View Barn, along with a link for them to leave a review on TripAdvisor. I'm still waiting. Let's hope that this next set of guests deem my newly opened holiday cottage worthy of a five-star review.

It's taken seven years to complete the renovation of the barn, seven years of having builders popping in and out to fit in with their schedule rather than mine. During that time, Joel was born, Daniel was promoted to consultant cardiothoracic surgeon and began working away more and more, his father died, and my parents moved to live nearer to us. Daniel assumed I would quit work, get a horse, and throw myself into country pursuits, join the Women's Institute or do whatever the other stay-at-home mums get up to. But I'm not like Alison,

Daniel's first wife. I've never sat on a horse and have no intention of ever doing so. The moment I laid eyes on the disintegrating barn, I realised here was my opportunity to fulfil a lifelong, nostalgic dream. Even more controversially, I had no intention of quitting work. But things change. I have changed.

Our home is a traditional stone cottage that has been extended over the years, with a large open-plan kitchen at one end and a living room with a master bedroom suite above at the other end. The barn sits to the right of our house, slightly lower on the hill, so that it doesn't impede our views. A driveway separates the two properties that share an extensive garden that curves around our house and the barn. The field adjacent to the barn, which is currently overgrown with grass and weeds, belongs to us, but all the other fields that surround the property are owned and farmed by the Mole family.

From the house's elevated position, I can see the front door to the barn and the first window, but it's not possible to look inside. Similar to the quaint cottage that my parents rented every summer, nestled at the foot of the South Downs, this isn't the sort of place you just stumble across. It's remote, up and down a narrow, potholed drive nearly one kilometre off the main road. The first time I drove along the track, my heart was in my throat; I didn't dare glance to the right in case my car tyres accidentally slipped over the sheer drop. But back then, I would have trekked across the world to be in my new lover's arms. The access is worth the trek just for the views, which are breathtaking, sweeping across seven counties, one hundred and eighty degrees of green fields dotted with woodlands and miniature towns that light up like constellations at night.

Daniel was already living in the house when we met. Alone. Alison moved out shortly after they bought it, and according to Daniel, their short marriage was over within three years. The bones of the main house were there, but the interiors are all mine. During a particularly vicious storm, when winds howled across the Atlantic, then across the Cheshire plain, slamming into our house on the first hillside of the Peak District, the central portion of the decrepit barn collapsed. The structural engineer told us we had to board the place up or renovate it. Fortunately, Daniel agreed to take the latter course of action.

Although I always saw the potential of turning the renovated barn into a holiday let, it has taken me seven years to persuade Daniel to turn my dreams into a reality. The drip, drip approach failed dismally. My husband doesn't take any notice of subtleties. His world is black and white: living or dying. But last year, our elderly neighbours, the Burts, were burgled. I got scared and begged Daniel to let us move to somewhere less isolated, somewhere nearer to his work. The answer was point-blank no. This is his home and he loves it; it represents his success. I suggested he let me have paying guests in the barn. Perhaps if I had neighbours, my subconscious would allow me to fully relax. I barely sleep when Daniel is away, and as he is in London or Manchester at least two nights a week, it's not doing me any good. To my delight, Daniel agreed, and now I have a holiday cottage.

'MUMMY! THEY'RE HERE!' Rosa is bouncing up and down.

We must be living too much of an isolated life if she's this excited about strangers coming to stay. The Joneses only booked a week ago, and they did it directly, using the form on my new website to request information. That suits me, as I don't have to pay any commission to a third-party booking site. I sent them the booking form, and they emailed it back, sending me payment for a week in advance and listing their names and address: Nadia, Mike and Kayleigh Jones from Sussex.

I stand back from the window. I don't want them to know that I'm on tenterhooks for their arrival, that they're only my second set of paying guests. An old-style Mercedes, the sort of saloon car that was popular in the 1990s, comes hurtling down the hill, clouds of dust billowing up from behind the car. The silver car comes to an abrupt halt in front of the barn, little pebbles spraying upwards and jingling against the rusted wheel hubs. The doors have dents in them, and the car is so mud-splattered, it's difficult to read the number plate.

'Can I go and say hello?' Rosa asks as Peanut jumps up and starts to bark. The shiny black hair on the back of the dog's neck and spine lift upwards.

'Let me go and welcome them first, please. You can hold onto Peanut.'

'Why?' Rosa has mastered the eye roll to perfection.

'In case they don't like dogs.'

'But everyone loves Peanut,' she says, throwing her arms around the black Labrador's neck, who stops barking and licks the cheeks of his favourite member of the family. I hurry down the stone steps to welcome my new guests. Mike Jones gets out of the car first, stretching his arms above his head and yawning, his yellow T-shirt lifting up to expose a gigantic hairy belly that hangs over the waistband of his beige shorts. Matched with green Crocs, it's not a stylish look. Peanut is barking wildly now, and as I turn back to look at the house, I see Rosa standing at the top of the steps, holding Peanut's pillar-box-red collar, but doing little else to keep him quiet.

'Rosa, take him inside, please!' I throw an embarrassed glance towards Mike Jones. 'Sorry. He's all bark and no bite. Welcome to Best View Barn.'

'Ta. Not a problem. We like dogs.'

I'm relieved.

The front passenger door opens, and a woman gets out. I assume she's my age, mid- to late thirties. She has blonde hair cut into a sharp bob and bright blue eyes enhanced by enormous fake eyelashes. Her face is heavily made up, cheekbones accentuated with a glittering bronzer, lips outlined in reddish brown a couple of shades darker than her lipstick. I wonder why she needs to wear so much makeup; she is attractive, with symmetrical features, but looks as if she's just had a free makeover at the beauty counter of a department store. She is wearing a black maxi-dress that swamps her small frame. Numerous gold bangles jingle around her slender wrists and up her forearms as she holds out her hand. The rings she wears on every finger dig painfully into mine as we shake hands.

'Hi. I'm Nadia, this is Mike, and in the back is Kayleigh.' She opens the rear passenger door and leans in. 'Wake up, babe. We're here.'

She stands up again and turns to me. 'The kid is grouchy today. I thought the sulky adolescent years were meant to start when they become teenagers, but our Kayleigh has begun young.'

'How old is your daughter?' I ask, trying to peer in through the car's blackened windows.

'Just turned nine.'

'She's a similar age to Rosa, who is eight.'

'Well, that's lovely. They'll be able to play together.'

Kayleigh emerges from the car, her long blonde hair messed up. She yawns without putting her hand in front of her mouth and blinks rapidly as her green eyes adjust to the sunlight. Unfortunately for Kayleigh, she appears to have inherited all of her father's features and none of her mother's.

'Say hello, Kayleigh,' Nadia instructs.

Kayleigh grunts. 'What is this place?'

Both her parents ignore her. Nadia leans back into the car and removes a boho fabric handbag embroidered with tiny circular mirror beads. Mike turns to me, an expectant look on his jowly face. His mid-brown hair is cut into a buzz cut, as if he has just left the army. 'Going to show us around, then?'

'With pleasure,' I say, jumping into my well-rehearsed script. 'Can I help with any luggage?'

'With puny arms like yours!' Mike laughs. He has a canine tooth made from gold that catches the light, and the rest of his teeth are yellowing. Either he's a heavy smoker or has never visited a dentist.

'Ignore him,' Nadia says. 'Let's have a look inside, and then we can come back for the bags.'

I step in front of the car and open the door to the barn. I take off my shoes on the doorstep, but the Jones family don't follow suit.

'This is the kitchen,' I say, standing to one side to let them through.

'Look, Mum, there's a cake!' Kayleigh points to my Victoria sponge.

'That's nice. Is it gluten-free?' Nadia asks.

'Um, no, sorry. I didn't know you were gluten intolerant.' I make a mental note to add food intolerances to my booking form, not that I offer food as a service. The welcome hamper and cake was just an idea to make my guests feel like they're getting great value for money. At £900 per week in high season, this is one of the most expensive holiday cottages in the area.

'It's our Kayleigh who is gluten intolerant. Gets the stinkiest of wind if she eats wheat, don't you, love? Sorry, Kales, you can't have any.'

The child pouts and slinks off into the living room. We follow her.

'The television controls are on the coffee table, and the Wi-Fi password is in the folder.' I point to my welcome folder, each page of information carefully laminated and labelled. I have detailed everything there is to know about the barn and the surrounding area. Mike sinks into the brown leather armchair and takes out a packet of Benson and Hedges from the pocket of his shorts. As he sticks a cigarette into his mouth, I try to control my grimace. I need to say something, but it won't be conducive to good relations with my newly arrived guests. Fortunately, Nadia beats me to it.

'It's a no-smoking place, Mike. I told you.'

'Sorry,' I say half-heartedly.

'I wish he'd bloody give up. Go outside if you want a smoke.' She gestures towards the patio doors that open up onto the wide terrace with some of the most stunning, expansive views in England. Mike hauls himself up with a grunt. His Crocs squeak on the mock-wood lino floor as he shuffles towards the doors.

'There's an Xbox, Mum!' Kayleigh says, leaning down in front of the large-screen television.

'Yeah, well, you won't be inside playing on that. You'll be getting fresh air this week.'

Kayleigh pouts.

I show Nadia the two bedrooms and bathrooms.

'You've done this up nicely. What are you, an interior designer?'

'No.' I laugh. 'I'm a music teacher. I teach the piano.'

'Yeah, you look like one!' Mike makes me jump. I hadn't realised he had followed us. He's removed his Crocs and is bare-footed, the unlit cigarette dangling between his lips. He snakes a chunky, hairy arm around Nadia's waist. 'That's a nice big sturdy bed, isn't it, Nads? It'll be getting plenty of action this week.'

I turn away so they can't see the reddening of my cheeks, as I cringe inside. I gesture towards the large arched window that faces the bed. 'You've got a great view of Manchester in the distance on a clear night.'

'It's beautiful here,' Nadia says as she gazes out of the window over the fields and towards the first hills of the Lake District in the very far distance.

'Any problems or questions, please don't hesitate to come

and find me. The kids and I are here most of the time. And I hope you have a lovely week.'

'Thanks, we will,' Nadia says. We walk together back along the corridor, through the open-plan living room and into the kitchen. The floor vibrates slightly as Mike lopes behind us.

'Are you sure I can't help you unload?' I ask as I hover by the front door.

'Quite sure,' Nadia says. I smile at her and try to avoid looking at Mike. I can sense his small black eyes roaming up and down my body, and it makes me feel uncomfortable. I know I shouldn't judge, but I wonder why someone as pretty as Nadia is with a man as loutish as him. But then again, Daniel and I are a strange match.

As I walk back along the gravel road and up the steep stone steps to our house, I think of Mike's words and wonder what the hell a music teacher is meant to look like.

Rosa and Joel are in the kitchen. Rosa looks up expectantly.

'I've got good news for you. Their daughter, Kayleigh, is nine years old.'

Rosa claps her hands. 'Can I go and say hello?'

My daughter's self-confidence and extroversion often takes me by surprise. She is so very different to how I was at her age.

'Maybe tomorrow morning. Let them unpack and settle in this evening. Anyway, we need to get ready for Daddy. He'll be home soon.'

I look out of the kitchen window, where I have a good view of our guests unloading the car. Rosa stands on a chair next to me. I hope they don't glance up and see us.

'How long are they staying?' she asks.

'A week.'

'So why have they got so much luggage?'

'I don't know.' I am thinking exactly the same thing.

. . .

AN HOUR AND A HALF LATER, Joel and Rosa have had a bath, and Joel is tucked up in bed, pretending to read a book. Coq au vin, Daniel's favourite dish, is in the oven. I'm planning a cheese soufflé as a starter, which hopefully will rise. I'll pop it in the oven when I hear Daniel's Range Rover pull up behind the house. Dessert is a pavlova, but no longer a perfect round. I gave in and cut Rosa and Joel each a slice for their tea; hopefully, Daniel won't mind.

Sometimes when I'm wiping down the kitchen and clearing away the dishes, I wonder what has happened to me. I had no domestic ambitions, largely kept out of the kitchen when I was growing up, because Mum is an excellent cook and didn't want her children from getting under her feet. All of my boyfriends had been good cooks, so it was a shock when I moved in with Daniel. He expected a meal on the table when he got home from work. At first, I bought ready-made meals from Marks and Spencer's and decanted them into our own dishes. But Daniel is a neat freak, and he found the packaging in the outside bins. Sometimes I wonder if he takes an inventory before putting out the rubbish. He laughed and hugged me tightly, telling me I never needed to pretend to be something or someone I wasn't. Two weeks later, it was the Easter holidays, and exhausted from teaching a long spring term, rather than taking me off to relax on a beach, Daniel enrolled me on an intensive cordon bleu cookery course in Central London. At first I was affronted, angry even, but when he gazed at me with those soulful, dark eyes and begged me to do it for him, I agreed. I was so in love with my older, debonair husband. These days, I look back and chastise myself for being such a pushover. I would never have described myself as a weak person, but back then Daniel was my superhero and my soulmate, and I would have done pretty much anything he requested of me.

Fast-forward ten years, and my life – our lives – are fundamentally different, and here I am, just like my mother was thirty years ago, undoing my apron and waiting for the return of my husband after a few nights away.

During the week, when he is home, Daniel and I always eat supper at 7.30 p.m. on the dot. He explained to me that he likes routine when he is at home because heart surgery is never routine; work requires him to be constantly hyper-alert. He needs the contrast between work and play. I'm the opposite. I would prefer spontaneity at home. My job as a teacher was all about routine, and I like my home life to be relaxed. I say was, because I am no longer working in a school. These days, I simply teach piano to a handful of students. Five pupils, to be precise. On the nights that Daniel is away, I often eat earlier with the children; other times I lounge on the sofa, watching television, trying not to drop crumbs on the pristine woollen beige living room carpet.

But now it's 7.35 p.m. and Daniel isn't home. I turn the oven down to stop the coq au vin drying out, and then Rosa pads into the kitchen wearing short pyjamas.

'Where's Daddy? I'm not going to sleep until he's said goodnight to me.'

'I'm sure he won't be long. Hop back to bed, and I'll send him up to read you a quick story.'

But Daniel doesn't appear. At 7.45 p.m. I call his mobile. It goes straight to voicemail. That's not surprising, as the hills here in the Peak District have notoriously poor mobile reception, but I leave a message just in case.

Three minutes later, the phone rings.

He sounds breathless. 'Sorry, darling. I've had the day from hell. Only just out of surgery. I'm still in London and aim to take the last train north. I won't be home until 1 a.m. I hope you didn't make me anything special.'

'It's fine,' I say. But it isn't fine. He knows I make a special meal to celebrate his return home after several nights away. I hope I successfully suppressed the annoyance in my voice. I appreciate when he's in a long surgery, he can't pop out to send me a text, but he might have asked a nurse or his secretary, Coleen, to let me know.

'Don't worry about food. I'll grab something here. What are the plans for the weekend? I'm playing golf with Gary tomorrow afternoon.' I try to answer his question, but he speaks over me. 'Anyway. Don't wait up. I'll be quiet when I get home. Kiss the kids for me.'

'Rosa's still up, if you'd like to say goodnight.' But my words fade into silence. Daniel has hung up.

2

I was in that bone-heavy stage between wakefulness and sleep when Daniel came to bed last night. I could sense his eyes on me, his breath hot on my neck as he tried to gauge whether I was awake, but I didn't turn over. I kept my breathing steady and my eyes closed.

This morning, despite having insufficient sleep, I'm up early, tiptoeing to the bathroom to make sure I don't wake him. Our pale silver bedroom curtains have blackout lining, but the light still seeps around the edges, and the birds start the dawn chorus early, followed not long after by the incessant baaing of sheep. I'm up by 6 a.m. most mornings in the summer. Our property lies in the heart of a farm owned by the Mole family, who live five miles away, true locals who have worked these lands for generations. Having been brought up in suburbia, on the outskirts of London, this rural location, with our nearest neighbours a kilometre away, is still alien to me. I have got used to the sheep, but my heart pounds when I hear the screeches of rabbits being caught by foxes, or I find a dead rodent in the house. Daniel says I'll always be a townie.

I can never linger because Peanut hears my footsteps and

starts moaning for his breakfast. So I hurry downstairs, feed him and let him out. It's another unseasonably warm and clear day, so I decide to give him a quick walk before the children get up.

The curtains are pulled across the bedroom windows in the barn, unsurprisingly for 6.30 a.m. on a Saturday morning, but by the time Peanut and I return twenty minutes later, Mike appears in front of me, seemingly out of nowhere. I jump and let out a little yelp.

'Sorry,' I say. 'I wasn't expecting to see anyone.'

He stares at me with those beady eyes. He's wearing the same shorts as yesterday but is bare on top, his massive belly on full display.

'Have you got any pills for a stomach upset?'

'Oh no! Are you ill?'

'Not me. Nadia's been up most of the night, coming out of both ends.'

'Poor thing. Has she got a bug?'

'No. She hasn't got a fever. Must have been something she ate. It's weird because we all ate the same yesterday. The only thing Nadia had that me and Kayleigh didn't was your cake. Shame, because she said it tasted good.'

I frown momentarily and then remember that these are my guests, so I tilt my head to one side with an expression of dismay. 'I'm so sorry, that's terrible. Let me go and see what pills we've got. Do you need a doctor? My husband, Daniel, is a cardiothoracic surgeon, and I'm sure he could help. He should be up soon.'

'Nah, don't bother him. Just give us something for the trots.'

I hurry back to the house. To blame my cake sounds like utter nonsense, and it irks me. Is it even possible to get sick from a home-baked cake? If the eggs had been off, I would have smelled them. In the kitchen, I fling open the fridge and take out the carton of twelve eggs, now holding just eight. The use-by date is a fortnight away, so they were not the culprit. I may not be the best cook, despite my cordon bleu crash-course tuition, but I've never made anyone ill through my food. It can't have been my cake. I groan. I need to suppress my annoyance. What's most important are my guests' online reviews. If the Jones family report that I poisoned them, that would be catastrophic for my fledgling business.

'Morning!' Daniel strides into the kitchen, wearing chinos and a polo shirt. He gives me a quick peck on the cheek. I am relieved that he appears to be in a good mood this morning.

'How was your journey home?' I ask.

'Uneventful. The train was on time for a change. What are the plans for today?'

'Would it be possible for you to take the kids for their riding lesson this morning? I'm teaching.' I hold my breath, awaiting his response.

'Really, Hannah? We discussed this only a couple of weeks ago! No teaching at the weekends. Our children must come first.'

I grit my teeth. 'I'm sorry, Daniel, but I don't have any choice. She's the girl who has been accepted into the specialist music school starting in September. Both her parents work, so Susie's mum can only bring her at the weekend. I'll only be giving her another couple of lessons.' I try to keep my voice level and soft, as Daniel responds so much better to quiet logic. He asked me to reduce the number of pupils I teach, but it's not as if I can do that overnight. Besides, he's so rarely at home, it's not like he's keeping track of how many lessons I'm giving.

He doesn't say anything as he takes an espresso cup out of the cupboard and then starts up the top-of-the-range coffee machine. I carry on putting the breakfast things on the table. He carries his white espresso cup to the table and sits down. I can feel his eyes on me as I take a carton of milk out of the fridge.

'What are you looking so uptight about?' he asks. 'I don't want to get into another discussion about your piano teaching.'

'It's not that. The barn guests think the cake I baked made them ill.'

He snorts. 'Unlikely.'

'But whether it's true or false, if they mention it in their reviews, it'll be disastrous.'

'Hardly a disaster, is it? Not worth worrying about.'

'Daddy!' Joel screeches as he races into the kitchen, throwing his arms around Daniel's legs. Daniel picks him up and swings him around the room. I smile. I'll process Daniel's barbed comments later. I love seeing my boys together.

AFTER RAIDING MY MEDICINE CUPBOARD, I take some paracetamol, Imodium and Buscopan around to the barn. I knock, but there's no answer. I hesitate before knocking again, a bit louder this time. And then the door is flung open.

'Can I meet your daughter?' Kayleigh asks. She's wearing a pink short-sleeved T-shirt with the word *princess* emblazoned in sequins on the front and grey leggings. Her toenails are painted a fluorescent pink, and they poke out the top of her silver sandals.

'Yes, of course. She'll be happy to have someone of her own age to play with. Please can you give these to your mum or dad?' I hand her the packets of pills, but she just chucks them onto the floor of the kitchen behind her.

'I'll come with you now,' she says, wrapping skinny arms around herself.

'Can you actually give the medicine to your mum?' I ask, pointing to the boxes on the floor.

'She's in the bathroom.'

'Perhaps you could pick them up and put them on the countertop?'

'No. It's good.' Kayleigh steps out of the barn door and shuts it behind her. I consider reprimanding her but dismiss it; she's not my child. Instead, I turn around and walk back to our house, the young girl trotting behind me, humming tonelessly.

Rosa is sitting at the large table, eating her cereal, when we walk through the kitchen's patio doors. She's still in her pyjamas, and her hair is mussed up. Kayleigh hovers in the doorway. Perhaps she's not as confident as I assumed.

Rosa lets her spoon clatter into her bowl and waves Kayleigh over.

'Would you like some Coco Pops?' she asks. Coco Pops are only allowed on a Saturday morning, so Rosa has piled her bowl up high. Kayleigh nods and settles on the chair next to her. Within a couple of minutes, the girls are giggling and whispering to each other. I leave them to it.

I TRY to avoid giving piano lessons when Daniel is at home because the sound annoys him. Our old farmhouse has thick stone walls, but even so, it's impossible to block out all noise. I have a beautiful Bluthner grand piano with a shining black lacquer exterior and three circular turned legs. With its warm tone and easy action, it is my pride and joy, given to me by Daniel on our wedding day. We turned the dining room into my music room, and although the space is much too small for my piano and the ceiling too low for good acoustics, my breath catches every time I open the door. It had been beyond my wildest dreams to own a grand piano, and to have a room just for making music is every musician's nirvana. Whenever I'm feeling low, I sit down on the leather stool and play Bach. Or if I'm feeling particularly miserable, I let tears flow during Chopin's Ballade No 1, my all-time favourite piano solo, which I play rather badly. I'm in front of the piano quite a lot these days. In the early years of our marriage, Daniel was concerned that my young piano pupils might fail to treat the expensive instrument with respect. He was wrong. Even beginners realise that my piano is special.

Eleven-year-old Susie is no beginner. She is a joy to teach, and her lessons are a highlight of my week. I'll be sad when she leaves me in September, but happy for her that she's got such a bright future ahead, studying at one of the country's most prestigious music schools. Daniel left an hour ago with the kids, driving them to their riding lesson, and now Susie and I are engrossed in analysing and breaking down a couple of complicated bars in Chopin's Nocturne in G minor. There's a loud rap on the window. I jump.

It's Nadia.

'Carry on practicing,' I tell Susie as I stand up from my stool and take a couple of steps to the window. I undo the latch and open the window wide.

'Sorry to disturb, but wondering if you've got some caster sugar I can have. I forgot to bring some.'

'Um, yes. But I'm just in the middle of teaching a lesson. Can I bring it over in half an hour?'

'Sure.'

'Are you feeling better?' I ask.

'Yes, thanks.'

I close the window.

'Carry on playing, Susie,' I say, but I remain standing there, watching Nadia as she saunters back to the barn, her shapeless grey linen dress billowing as she walks, skimming her slim ankles and wrists. She has a strange-looking black tattoo on the back of her left ankle, shaped like a crescent moon, or perhaps it's a curved clawlike knife. For someone who was supposedly ill last night, she looks the picture of health. Perhaps that is courtesy of the application of heavy makeup and the quick effects of the medicine. Or maybe Mike was exaggerating her symptoms. When Nadia disappears inside the barn, I turn my attention to Susie and once again get lost in the lesson.

Forty minutes later, I have waved goodbye to Susie and her mother, and I find a three-quarters full bag of caster sugar in my walk-in pantry. I take it over to the barn. Loud pop music is thumping through the walls. I knock on the door, but there is no answer; unsurprising, as no one will be able to hear over the heavy beat. I don't want to leave the sugar on the doorstep in case Peanut takes a fancy to it, so cautiously, I open the door and poke my head around.

'Hello!' I shout. There is no answer. I walk into the kitchen, and my heart sinks when I see the mess. It looks like they have emptied the contents of my cupboards and dirtied every dish, leaving them on the work surface and piled high in the sink. I turn to look at the living room, and here it is as if they have upended the full contents of their wardrobes and scattered everything across the living room. Mike is lounging on the sofa, his bare feet, with filthy, calloused soles, leaning on the coffee table, his face turned away from me. The television is turned up so loud it hurts my ears. Kayleigh is sitting in the middle of the chaos, playing games on an iPad. She jumps up when she sees me.

'I've brought some sugar for your mum.'

Mike doesn't acknowledge me, and I wonder if he even knows I'm standing just a metre away from him.

And then Nadia floats into the living room from the hall at the far end. She grabs the remote control off the sofa and presses the mute button.

'Oi! Why did you do that?' Mike snaps. He glowers at her.

'Sorry to disturb you,' I say as I hand her the sugar. 'I hope you're fully recovered.'

'Yeah. Thanks.'

'Where are your kids?' she asks.

I try not to show my surprise by the question. 'My husband took them for a riding lesson.'

She nods. 'Our Kayleigh was hoping she could play with Rosa again this afternoon, weren't you, love?' She puts a hand on her daughter's shoulder. Her fingernails are painted black with a little glistening diamante crystal embedded into the centre of each nail.

'Of course she can. Why don't you come over after lunch, Kayleigh? About 2 p.m.'

'I'm off for a game of golf with Gary,' Daniel announces as we're clearing up the lunch things. Gary Abelman has been Daniel's best friend since medical school. A couple of years ago, I might have tried to persuade Daniel to stay at home and spend more time with us, his family. But something has shifted inside me. I'm almost relieved that he will be out for a few hours, as it means I won't need to tread on eggshells. The most important thing for me is that Daniel spends time with the children, and at least he took them for their riding lesson this morning and will be home in time for their tea and bedtime.

A few weeks ago, Amber asked me if I still loved Daniel. I said yes, of course, but it got me thinking. I am grateful to Daniel. Grateful that the kids and I live in this house, with no money worries. Grateful that he is a good father, when he's around. But it's difficult to love someone who puts you down all the time, who takes you for granted, who shows no true affection and respect.

The transition has been gradual. Sometimes I think I'm lonelier when Daniel is at home than when he's away. Is this what happens with all marriages? That we gradually diverge, travelling on our own trajectories, in the same direction, but apart. I don't want to give up on our marriage, but I do want to try to fix it, I just need to work out how. But in the meantime, if I can make the holiday cottage into a viable business, I am sure that Daniel will be proud of me. And even if he isn't, at least I'll have proven something to myself.

After I have cleared up the lunch things and Daniel has left, I join the children in the garden. Rosa and Kayleigh are seated on our wooden garden furniture, giggling conspiratorially, making beaded jewellery. Joel is playing with his dinosaurs, fully engrossed in a prehistoric world of his own making. He's sitting on the grass at my feet whilst I try and fail to read the weekend newspapers that Daniel picked up this morning. I'm flicking through a magazine when Nadia startles me.

'How are you doing, little man?' she asks Joel as she crouches down next to him. Joel inches away from her, throwing me a startled look. My little boy doesn't have the confidence of his older sister and is wary of strangers.

'Is everything all right?' I ask Nadia.

'Hunky-dory. Just thought I'd come and have a little chat with you.' She drags one of our wooden chairs and positions it right next to me. 'The views are amazing. How did you find this place?' She's wearing dark sunglasses that make it impossible to see her eyes.

'Daniel, my husband, was brought up in south Manchester. He always dreamed of living in the hills.' I don't tell her that the house came with my husband.

'I guess dreams come true for some people.' She gazes off into the distance, and I wonder why she's here, acting as if we're friends. Or is this normal for holiday guests? Being a new host, I don't have a benchmark. 'Where is your Daniel? We haven't met him yet.'

'He's playing golf.'

'Oh. Which way did he go?'

'I'm not sure. Why?' It's a strange question. She could have asked which golf course he frequented, but why would she be interested in how he drove to a location she doesn't know about?

She shakes her head vigorously and murmurs, 'Never mind. Anyway, tell me about the holiday cottage.'

'You're our second guests. I only set it up last month.'

'That explains why everything is so pristine.' She bashes the heel of her hand into her forehead. 'Of course I knew that. I'd forgotten. I read the article in the papers.'

I smile and feel a sense of pride. I wrote a press release and sent it to the editor of the local newspaper. They wrote a lovely piece on me and Best View Barn.

'I'm surprised you saw it. I thought you lived in the south of England.'

'I've got a friend who told me about this place. Did you do all the renovations, or was the barn like that when you got it?'

'It was a derelict wreck. We either had to board it up or renovate it, so we found a couple of local builders, and they took years to turn it into what it is today.'

'Well, you've done a great job.' She shifts in her chair as if she's about to get up. 'Is it ok if I help myself to a glass of water?'

'I'll get one for you.' I jump up, remembering that Nadia is my guest.

When I return with a glass, she is leaning down talking to Joel. He throws me a look of relief when I settle back into my chair.

'So you're a piano teacher?'

'Yes. I used to teach music in a secondary school, but I gave that up after the children were born. I have a few private pupils that I teach piano. What about you? Do you work?'

'I wanted Kayleigh to have music lessons, but with one thing and another... Anyway, what does your husband do?'

'He's a cardiothoracic surgeon.'

She frowns momentarily, and I wonder if she knows what the word means.

'A heart doctor,' I say.

'Of course. Wow. We'll have to watch ourselves. Don't want to misbehave around a man who cuts people's hearts out for a living.' She plays with the numerous amulets hanging from a silver bracelet.

'He doesn't exactly–'

'But he must be pretty good with a knife in a job like that.'

I shift uneasily. When I think of Daniel's work, I feel a sense of pride that my husband saves people's lives. I try not to dwell on the gory side of his profession.

'What does Mike do?'

'This and that. We get by, well enough to rent your beautiful place, anyway. It's not cheap. I wonder if people will pay that much going forwards.'

I thought the same thing myself, but as Dad suggested, we can always lower the prices; it's much harder to put them up. Dad, who used to run his own small chain of hardware shops, is blessed with common sense.

'How did you and Daniel meet?'

This isn't a story that I share readily. 'Through mutual friends,' I lie.

'Love at first sight, was it?'

I smile. We sit in silence for a few long moments, me wishing she would go and leave me in peace. I know she's trying to be friendly, but her presence is making me feel uncomfortable, as if she's invading my personal space. I try not to stare at all her jewellery. There are a lot of emblems and charms in strange shapes, little nuggets of coloured stones wrapped with silver wires, evil eyes and five-pointed stars. She must have six or seven bracelets on each wrist and rings on every finger. I pick up the newspaper from the ground, but she doesn't get the hint.

'It's lovely how the girls have taken to each other,' she says.

I look over to where they are playing, their heads so close

together, Kayleigh's long blonde hair appears tangled in Rosa's dark brown locks. 'Rosa must be special, because Kayleigh doesn't normally take easily to other children. She can be a bit of a loner. You're lucky to have two children.'

'Are there any places you want to explore around here?' I ask, hopeful that she may decide to have days out. 'Chatsworth House is only forty-five minutes' drive away.'

'Nah. We're not into historic buildings.'

'There are some fabulous walks. I've got some maps I can lend you,' I suggest.

Nadia shakes her head. 'We just want to chill. We'll be staying here and enjoying these lovely views.'

My heart sinks.

3

My parents come over for Sunday lunch at least once a month. Today, I've made roast beef with Yorkshire puddings, and we're seated at the kitchen table, in our regular places. Daniel at one end and my dad at the other. Both the kids love their grandparents, who spoil them rotten. I suppose my parents feel they need to make up for the lack of grandparents on Daniel's side. His mother died long before I met Daniel, and his father passed away three years ago.

Mum and Dad moved to live closer to us when Joel was one. In the early years of our marriage, it used to irk Daniel that I spent so much time on the phone to Mum, and that I referred any major life decisions to Dad. He's never really understood how I can be so close to my parents. So when they moved up north, buying a modern house on a small new development on the far side of Macclesfield, I was both delighted and worried. These days my parents couldn't be more complimentary about their son-in-law, chests puffing up with pride when they talk about his achievements and what a wonderful husband and father he is.

In turn, Daniel has mellowed towards them, grateful, I assume, that they make my life easier and allow him to work away from home. But they only see Daniel on the occasional Sunday, and whereas I used to share everything with them, these days I am more recalcitrant. If push came to shove, I sometimes think they would side with my husband over me. When Daniel accepted the consultant cardiothoracic surgeon position that would require him to work away, spending nights both in London and Manchester, he reminded me that my parents were on the doorstep for that very reason: to step in during his absence. Mum had a mini-stroke last year. It was ironic that Daniel was in London and not at hand to oversee her care. Fortunately, other than being a little less steady on her feet, she's back to her old self.

'Please, can you pass me the horseradish,' Mum asks. I hand it to her. Daniel is regaling us with details of an aortic valve replacement that he undertook last week, which proved more complex than he anticipated, and Dad is asking all sorts of questions about valves.

'They're not your kind of valves, Dad,' I joke. I realise how lucky I am, having a father who can fix any problem around the house and a husband who can diagnose, if not fix, most medical issues. Rosa has her fingers in her ears, as she hates anything to do with blood. I can't see my daughter taking in her father's footsteps. She hasn't touched her vegetables.

'Eat up,' I reprimand her. She scowls.

'Delicious Yorkshire puds, as normal, darling,' Mum says. 'I don't know how you have time with teaching, bringing up our grandchildren, and the new business. How's the barn going?'

'We've got our second lot of guests in. They arrived yesterday.'

'Kayleigh's my friend. She's six months older than me,' Rosa says.

There's a knock on the glass of the patio doors. We all jump.

I am pouring some gravy over my plate and spill it onto the pale green tablecloth.

'Hannah!' Daniel says, rolling his eyes before he stares at the mess. I grab my table napkin and soak up the brown splodge.

'Who's that?' Mum asks quietly. She and I are facing the window. The kids have their backs to it.

'Nadia Jones. Our current guest.' I take Mum's napkin and wipe the wooden table under the cloth. Nadia points towards the side of the house and starts walking away. I push my chair back and stand up.

'Hannah!' Daniel frowns at me. 'We're in the middle of lunch.'

I grit my teeth. I've noticed that he has an increasing tendency to talk to me in the tone he addresses the kids. 'I won't be a moment.'

I walk to the sink and pick up a roll of kitchen towel. As I turn around, I jump again. Nadia is in our kitchen. She must have walked around the house and let herself in through the back door.

'I'm so sorry for interrupting.' She smiles at everyone, her gaze lingering on Daniel's eyes. I notice how his pupils dilate, but that isn't surprising. Nadia is attractive, and today particularly so, with cherry red plump lips and those clear blue eyes surrounded by dark lashes. I suppose he thought that our guests would all be similar to the last couple, middle-aged and nondescript.

Daniel stands up and puts out his hand. Nadia steps forwards to shake it.

'Pleasure to meet you.' Daniel smiles. She nods and briefly licks her lips, then turns to smile at my parents.

'I hope you're enjoying your lunch. We're going for a walk, and I was wondering whether you'd like us to take Peanut with us? Kayleigh has taken quite a shine to him, and he seems like such a lovely dog.'

Peanut, who was lying on the floor next to Joel, a strategic spot where he is most likely to catch falling food, stands up and wags his tail. I know Labradors are clever dogs, but sometimes I think he understands too much.

'We're thinking of buying a puppy, and it would be lovely to see how Kayleigh is with Peanut. Is that ok?'

Daniel and I speak at the same time.

'Yes, that's fine,' he says, smiling broadly at Nadia.

I say, 'I'm sorry, but–'

Nadia laughs. I realise it's the first time I've heard her laugh, and it's deep and throaty. 'Is that how it normally is in this household? Dad says yes and Mum says no?'

I redden and hurry to explain myself. 'It's just that Peanut isn't used to going for walks with strangers, and I'm worried that he might run off. He's not great on the lead, and we haven't been very diligent in training him.'

Daniel frowns at me. That's a complete lie. I took him to puppy classes every week for six months, and although it's true that he is more used to being off than on the lead, he is an extraordinarily obedient dog. The truth is, I don't want these people I don't know taking our dog for a walk.

'I can go with you!' Rosa says. She hurriedly shovels a forkful into her mouth.

'No, Rosa,' I say, a little too firmly. 'We are having Sunday lunch with your grandparents. Sit back down.' She scowls at me.

'I'm very sorry to interrupt,' Nadia says, taking a step backwards. 'I'm sure you're right. It's not a good idea for us to take Peanut, not without one of you. Perhaps another time?' She turns around. 'Enjoy your lunch.' She hurries out of the kitchen. We sit in silence as the back door closes gently behind her.

Rosa speaks first. 'You're so mean!'

'Now, now, don't talk to your mum like that,' Dad says, patting Rosa's hand. 'She was only trying to protect Peanut.' But the relaxed and easy banter has dissipated, and although my parents try to keep chatting, Daniel and I are monosyllabic.

After lunch, Dad and Daniel drink coffee outside while Mum and I fill up the dishwasher and clean the pots and pans.

'Is everything all right, love? It's just you seem a bit tense at the moment. Is running a new business taking its toll?'

I'm surprised by the question. Yes, I feel stressed; I don't feel that comfortable around Nadia and Mike, but the real reason I'm on edge is because of Daniel. I used to think that nothing could come between Daniel and me, that he was my soulmate, but these days, I wonder. Sometimes, at the end of a long day when I haven't had a single conversation with an adult, I wish he were at home by my side. I feel resentful that he's only with us two or three nights a week, that he barely has any input into the children's upbringing, that all we talk about are the practical minutiae of life, and the extent of our physical contact is the grazing of lips on a forehead. But when he's home, he is increasingly critical of me, belittling, questioning the decisions I make in his absence. As if he can't quite decide whether he wants to be at home with me or not. And that scares me because I don't know how to make it right.

AFTER MY PARENTS have left and the children have gone to bed, Daniel takes me by surprise. 'Fancy sitting outside to watch the sun set?'

I smile and that heavy sense of unease instantly dissipates. Perhaps I've been worrying about nothing. This is what we used to do the first year I lived here. Whenever there was a hint of a sunset, we would huddle together on the oak bench at the front of the house, clutching glasses of wine, and marvel as the sky turned from blue to shades of orange, pink, purples and indigo, discussing what our future children would look like, where we would travel on luxury holidays. Even in the depth of winter, when there was snow on the ground and icicles hanging from the gutters, we would dress up in thick coats and wrap ourselves in blankets, swapping glasses of wine for hot toddies or vin chaud. It's been years since we did that.

Daniel opens a bottle of Bordeaux, and I collect two glasses. He grabs his pair of binoculars, and we sit side by side on the bench in companionable silence, listening to the birds sing and the sheep baa.

'I saw a peregrine falcon earlier. It was such a joy to see, especially as they were nearly all wiped out from the UK a few decades ago. Did you know that they're the fastest animal on the planet?'

I laugh. 'Yes, you might have told me a few times before.' When I first discovered that Daniel was a passionate bird-watcher, particularly of raptors (and I have to admit that I didn't even know a raptor was a bird of prey), I found it a bit weird. I imagined all twitchers were retired men in dodgy macs who had nothing better to do. Shows how wrong one can be when thinking in stereotypes. The fact that Daniel is obsessed with carnivorous, vicious birds initially made me uncomfortable. But then he explained to me that raptors include owls, and he wasn't just a twitcher but an activist for the protection and welfare of all birds of prey. I was somewhat appeased. These days Daniel doesn't contribute much to the raptor-monitoring group, but his passion for conservation hasn't waned, and he's doing his best to encourage our children to show an interest in nature and conservation.

'I don't think I'll ever tire of this view.' Daniel sighs. 'I miss it when I'm in Manchester and London.'

'And we miss you,' I say.

'I've got no choice.' Daniel's back stiffens, and imperceptibly, he edges away from me.

'Is it too much strain working such long hours in London?'

'Of course it's a strain, Hannah, but it's my job. What choice do I have?'

I grab his left hand. 'But I thought you enjoyed your job, that it is what you wanted?'

He gazes off into the distance. 'It is.' Tension ripples through his back.

I am leaning towards him to place a kiss on his cheek when I glimpse movement. The barn door opens, and Mike and Nadia walk out, carrying six cans of beer and a bottle of wine. I will them to walk in the opposite direction towards their car, but they don't. Mike catches sight of us and waves his arm high up in the air, a wide smile on his unshaven face. I nudge Daniel in the ribs.

'Looks like we've got company.' I moan quietly. 'Do you mind?'

'Not at all. Could be fun,' he says. So much for a quiet evening with my husband. And then I wonder whether Daniel is in fact relieved that we're not faced with a few hours alone. I don't have long to ponder my thoughts. Mike steps onto the patio, and Daniel stands up, extending his hand. 'Welcome to the best view in Britain.'

Mike shifts the cans of beer into his left hand and pumps Daniel's hand. He is wearing shorts that stop just under his knees and a black T-shirt that is too tight for his girth; the combination makes him look as if he's outgrown his clothes on top whilst his legs are stunted.

'Just wanted to say thanks for letting us stay here and brought a few bevvies over to share.'

'That's very kind of you, but you don't have to thank us.' Daniel laughs. 'You've paid for the privilege.'

'Yeah, even so, you don't always get what you see in the

pictures, do you? This place is nicer than your website suggests.'

'Hi, Hannah,' Nadia says almost coyly. I wonder if she feels uncomfortable about imposing herself on us, especially since the awkward scene at lunchtime. She stands next to Mike, dressed in another of her oversized dresses, a dark burgundy linen dress this time, matched with a black old-fashioned crocheted shawl over her shoulders. For someone of her age and the evident effort she makes in applying her make-up, she has the strangest dress sense. She holds out the bottle of wine.

'There's really no need for this, but lovely anyway,' Daniel says. As he reads the label on the wine, his lips straighten out ever so slightly. Daniel's a wine snob and happy to admit it, and from his fleeting glance, I deduce this is a bottle of plonk.

'Let me grab a couple of chairs while Hannah gets you some glasses. We won't be a moment,' Daniel says.

I try to catch my husband's eye, but Daniel turns his back on me and strides around the side of the house to the shed where we keep our garden furniture. Whilst Nadia and Mike stand side by side on the patio, gazing at the setting sun, I grab a couple of wine glasses and the corkscrew, opening the bottle that they brought. I pour it into the glasses and carry them back outside.

Nadia sits on the chair next to Daniel, shifting it so she's just a couple of inches away from him. Mike is on my side.

I proffer him a glass of wine. 'I'll have a beer. Not keen on the vino,' Mike says, peeling off a can from the six-pack and snapping open the lid.

'Would you like a glass?' I ask.

He laughs at me, little droplets of spittle flying across the still evening air. 'Who drinks beer out of glasses?'

'Hannah says you're a doctor.' Nadia flutters her fake eyelashes at my husband. 'All the doctors I know work so hard.

I don't suppose you have much time to enjoy your beautiful home.'

'You're right. Sometimes it feels that way.'

'If this place were mine, I'd never go out to work,' Mike says, taking a swig of beer from the can. 'Must have cost a pretty packet to do up.'

Daniel and Nadia speak at the same time. She laughs. 'Ladies first,' Daniel says.

'We were curious as to why you're running a holiday cottage.'

'Yeah. Can't imagine you're doing it for the money,' Mike interjects. 'But a damn fine job you've done.'

'It's Hannah's project,' Daniel says. 'I'm away quite a lot, so it's good to know she's not living out here in the sticks all alone with the kids.'

'It's a lovely place for a holiday, but not sure I could live here full time.' Mike sniffs. 'We're used to having neighbours and being able to walk to the pub.'

'Where do you live?' Daniel asks.

Nadia ignores Daniel's question. 'I'd love to live somewhere as remote as this. But I don't think I'd want strangers staying in my home. I'd keep the barn for friends and family or set it up as a studio.'

'That's what I said to Hannah.' Daniel smiles at Nadia. 'But she was adamant she wanted to run a little hobby business.'

I bristle at Daniel's terminology. Is that how he sees it?

'I don't know how you do it, Hannah.' Nadia shakes her head in what seems to me to be a fake expression of admiration. 'And you're a piano teacher. It's amazing. Didn't you want to give up teaching?'

'No. Music is my life, and I want to share that love and skill with as many people as I can.' I'm about to launch into my pet subject of how music is so undervalued, particularly in schools, and that we're in danger of depriving a whole generation of

self-expression, creativity and teamwork, but Daniel cuts
me off.

'I'm sure Nadia and Mike aren't interested in your philoso-
phies on music education, Hannah.'

'Actually, I wanted Kayleigh to learn an instrument, but it
never happened.'

'It's not too late,' I say, trying to stifle my annoyance towards
Daniel for being so condescending towards me.

'Would you give her a lesson this week?' Nadia leans
forwards with her elbows on her knees. I notice that she has
barely sipped her wine, whereas Mike is already onto his
second beer.

I hesitate.

'Please.' She tilts her head to one side. 'Can you persuade
your wife?' she asks Daniel, placing a hand briefly on his
forearm.

'Well, Hannah?' Daniel nudges me.

'Of course I can,' I say tightly.

But all I hear are Daniel's disparaging words. *A little hobby
business.*

4

The sun disappears, but there are clouds on the horizon, and the magical sunset I was hoping for doesn't materialise. It turns cold quickly.

'Are you warm enough?' I ask Nadia, hoping that the plummeting temperature will spur her to leave us alone.

'I don't feel the cold,' she says. 'It's all in the mind. If you think you're warm, you are.'

I wait for my learned doctor husband to dispute the statement, but he doesn't. He gazes at Nadia and lets her do all the talking. She asks Daniel questions about his work, finds out about our lives, but whenever we ask her any questions, she deflects them.

The moon rises and the sky is magnificent with galaxies and flickering pin lights. Mike and Nadia seem quite content to sit on our patio, admiring the sky for hours, but I want them gone.

In the end, it is Daniel who stands up.

'It was great to chat to you, but I'm afraid I need to go to bed. I've got an early start in the morning.'

'We mustn't stop the doctor from getting his beauty sleep,'

Nadia says, standing up. Mike accidentally kicks one of his empty beer cans, and it rolls across the patio. Daniel races after it and then leans down to collect the other five empty cans. I'm surprised Mike's bladder can hold so much beer.

We wish them goodnight, and I carry the empty glasses inside. Daniel drops the beer cans into the outside recycling bin.

'I'm not sure about those two,' I say as Daniel reappears in the kitchen. I place the glasses in the dishwasher.

'They're all right. Mike's a bit of a rough diamond, but they're entertaining enough.' He picks up the empty wine bottles and takes them outside. I hear the clatter of glass as he places them in the recycling bin. A few moments later, Daniel walks back into the kitchen, locks the door, and takes Peanut's collar off. We walk upstairs together.

'I'm just a little annoyed that I couldn't have my husband all to myself this evening,' I say in a whisper, so as not to wake the children.

Daniel doesn't answer.

When we're in bed, I lean over and try to kiss him. Perhaps if I try to initiate some intimacy, it might make things better.

'Not tonight, Hannah. I'm knackered, and I've got to be up at 5.30 a.m. tomorrow.' He turns over, his back towards me.

My initial reaction is relief. And then the guilt comes rushing through my veins. I should want to be in his arms. My husband is an attractive man, and I only had to see how Nadia looked at him this evening to realise that. I listen as his breathing slows and steadies, and then it hits me. What is wrong is how he makes me feel about myself. Dowdy, mediocre and put-upon. Something is going to have to change, but what, I don't know.

. . .

IT'S AN UNSEASONABLY HOT DAY, and I have all of the windows and doors open. Although we live in a beautiful spot, it's not renowned for its fine weather, so I'm grateful for the sunshine. Kayleigh and Rosa are outside sitting on the lawn, making friendship bracelets, and Joel is harassing Peanut. I am doing some ironing in the kitchen.

I see Nadia walking over towards the girls. She's wearing a white long-sleeved flowing dress today. A few moments later, Rosa comes careering into the kitchen; Kayleigh hovers at the door.

'Mum! Mum! Kayleigh's mum has asked me if I'd like to go to the lake with them today. They're taking a picnic and renting a boat. It's so exciting!'

'Slow down,' I say. I glance at Kayleigh, who is staring at me with big blue eyes, and then revert my gaze to Rosa. 'I don't think it's appropriate.'

'What! No, Mummy! I want to go. Please!' Rosa is jumping up and down.

'We don't know the Joneses very well, and I'm sure they don't want another child to look after.' I try to speak quietly, but it's impossible for Kayleigh not to overhear us.

'It's fine,' Kayleigh says quietly. 'Mum suggested it.'

I feel as if I've been wedged into a tight corner. Of course I don't want these strangers taking my daughter out for the day. Rosa runs over to Kayleigh and grabs her hand.

'We're going to be blood sisters,' she says. Kayleigh smiles and hugs Rosa to her side. She is almost half a head taller than my daughter.

I shiver. I wonder if Rosa understands what she's saying. I remember when I was young, how best friends pricked their fingers and mingled their blood on a page, promising to be best friends for ever. I had hoped that such rituals might have died out. Just as I'm desperately trying to work out how to deal with this, Nadia appears.

'Knock, knock!' she says as she puts her head around the open patio door. 'We'd love Rosa to join us today. We thought we'd hang around Rudyard Lake and perhaps nip over to Tittesworth Reservoir. Can Rosa bring a swimming costume and a towel?'

'Titty!' Kayleigh says. Rosa convulses with laughter, and then Joel starts saying the word over and over again. Nadia grins.

'It's very kind of you to offer to take Rosa, but we already have plans for today.'

'I don't, Mum!' Rosa says, her hands on her hips, a look of outrage on her face. It's true that Rosa has an empty day ahead. I have a piano lesson to give this afternoon, and my friend Amber is coming over with her son, Billy, to collect Joel so that the two boys, who are in the same Reception class, can spend the afternoon together. 'I want to go! You've got to let me.'

'Rosa, don't be rude.'

'It's not fair!' Tears start welling up in her eyes, and to my dismay, I see that Kayleigh's bottom lip is quivering too.

'Any chance you could change your plans?' Nadia asks, her head tilted to the side. 'The forecast for today is glorious, and it looks like the weather is going to break later in the week. Perhaps you and Joel could come along too?'

'I'm sorry, but I'm teaching later.'

'Please, Mummy!'

I have three sets of pleading eyes staring at me.

'Okay,' I say eventually. But I don't feel good about it.

'You've got my phone number on the booking form, but why don't I give it to you again. You can call us any time. Mike and I will make sure the girls are safe and have a lovely time. Ice cream, boats... it'll be great.' Nadia airdrops her phone number to me.

'Rosa isn't a strong swimmer,' I say. 'And she burns easily.'

Nadia tilts her head to one side, her straight blonde hair

shimmering like a wave. 'Don't worry, Hannah. I'll look after Rosa as if she were my own child.' She lowers her voice. 'Better even.'

Rosa runs upstairs, followed by Kayleigh. A few moments later, she has reappeared with her swimming costume and a large towel.

'You'll need suntan lotion as well,' I tell her.

'Don't worry about that. We've got plenty, haven't we, Kayleigh?'

'Can I give you some money for ice cream and lunch?' I ask.

'Absolutely not! It's our treat. Come on, girls, let's get going.'

I blow Rosa a kiss, but she's already out of the house, racing towards the barn, where Mike's car is idling, fumes belching from the old Mercedes' exhaust. I watch the car as it drives up the hill and disappears over the brow. My stomach clenches, and I realise I've been holding my breath for much too long.

'What are you staring at?' Joel appears at my side.

'Nothing, sweetheart. I'll do this ironing later. Why don't we take Peanut for a walk?'

AMBER AND HER SON, Billy, arrive just before lunch.

'Where's Rosa?' Amber asks, giving me a kiss on the cheek.

'She's gone out for the day with the guests staying in the barn.'

Amber raises an eyebrow, and I get that lurch again in my stomach. Rosa adores Amber, thinking she's the coolest adult she knows, and I remember now that Amber had promised to braid Rosa's hair. I give the boys fish fingers and chips on the proviso that they eat a healthy portion of salad, and Amber and I eat cold Gazpacho and chunky bread.

After shovelling in their lunch, the boys race around the house and garden at an exhausting pace. I then get the chance to look at Amber properly. Her pale-yellow sundress looks crumpled, and there is a stain on the front. Her afro hair, which is normally tied back in neat cornrows, is frizzy and on end. I'm surprised. She is normally well-turned-out.

'I need a double espresso,' she says, sinking back into her chair.

'Coming right up. You look tired. What's up?'

'I am tired. I haven't been sleeping well. No obvious reason.'

Amber and I are the outsiders; she because of the colour of her skin, me because I was such a townie. We live in the midst of a very white, old English farming community, and until Jonathan married Amber, there were no black faces. It was one of the things that struck me most when I first moved here. I am used to living in a city with friends of every race, religion and ethnicity. It seemed to me that everyone was the same here, and unless you were fourth or fifth generation from the locality, you would never be accepted as a local. Daniel just about fitted in because at least he was from the north-west; I didn't. When I met Amber at antenatal classes, I felt a magnetic pull towards her. She's funny and smart and ballsy, not fearful of standing up to anyone. I've never seen her this low. Unfortunately, we haven't got long to chat because I have a pupil coming at 2 p.m., so after finishing her coffee, Amber hustles Joel and Billy into her car, and they drive away for an afternoon of fun.

For a moment, I stand on the doorstep, listening. All I can hear is the rustle of long grass, the chirruping of crickets, and the birds singing. Without the children, it is so peaceful. Although I relish the silence, it makes me miss them. I know that Joel is safe with Amber, but is Rosa safe with Mike and Nadia? There is nothing to suggest she's not, except that nagging feeling in my belly.

I quickly tidy up the kitchen and then, on the dot of 2 p.m., Ellen Snow arrives with her son, Cameron. If I could write a character description of the nightmare pushy mother, Ellen Snow would tick every box. Perhaps ten years older than me,

Ellen has never hidden her grand ambitions for her son, Cameron. Whether the boy likes it or not, she is convinced that he will be the next Lang Lang, a classical pianist superstar. Fortunately for her, Cameron has both the talent and the ambition, so on the face of it, her dream may be realised. But I've seen this before. A child is pushed hard, their talent recognised at a young age, but when they reach fifteen or sixteen, they bail out. It's all too much pressure. Or perhaps they stick at it and make it to conservatoire, but now they are faced with the fiercest competition. They are no longer special. Destruction comes about either through arrogance and the belief that they are owed success, or they wither away in the face of the competition, becoming disillusioned and overwhelmed with self-doubt, fading into obscurity. To maintain a love of the instrument, the commitment of practice, the confidence of performance, and rise above the competition is a very tall order indeed.

When Ellen first contacted me, she told me that her ambition was for eight-year-old Cameron to be accepted into one of the four specialist music schools in the country. She had heard that I had had success with two previous pupils, one who was accepted by Chetham's School of Music and the other by the Yehudi Menuhin School. She insisted that I listen to Cameron play, and when I did, I was astounded. He is a natural pianist with a sensitivity and musicality far beyond his years. I agreed to teach him; in fact, it is an honour to teach him, and I have little doubt that he will achieve his mother's first objective, of getting into a specialist music school. Whether it is his dream too is still to be uncovered. Whilst Cameron is a joy to have around, I can't say the same about Ellen. It has taken me three months to get her to agree that she doesn't need to sit in on his lessons. As a non-musician, her constant interruptions were inhibiting both Cameron and myself.

'Would you like a cold drink?' I ask, leading her into our

living room, where she normally reads the newspapers. Cameron, who is small for his age, lurks in the doorway.

'No, thank you. A herbal tea is much more refreshing in the hot weather.'

'What flavour would you like?'

'Tulsi.'

'I'm sorry, but I think we only have mint or lemon and ginger.'

'I'll pass. I want Cameron to be entered into a competition. I was thinking–'

'No.' Cameron speaks quietly but emphatically.

'I am talking to your teacher!' Ellen snaps, jabbing her finger at her son.

'Why don't we have this discussion by phone at a later date?' I suggest. I guide Cameron out of the room and along the corridor to my music room. I shut the door.

'I don't want to take part in a competition,' Cameron says as he settles on the piano stool.

'In which case you won't.'

'But what about Mum?'

'Leave your mother to me.'

AFTER CAMERON LEAVES, I spend the rest of the afternoon cleaning the house. Amber calls to say that she'll be bringing Joel home at 7 p.m. I play the piano for half an hour or so, but I'm restless, constantly checking to see if I've had any missed calls from Nadia.

I give Peanut his tea and throw him a couple of balls. By 6 p.m., I am very twitchy. Mike and Nadia have been out for hours, and there isn't that much to do at the various lakes. I suppose they might have gone into Leek for a spot of shopping or perhaps they went further afield. Rosa should have eaten her tea by now, and she'll be starving if they haven't fed her. I find myself pacing around the house, running a duster over surfaces that are spotless. I call Nadia's phone, but it goes straight to voicemail. I leave a message, trying to make my voice sound upbeat. 'Hi, it's Hannah. Just wanted to find out when you'll be home.' Mobile reception is lousy in the hills, and the chances are they're driving somewhere with no coverage.

By 7 p.m. my stomach is churning and I feel nauseous. I call Nadia every fifteen minutes, and each time it goes straight to voicemail. I wish I had relented and given Rosa a mobile phone. Some of her friends have them already, but I have told her she will need to be at least ten years old before she gets one.

Amber arrives with the boys.

'Can't stop,' she shouts as she hustles Joel out of the car. 'I've got a chicken in the oven.'

And so I don't tell her that Rosa isn't home yet. She didn't seem to judge me too harshly earlier when I explained that I had let my daughter go out for the day with strangers, but now I feel a gut-wrenching terror combined with shame. I've tried so hard to be a good mother, but today I've totally failed.

I know I should call Daniel, but I don't want to. At 7.20 p.m. I pick up the courage and ring his mobile.

'I let Rosa go out for the day with Mike and Nadia. They're not home yet, and Nadia's mobile phone is switched off.'

'You what!' Daniel erupts. I'm not surprised. I would have the same reaction if the shoe was on the other foot. I suppose I've given him yet more ammunition, but he is Rosa's father. He deserves to know. 'Have you rung the police?'

'No, not yet. I thought it might be a bit soon.'

'For God's sake, Hannah. Call the bloody police and call me back as soon as you know anything.' He hangs up on me.

I pace the kitchen a few times, the phone clutched in my hand. What choice do I have? They could have been in an accident, or worse.

I dial 999.

'Which service?'

'Police.'

And then I hear the slamming of car doors. I rush to the window and look outside.

'I'm sorry. Emergency over.' I hang up the phone and send Daniel a quick text. 'She's home safe and sound.'

The girls are clambering out of the car, their faces red from too much time spent in the sun. I want to yell at Nadia, ask her how she would feel if strangers took off with her daughter and didn't make contact. But I don't. I stand at the top of the steps, my arms crossed. 'Did you have a nice day?'

'It was such fun, Mum!' Rosa comes skipping over to me. She has ice-cream stains down the front of her T-shirt.

'Thank you for having her,' I say tightly.

Nadia looks amused but doesn't speak. Mike is already inside the barn.

'See you tomorrow, Rosa!' Kayleigh shouts.

When we get into the kitchen and out of sight, I fling my arms around Rosa, hugging her so tightly, she squeals.

5

After their hectic days yesterday, both the children sleep in much longer than normal. I take advantage of the tranquillity by practising the piano. I used to worry that the music would wake them, but Rosa and Joel are so used to hearing me play, I think it's just a comforting backdrop or normal ambient sound to them. They never complain. I slept badly last night thinking about all the what-ifs. It didn't help that Daniel sent me a litany of texts saying how livid he was that I let Rosa go out for the day with virtual strangers. He criticises me for many things, but he has never, until now, said I was a bad mother. I have to agree with him; yesterday, I was.

I am practising Chopin's Ballade Number One when Peanut starts barking. Sighing, I gently close the lid on my beautiful Bluthner grand piano and hurry to the kitchen. Mike is standing at the door, and my heart sinks.

As I open the door, he yawns noisily, without putting his hand over his mouth. He leans a shoulder against the door frame.

'Good morning!' I say in a more cheerful tone than I feel.

'Isn't for me. I slept badly.'

'I'm sorry to hear that.'

'I can't sleep under all those feathers.'

I frown.

'The duvet and pillows are filled with feathers, aren't they?'

I nod, thinking about the extremely expensive, top-of-the-range duvet and pillows filled with Hungarian goose down and feathers. As I am charging nearly a thousand pounds a week for renting the barn, I chose the very best of everything, including the bed and bedding.

'They give me allergies, and they're too light. I need to feel as if I've got something over me at night. Can you get us a synthetic duvet and pillows?'

'Yes,' I say, my heart sinking. I suppose if he is allergic to natural materials, I have no choice, but it annoys me.

'And the bed is too hard. I've got a bad back, and it's doing me no favours. Can you get one of them mattress toppers to soften it up? Gotta sleep well on holiday.'

'Yes, of course. I'll do my best.'

'Nadia didn't want me to bother you, but I said you wouldn't mind. I was right, wasn't I?' He grins at me, the gold-capped tooth catching the light. He turns around and waddles back towards the barn.

I swear under my breath. That will be an expensive mission. Daniel won't be happy; he thinks I've already overspent on the interior of the barn. But I have no choice. If I don't keep the guests happy, I won't get good reviews, and then I won't be able to build a sustainable business. Now I know that Daniel views it as a little hobby business, I am even more determined that it must be a success. I've read several books and lots of online advice about running a holiday let business profitably, and the key to success is all about guest satisfaction, providing a personalised service, and racking up great reviews online. Thanks to Mike Jones, I'll have to go shopping today, probably to John Lewis in Cheadle. So much for a quiet day at home, pottering with the kids.

IN THE END, we make an outing of my shopping trip. We have lunch in a trendy cafe in Wilmslow, I buy the bedding, and we're not back home until nearly 4 p.m. The moment our car pulls up behind the house, Kayleigh comes running towards us. It's as if she's been sitting there waiting for Rosa to return all day, much like Peanut does when we're out. Rosa dashes out of the car, and the girls fling their arms around each other, as if they're best friends who have been apart for years. It's heartwarming to see, but at the same time, it worries me. Rosa will be upset when Kayleigh leaves at the end of the week.

'I've got some bedding for your parents,' I tell Kayleigh, lugging the large bags out of the boot of my Toyota Rav. 'Would you girls like to give me a hand?'

Joel insists on carrying a bag too, so we all traipse around the house. Just as we're passing the bins and the log store, Joel trips and lands on his bottom, landing neatly on top of a bag of pillows. It's one of those comical moments that fail in the retelling, but it has all of us in stitches.

'You're such a little klutz,' I say as I help him to his feet.

'What does that mean?' he asks.

'Butterfingers,' I say.

'Stumblebum.' Kayleigh giggles. And then the kids are in hysterics again.

'We'll be able to watch ourselves.' Rosa hiccups.

'What do you mean?' Kayleigh asks.

'The bird camera, it's up there by the drainpipe.' She points to the guttering. 'It's Dad's wildlife camera. We watched the baby birds leave their nest in the spring.'

'Wow, that's so cool.' Kayleigh stands on tiptoes, trying to spot the camera, but it's camouflaged and well hidden. 'I can't see it?'

'It's so well hidden, if you didn't know it's there, you'd never find it,' I say.

'Did you see the eggs hatch?' Kayleigh asks.

Rosa nods.

'Shit. That's so cool!' Kayleigh says. 'I wish I could see that.' I bristle at the use of a swear word but choose to ignore it. Unfortunately, Joel doesn't.

'Kayleigh just said shit!' he says excitedly. 'She just used a naughty word.'

'It's not that naughty,' Kayleigh retorts. 'I know way worse ones than that.'

'Like what?' Joel bounces up and down next to her whilst Rosa stares at her new friend with a look of admiration. I need to shut this conversation down now.

'You can see the chicks,' I say. 'We've still got the footage. I can show you later.'

'Dope,' Kayleigh says, smiling, and we carry on walking around the house and down the steps to the barn.

Kayleigh opens the barn's door, shouting, 'They're back!' The television is turned up to full volume, and from the sound of the commentary, it's evident that Mike is watching a game of football.

Before I or the kids can step inside, Mike appears. 'Got the bedding, then?' he says, holding out stubby fingers to take the bags.

'Would you like me to change the beds for you and remove the feather duvet and pillows?' I ask.

'No. Nadia will do it. She's having a rest right now.'

I wonder how she can get any sleep over the excited commentary and the racket of the roaring crowds on the television.

Joel and I stroll back to the house while Rosa and Kayleigh walk arm in arm into the garden.

HALF AN HOUR LATER, I take my cup of tea and sit on the bench outside to read a book. The girls have allowed Joel to join them, and the three kids are sitting in the long grass, examining bugs.

I look up as a shadow falls over me. It's Nadia. She is wearing black harem trousers and a pale grey, loose-fitting, long-sleeved linen blouse. Her dark sunglasses are much too large for her petite face and make her look bug-eyed.

'Thanks for buying the bedding. Mike's an old softie, and he needs his creature comforts. Do you mind if I join you?'

She doesn't wait for an answer and plonks herself down next to me. The air becomes heavy with her strong perfume, a scent that reminds me of incense sticks.

'He's watching the footie, and it's doing my head in. I need some peace and quiet.'

I feel like saying, *We live in the middle of nowhere. You are surrounded by peace and quiet, so leave me alone.* Instead, I smile tightly.

'What are you reading?' she asks.

I show her the front cover of my novel.

'I don't suppose you get much time for reading with everything that you do.'

I glance at her, surprised at her empathy.

'No. It's been very full-on lately.'

'Can I take you up on that offer to give our Kayleigh a piano lesson?'

I nod, although I recall it was her request rather than my offer.

'What did you have to do to train as a music teacher?'

'I studied music at university and then did a teacher training course.'

'You never wanted to be a performer?'

It's been years since anyone has asked me that question, and I'm touched by Nadia's perceptive interest. 'I would have liked to have been, but I wasn't good enough, and I realised that early on. I've always loved kids, so it never felt second best becoming a teacher.'

'That's good. Resentment can eat you up.'

'And what about you?' I ask. 'You haven't told me what you do, if you work?'

'It's a vocation, a calling, a bit like yours. I've known since I was a kid that I had the gift. I'm a psychic.'

I know I'm gawping, but I wasn't expecting that. I'm so glad Daniel isn't here, otherwise he would have caught my eye, and we would be on the floor convulsed with laughter.

'You're not a believer, are you?' She takes her dark glasses off and peers at me.

It makes me feel awkward, as if she's gazing into my brain.

'I'm one of the best, Hannah. Good enough to pay for holidays in nice places like this.'

'I've never met a psychic before,' I say hastily, eager to dissipate any awkwardness.

'No, people like you never have.' She shoves her sunglasses on top of her head and claps her hands together. 'How about I give you a reading? My treat as a thank you for giving Kayleigh a piano lesson.'

'Um, thanks, but that's really not necessary.'

'I'm not taking no for an answer. I insist. What time do your children go to bed?'

'Um, Rosa's lights out is at 8.30 p.m.'

'And what time does your husband get back tonight?'

'Daniel's away this week.'

'That's perfect. We won't be disturbed. I'll pop over at 9 p.m. and give you a reading. It will change your life. I guarantee that!' Nadia stands up.

'Really, I don't–'

'I insist. It's my treat.'

I groan to myself. I don't need a bloody reading. I recall how a friend of mine visited a fortune teller during a trip to India. She was told that she would fall in love in her early twenties and get married. Within two years, the marriage would fall apart. She would then meet the true love of her life and have their first baby aged thirty. It was a self-fulfilling prophecy, almost as if she subconsciously willed that first marriage to break down in order to fulfil the destiny prescribed by the fortune teller. As predicted, her first child was born a month before her thirty-first birthday. I'm not sure what I believe in. There probably is a higher power, an energy that we can't see, but I am doubtful of psychics and have never so much as studied the lines on my palms, let alone have had a tarot reading. I suppose with my sceptical attitude, it can't do much harm. Better to accept it gracefully and take it with a pinch of salt.

BY 8.30 P.M., the weather has turned. Before living here, I didn't fully appreciate the weather. Typical to many Brits, it was always a topic of conversation, but I never felt I lived with the weather in the way that I do in this place. With such expansive views, we can watch the clouds descend, or rain clouds sweep across the Cheshire plain, curtains of rain sweeping towards us. My favourite days are when our house sits above the clouds, replacing our view of green fields and speckled towns with a carpet of white fluffiness and a bright blue sky above. Tonight, rain clouds have gathered, and the sky flashes in the distance as a storm approaches. I close all the windows and doors and hunker down. Ten minutes later, rain is slashing the house and a wind has whipped up. I am hoping that the weather will put off Nadia from making the short walk from the barn to the house.

I am disappointed.

She raps hard on the back door at 8.50 p.m., wearing a large plastic cape that she shrugs off at the door. Water drops off it in rivulets.

'Does the weather always change that quickly up here?'

I take the wet cape from her and hang it up on a peg in the utility room. She removes her black ankle boots. Her toenails are painted in the same dark colour as her nails, minus the diamantes.

'It can do. It'll probably be fresher tomorrow, which is a good thing.'

She follows me into the kitchen and places her sequin-encrusted bag on the table.

'What can I get you to drink?' I ask.

'Just water, please. I don't drink alcohol when I'm doing a reading. The spirits don't like it.'

I bite my lip to stop myself from grinning. I pour her a glass and hand it to her, then pull out a chair at the table. Nadia remains standing.

'Um, this isn't the best place to do a reading. It would be better to do it in a more intimate room, somewhere that has special meaning for you. I was thinking your piano room might work well. Do you have a small table we can use, like a card table?'

I shake my head. For some reason, I don't want Nadia in my piano room. But she's right about one thing; it is my special place.

'No worries. We can sit on the floor.'

'How about in the living room?' I suggest.

'No. We need to do it in the piano room. I can feel the strength of that space from here.'

I stop myself from rolling my eyes, pick up my glass of white wine, which hopefully the spirits won't mind too much, and Nadia follows me along the short corridor to my music room. It's not really a large enough space for my grand piano, but I am so grateful to have a unique space to play it, I don't worry too much about the cramped surroundings and less than ideal acoustics.

Nadia sits down on the carpet, but not before I have seen a livid, purple bruise on the back of her shin, just above her strange-looking tattoo. There isn't much space for me, so I sit opposite her, my back against a piano leg. She takes out various items from her bag, including a crystal ball, a pack of cards, crystals and stones in different colours, and a large candle sitting on a copper plate. She lights the candle with a diamond-encrusted lighter and then places the stones around her in a semicircle.

'It's not dark enough in here. Can you turn the main light off and pull the blind?'

I would like to tell her to take a running jump, that I don't want her here, and the last thing I need to be told is some nonsense about what might or might not happen to me in the future. But I stay silent and haul myself up and do as instructed, switching on a table lamp and turning off the over-head lights. There is a low glow in the room now, and the flame from the candle creates dancing shadows on the ceiling. I resume my place on the floor.

Nadia shifts herself so that she is sitting cross-legged, her billowing dress hiding her legs, with just her feet poking out. She shuts her eyes and murmurs something unintelligible under her breath. She inhales and exhales very deeply several times and then opens her eyes and turns towards me. She stares at me, unblinking, and then reaches forward and grabs a purple-coloured stone.

'This is for you. It's an agate.' She holds it out in the palm of her hand. 'Please take it.' Reluctantly, I take it from her and clutch it in my right hand.

'Agate is a stone of strength and courage, and it will help you accept yourself and to see the truth. It cleanses negative energy and calms the mind, body and spirit. Close your eyes, Hannah, and really feel it in your palm.'

I do as she tells me and clasp my fingers around the smooth, cool stone. I'm not sure what I'm meant to be feeling or doing, so after a long period of silence, I open my eyes. Nadia is sitting totally still, staring at me. It is almost creepy; it's like she's looking at me but not seeing, not blinking. I have to glance away.

'What do you know about Tarot cards, Hannah?'

'Nothing,' I admit. I place the purple stone on the carpet next to me.

She holds up an oversized deck of cards. 'I have here seventy-eight cards, each with its own imagery, story and symbolism. There are twenty-two Major Arcana cards that represent life's karmic and spiritual lessons, and they are related to the twenty-two letters of the Hebrew alphabet and the twenty-two branches of the Tree of Life, which has a very prominent place in the Kabbala. They tend to represent forces outside of our control. The fifty-six Minor Arcana cards are divided up into four suits: cups, swords, pentacles and wands. They show us our daily trials and tribulations, and we have the power to change these. For me, the Tarot is the storybook of our lives, the mirror to our souls, the key to our inner wisdom. They allow me to connect with higher spirits and my own deep intuition. They have never failed me. Before we begin, I would like you to do some deep breathing with me. Shut your eyes. Now take a slow breath in and a slow breath out. As you release your next breath, feel your tail bone sinking into the floor and your body becoming heavier.' Her voice becomes slower and deeper. 'You are now totally relaxed and ready to receive the wisdom of the cards. Open your eyes.'

I do as instructed and nearly jump off the ground as a massive clap of thunder echoes in the sky above. I hope it doesn't wake the children, as both are scared of storms. Nadia, however, appears totally unaware of it. She shuffles the pack of oversized cards.

'How good are you at shuffling cards?' she asks.

'Not very.'

'Lay your right hand over the pack of cards, shut your eyes and feel the cards, allowing that sensation to run through your body as an uninterrupted tingle.'

I do as she says but feel absolutely nothing. My eyes flicker open, but she is staring at me, so I close them again.

'Inhale in and out. Good. Now open your eyes.' Her voice sounds languid.

She removes one card from the deck and places it face down on the ground. She then shuffles the cards, quickly and expertly, before placing the pack onto the ground in front of me.

'Using your left hand, cut the pack of cards into five piles, setting each pile down to the left of the one before.'

I do as instructed. I know it's silly, but I feel a tremor of excitement, or is it nervousness? Despite being a rational non-believer, now I am curious to know what my future holds. Nadia is so composed and serious, it's hard for some of that not to rub off on me.

She selects a card from the top of each pile and places the five cards on the floor in the shape of a cross, with three cards on the horizontal, one card above the central card, and one card below it.

The first card she turns over features the picture of a tower, with lightning striking the top of it. The picture is facing away from me. Nadia knots her eyebrows together. The following card depicts three swords, the third card is of the devil, the fourth card is the five of pentacles, and the fifth card says death. Nadia shivers and places the pack of cards on the floor next to her. She bites the side of her bottom lip and then glances up at me, her eyes wide. When she speaks, her voice sounds hoarse and tremulous.

'I'm sorry, Hannah, but I can't do this reading.'

'What do you mean?' I say, shifting on the floor.

'I've never had all the worst cards show up together. Never. To be honest, it scares me. This is a truly terrible reading.' Her hand is shaking as she sweeps up the cards from the floor.

'What does it mean?' I ask.

She shakes her head and picks up a couple of the crystals from the ground, holding one against her solar plexus and another to her forehead. She closes her eyes and mutters something weird under her breath. Then she stands up and shakes herself violently, much like a dog does when it comes out of a river.

'I can't tell you exactly. All I can say is that something terrible is going to happen. You are going to have to be very, very careful.'

For a moment, I wonder if she's taking the micky. I snigger, but the look of horror on Nadia's face tells me I've got it wrong. I might think it's a joke, but she doesn't.

'Can you switch the main light on, please?' she asks, her voice wobbly.

With creaking limbs, I stand up and switch the light on just as she blows the candle out.

'I need to go now,' Nadia says, quickly shoving all of her things into her bag. 'But be careful, Hannah. Be very careful. The cards are never wrong.'

6

M y sleep is interrupted with nightmares that jerk me awake in the middle of the night, my heart pounding, adrenaline rushing through my limbs, and Nadia's words ringing in my ears. This morning, her card reading – or rather, her abbreviated card reading – still plays heavily on my mind. I wish I could tell Daniel about it, but he ridicules anything vaguely other-worldly or spiritual, not surprising really for someone with such a scientific, logical brain and an intimate knowledge of how the body works. I need to discuss it with someone, though, so I call Amber.

'Come on, Hannah. The woman must be a charlatan. Surely you don't believe in rubbish like that?'

'I don't. It's just that she shuffled the pack really well, and I cut the cards, so how did those horrible cards come up?'

'Sleight of hand, I assume. It's not difficult if you practice and know what you're doing.'

Amber's rational explanation soothes me somewhat, but it still leaves question marks in my brain. Nadia would have to be very skilled to select those cards, or perhaps she has a special pack, like the packs of fake cards found in a children's box of magic tricks. Maybe all Nadia wanted to do was scare me, but why? Or perhaps it was a genuine hand and she is truly scared. Even though I am not a believer, it has still planted a seed of doubt in my mind. I don't believe in coincidences, but that very thought doesn't sit comfortably with my disbelief about fortune telling. Perhaps that's exactly what Nadia wants to achieve – to cause confusion and doubt. Perhaps it makes her feel powerful, boosts her confidence, makes her feel superior to others. Quite why she feels the need to prove anything to me, I don't know. Whatever the result of the reading, I resolve to stay out of Nadia's way.

Last night's storm has left behind a grey and drizzling day, so the children potter around in the house. I play with Joel for a while, and the three of us make a cake. Eventually, I manage to shake off that uneasy clenching in my sternum. Late morning, there is a loud knock on the door. We have a bell that rings, and I don't know why people fail to use it. I take a deep breath and walk to the door. I am relieved that it's Mike and not Nadia.

He doesn't say hello or good morning. 'One of the taps in the bathroom is leaking. Wondering if Daniel could pop over to fix it? He's a kind of plumber isn't he, doing valves and stuff in his heart surgery.'

I try not to smirk. I can't see Daniel fixing any bathroom leaks, and I don't suppose he'd appreciate being referred to as a plumber.

'Unfortunately, Daniel won't be home until Friday. I can call out a plumber to sort it.' I think of asking Dad, but I don't want to disturb him.

'Nah. Don't bother, it's just a drip and not that much of a big deal. I'm more bothered by the bloody baaing of the sheep. Woke me up at 4 a.m. F-ing nightmare.'

I can't think of a suitable response, as there is absolutely nothing I can do about the sheep. We live in the middle of an upland sheep farm, and there are hundreds in the fields that surround our property. There is no way that I can ask Jamie Mole to shift his flocks into faraway fields. I clench my jaw at the thought of Mike and Nadia leaving a lousy review about the sheep. It would be comical if it didn't matter so much to me.

Fortunately, I don't need to make any further conversation, as Mike turns around and slinks back towards the barn.

AFTER LUNCH, Rosa begs me to let Kayleigh come over to play. It seems churlish to say no. Just because I'm wary of her parents doesn't justify me stopping Rosa from playing with their daughter.

The girls sit at the kitchen table, and I supply them with materials for papier maché, then leave them to it whilst I prepare supper.

'You live in a very big house,' Kayleigh says. I busy myself cutting vegetables and pretend I'm not listening to their conversation.

'Mmm. I suppose so,' Rosa replies.

'We used to live in a big house, but not for long. Before that we lived in a foreign country.'

'That's cool. Where did you live?'

'Wales.'

I swallow my snigger and am grateful that Rosa doesn't point out that Wales is still part of the United Kingdom and not a 'foreign' country.

'I couldn't understand what the people said a lot of the time, and the road signs are in another language. Really long words.'

'If you couldn't understand them, what happened at school? Did you understand what the teachers were saying?'

'I don't go to school.'

Rosa drops her papier maché balloon and it skirts across

the floor. She chases after it. 'How come you don't go to school? Everyone has to go to school!'

'Not if you're homeschooled.'

'What, like in the olden days when a governess comes over and teaches you at home? Is it like in *The King and I*?'

'What?'

'*The King and I*. It's a musical.'

Kayleigh shrugs. 'Don't watch any crap like that.'

I inhale a little too loudly, but the children don't seem to notice.

'So who teaches you?'

'Mum. Other people.'

I am very surprised. I didn't have Nadia down as the home-educating type, but then who am I to judge? I take my hat off to anyone who chooses to home educate. I can't even manage to teach my own children the piano. That reminds me about my promise to give Kayleigh a lesson.

'Kayleigh, your mum suggested you might like a piano lesson. We could do that when you've finished the papier maché if you'd like.'

'Nah.'

'I think your mum would like you to have a lesson.'

'I don't want one, and I'm not having one.' She doesn't glance up from painting glue over the paper. Her tone of voice is calm without any hint of indignance, as would be evident if I asked Rosa to do something she didn't want to do. 'Thanks anyway,' she says as a surprisingly polite afterthought.

I don't argue. I feel as if I've been put firmly in my place by a nine-year-old. She is a strange girl, sometimes sounding polite and more mature than her years, and other times swearing like a trooper.

. . .

BY LATE AFTERNOON, the weather has cleared and the sun is shining, mist rising from the damp fields to create the kind of vistas I associate with Tuscany: long, orange rays of sunshine, low fog creeping around the base of trees, and the promise of a beautiful summer's evening.

'Hello!'

I jump at the sound of Nadia's voice.

'Hannah, as the girls are getting along so well, I was wondering if they'd like to do a sleepover?'

Both Kayleigh and Rosa jump into the air and clap their hands.

I open my mouth and shut it again. I do not want Rosa sleeping in the barn with Nadia and Mike. They are too weird for my liking. What if Nadia decides to look into the crystal ball and predict Rosa's life. It could be devastating. I'm trying to formulate a response when Nadia speaks.

'I was wondering whether Kayleigh could stay here with you. Only if that's convenient, of course, and if you have the room.'

She must know perfectly well that we have enough space. Rosa has already shown Kayleigh around the house, as well as demonstrating how the pull-out bed works underneath her own.

'That's fine,' I say, eager for Nadia to leave.

'Pop over and collect your night things, Kayleigh,' Nadia says.

'Can Kayleigh stay for tea?' Rosa asks me, holding her hands together in mock prayer.

'Yes,' I say.

'Afterwards, we can watch the video of the baby birds!' Rosa claps her hands together.

'Thanks, Hannah, you're a star.' Nadia turns around and then swivels back to face me. She speaks in a low whisper. 'Take care, Hannah. Real care.'

I shiver as she walks away.

At 5.30 p.m. I am just about to serve up shepherd's pie when I remember Kayleigh's food intolerance.

'Kayleigh, you can't eat gluten, can you?'

She shrugs. 'I think it's fine. Mum just says things sometimes.'

I am holding the serving spoon in mid-air. 'What happens when you eat bread? Do you get a tummy ache?'

'No.'

I find this very strange, recalling how Nadia said Kayleigh couldn't eat the cake I left them because it wasn't gluten-free. I try to think if there is any gluten in my home-made shepherd's pie, but I reckon it's safe. I ladle it up. Kayleigh eats with such gusto, it makes me wonder what Nadia feeds her.

There is a lot of light-hearted banter around the table, but then Joel accidentally spills his glass of water onto Kayleigh's plate of food.

'What the fuck!' she screeches.

My children turn and stare at her. I am dumbfounded.

'We don't use language like that in this household,' I say sharply, sounding like a prudish headmistress. I wonder if Kayleigh will burst into tears and flee back to her parents, but she doesn't. She holds my gaze, almost brazenly.

'Mum and Dad say fuck all the time.'

'That may be the case, but we don't swear in this family.'

'Okay,' she says in a sing-song voice, as if me rebuking her was perfectly normal. It certainly isn't ordinary for us. I am uneasy about reprimanding other people's children, but swearing like that leaves me no option.

'Would you like some more?' I ask as I pick up her plate and carry it to the sink. I pour the spilled water off the plate and rinse off the remaining morsels of soggy food.

'Yes, please,' she says eagerly.

'Mum, can you get the film of the baby birds? I want to show it to Kayleigh.'

'Yes, after tea,' I promise.

JOEL IS TUCKED up in bed, and the girls are in their night-clothes, huddled together on the sofa in the living room, watching the video we captured of the little house sparrows flying out of their nest, and the cheeky deer that came right up to the side of the house and nibbled the tops of the rose bushes, and the fox that managed to topple over the rubbish bin. I never get tired of watching the footage. Daniel bought the smallest top-of-the-range night-vision motion-activated camera about eighteen months ago, and it has brought us hours of pleasure. And then we are interrupted by what sounds like rapid gunfire. I jump up in terror and rush to the window. No one is standing outside holding an automatic rifle; instead there is a black Volkswagen Golf driving towards the house, its souped-up exhaust roaring and popping at a deafening level. The engine is switched off, and two couples climb out of the car, the men in shorts and T-shirts, one woman, with lurid orange skin, wearing leopard-print leggings, the other woman smartly dressed in a leather miniskirt and shimmering long-sleeved top. They are carrying cases of beer and boxes of wine. Nadia and Mike greet them noisily, with lots of shouts, arm flinging and back slapping. I pull away from the window.

'What's going on?' Rosa asks.

'Kayleigh's parents have some visitors.'

So that is why Nadia suggested a sleepover. They wanted to get their daughter out of the house for the night. Kayleigh seems totally disinterested. I recall my carefully worded terms and conditions that states that guests are not allowed to have parties, but six people doesn't constitute a party. With all that booze, I expect they'll be making lots of noise; on the other hand, I have no desire to rebuke our guests.

It isn't long before smoke starts billowing towards the house. It smells like charcoal and burning grease and suggests they're having a BBQ. I shut the windows to stop the reek from wafting inside. After saying goodnight to the girls and asking them not to talk for too long, I return to the living room and switch on the television. But I can't concentrate. The Joneses and their guests are making such a racket outside, with music turned up loud and the *boom, boom* of the base vibrating through the house. It's just as well we don't have any neighbours, as they would definitely be complaining.

After a while, I have a bath and get ready for bed. But still the music is pulsating and there are shrieks of laughter. I tiptoe to Rosa's room and put my ear against the door. I don't hear anything. It's a relief that the children are such heavy sleepers. Daniel calls me, as he does most nights he is away. When he first took the consultant's job, he used to call us every evening, early enough to wish the children goodnight, and often he and I would speak again later before bed. That's changed now. A few months ago, he explained that it's better if he calls us once his surgery is finished for the day. Me calling him was a distraction, apparently. The result is, these days, he rarely calls early enough to say goodnight to the kids. And our conversations are perfunctory.

'Everything all right at home?' he asks.

'Mike and Nadia have friends over, and they're making a racket.'

'You should try taking a kip in a hospital like I have to do, and you'll soon learn how to sleep through noise.'

I suppose it was foolish of me to expect any sympathy.

'How was your day?' I ask.

'Normal. Stressful. Intense.'

This is a typical response. I've tried questioning whether he should relinquish one of his jobs, whether he needs to travel so much, whether I can go back to work to bring in some more money. His replies are either cutting and sarcastic, or belittling. I've given up asking, and instead, I just offer platitudes.

'I hope you sleep well, anyway.'

He grunts. 'Goodnight. Send my love to the kids.'

And that is the end of the conversation. I lie down on the bed and close my eyes; the tears seep out anyway. Daniel and I need to sort things out, but I simply don't know how. If I suggest counselling, I know for sure he'll laugh in my face. I miss the old Daniel, the man who would hold me close at night and tell me what an amazing mother I was. The husband who was my cheerleader and not my chief critic. Living apart like this isn't sustainable, and I need Daniel to realise that too.

Eventually, I get ready for bed, read a book, and switch off my bedside light, but it's impossible to sleep. The noise is incessant and it's making me increasingly agitated. I try reading again, but then I'm clock-watching and thinking about how tired I'll be in the morning. By 1 a.m., I've had enough. I dig out Nadia's mobile number and call it. It goes straight to voicemail. I debate getting dressed and going over there to complain, but in the end, I decide against it. Eventually, I fall asleep.

7

W
e are having a late breakfast. Joel was the first one up, and at 9 a.m., I woke the girls. Perhaps they were kept awake by Mike and Nadia's raucous behaviour, but more likely they had been pretending to be asleep when I listened outside Rosa's door. No doubt, the creaking floorboards gave them advance warning of my approach. When I glance out of the window, I'm relieved that the Joneses' visitors' car has gone and all is quiet.

We are finishing eating toast when there is a hammering on the back door. I hurry through into the utility room. It is Nadia and she looks as if she's been dragged through a bush backwards. As soon as I open the door, it's obvious she's in a total panic. She's wearing a grey sweatshirt pulled over a pair of pyjamas. Her feet are wedged into old, mucky trainers, and her hair is all messed up, her face blotchy with mascara rubbed around her eyes. It looks like she forgot to remove her makeup last night.

'Where's the nearest hospital?' she asks breathlessly.

'What's happened?' My heart sinks.

'Mike went out for a smoke and tripped over a loose paving

stone on the patio. He's done something terrible to his leg.' She lets out a little cry, her hand rushing to cover her mouth.

I remind myself that I am calm in a crisis. This will be fine. I take a deep breath. 'Have you called for an ambulance?'

'Is there a hospital in Macclesfield?'

'Yes, there's a big hospital with an accident and emergency department.'

'Ok. It'll be faster for me to drive him to the hospital. Can you give me directions?'

'Of course.'

The children congregate at the door behind me.

'What's happened?' Rosa asks, her eyes wide.

'Kayleigh's dad has hurt himself. I'm sure it will be fine. You stay here and finish your breakfast.'

I race after Nadia, who runs around the house, down the steps and across the drive and around the side of the barn to the patio area. Mike is sitting on the ground, one leg stretched out in front of him. Wearing grey jogging bottoms and a white sweatshirt covered in stains, he is groaning and rocking his body backwards and forwards. There is a shine of sweat on his forehead, and he is so pale, I'm fearful he's going to pass out.

'I think it's broken,' he moans. 'It's fucking painful. Unbearable.'

'How far is it to the hospital?' Nadia asks.

'Ten to fifteen minutes in the car,' I say.

Nadia crouches down in front of her husband. 'Right. We'll get you to the hospital, Mikey. It'll be faster for me to take you than to wait for an ambulance.'

Fortunately, we've never had to call for an ambulance, but I fear that Nadia might be right.

'Hannah and me will help you get up. Put all your weight on us and keep that foot off the ground.'

Somehow or other, we heave Mike into a standing position, with me holding his left arm and Nadia standing behind him.

Very slowly, we help him hop to the car, his moans and groans becoming increasingly loud. Nadia opens the car door, and we support Mike as he edges in with his large bottom first. Then Nadia bends down to help him swing his feet inside. He yelps when she touches the ankle he thinks he's broken. Mike isn't the only one hurt. As Nadia stands up, I see that she has a livid bruise on her forearm, but when she sees me looking at it, she tugs her sweatshirt sleeve right down.

It's at times like this I wish I'd learned first aid, and I make a promise to myself that I will go on a course. Being married to a doctor has made me complacent. If only Daniel were at home right now, he would take control and probably drive them to the hospital himself. When Nadia shuts the car door, I glance behind me and see the children standing in a tight huddle at the bottom of the steps.

'I'll just grab some clothes and my bag,' Nadia says.

'What can I do?' I ask.

'Look after our Kayleigh so I can get Mike to the hospital.' She hurries over to her daughter and gives her a cursory kiss on the top of her head, whispering something into her ear.

'Right, kids, let's finish our breakfast,' I say, trying to herd them back up the steps.

'Is Kayleigh's daddy going to be all right?' Rosa asks, her eyes wide and her face pale.

'Yes. At worst he's broken a bone, and bones heal. Hopefully, it's just a sprain.'

'Will they chop his foot off?' Joel asks.

'No. Definitely not.'

'Do you think it hurts very, very much?' he asks.

'Probably, but Mike is being brave.'

'Like a soldier,' Joel says.

I nod. I hustle them back into the house.

It isn't until we've finished breakfast and I've sent the kids upstairs to brush their teeth that I realise what was so odd. My children seemed deeply concerned about Mike's injury. Kayleigh was bizarrely unworried. In fact, she's hardly said a word.

ONCE I HAVE CLEARED up the breakfast things, I nip over to the barn to look at the patio. The patio extends from the double doors of the living room to the edge of the lawn, a sizeable area, with enough space for the circular wooden table and chairs for four and two sun loungers, as well as a standard-size BBQ, which is up against the wall and was obviously put to good use last night. It is filthy. There are empty bottles and glasses on the table and an ashtray full of cigarette stubs. But it's the patio I need to examine.

The pale paving stones are all well grouted in, making the patio quite smooth, with the exception of one smaller stone that is obviously raised above the others. Gently, I put my foot on it, and it moves. I groan. How did this happen? The patio was only laid last year, and I certainly never noticed anything odd about it. But I have to admit, to myself at least, that other than making sure the garden furniture was clean and tidy, I didn't check the patio stones. Should I have done? Hand on heart, I can't be sure whether this stone was loose last week or not. Could they have done this whilst they were partying last night? And now what am I meant to do? Check each stone before every set of new guests arrive? I suspect that Mike was massively hung-over this morning, still drunk probably, based upon the amount of alcohol consumed, and simply wasn't looking where he was going. I glance through the glass patio doors to inside the barn, and it is in a terrible state. Their belongings strewn everywhere, dirty plates and glasses on the floor and on the table. I can't bear to look. My neat-freak husband, Daniel, would go apoplectic if he saw this.

· · ·

NADIA AND MIKE return early afternoon. Their car pulls up in front of the barn's door, and I hurry down to help them. Nadia is trying to get Mike out of the car.

'How are you?' I ask.

'I've got a broken bloody ankle thanks to your paving stone,' Mike snarls. Nadia leans into the back of the car and takes out a pair of crutches. Mike groans and pants as he levers himself out of the car and hobbles precariously as he attempts to walk using the crutches. His ankle and foot are in a cast.

'Can I help?' I ask, feeling rather futile.

'This is your fault.' Mike's upper lip curls as he speaks. 'They said I might need an operation and a titanium implant, all because of your paving stone.'

'I'm really sorry,' I say.

Nadia takes a Tesco carrier bag out of the back of the car. She is looking everywhere except at me.

'We're going to have to stay another week,' Mike says as he hauls himself up the step into the barn.

My heart sinks. This cannot be happening. 'I'm very sorry, but that won't be possible. I have other guests arriving on Saturday.'

Mike turns around and leans against the wall, the crutches dangling off his thick wrists.

'You can't chuck us out. It's your bloody fault we're stuck here. If you'd maintained your property properly, none of this would have happened. It's ruined our f-ing holiday, and if I've got to have an operation, it might ruin my whole bloody life. Just think about that. Me in pain for years to come because you didn't check your paving stones.' He turns his back on me, and I'm grateful that he appears to be making his way inside, but then he stops and swings around again. 'We're going to have to sue you for damages. Not right that I should have to suffer.' He moans and groans as he hobbles inside. Nadia squeezes past me, throwing me an embarrassed look.

'It'll be all right, Mike,' she says.

'Don't you fucking tell me it'll be all right, because it isn't. You don't know how painful it is, and I've got a really high pain threshold.'

'I know, love. Let's get you sitting down and prop your leg up as the doctor said.' There are more moans, and I wonder if I should make myself scarce. Just as I turn to walk away, Nadia calls out, 'Hannah!'

I turn and step back towards the door. She steps outside to face me and speaks in a low, quiet voice.

'Please let us stay, Hannah. It's impossible for us to go home. We've got a really steep staircase, and he'll never get up the steps in this state. The barn is perfect because it's all on one level.'

'I can't–'

Nadia interrupts me. She clutches at a pointed crystal that is attached to a leather cord around her neck. I don't recall seeing her wearing it earlier.

'The other thing is, the consultant we saw at Macclesfield hospital was great with Mikey. You've seen how my husband is; he's a grouchy old thing, especially when he's in pain, and that doctor really got the measure of him. Normally, Mike hates doctors, won't listen to them, thinks he knows best. But he listened to this man. And we need to go back in again next week for a follow-up consultation and a further X-ray. If we go home, we'd have to find a new doctor, and that would be a nightmare, too.'

Nadia wrings her hands in front of her, the numerous bracelets and bangles jingling. Her make-up-free face is creased with concern. It's evident that she's really worried about Mike, and I suppose I would be too, if I were in her position. 'I'm sure your other guests will understand,' she says. 'I can speak to them for you if you'd like?'

I bite my lower lip. I can see why Nadia and Mike want to

stay on, and I suppose it won't harm to at least ask my incoming guests if they wouldn't mind transferring their stay to another week. I seem to recall that they're an older couple, so perhaps they are more flexible than people who have to take time off work. It's a horrible situation.

'We'll give you the best ever reviews all over the internet,' Nadia says. 'Trust me, they'll be glowing.'

I swallow. I guess the implication is, if I say no, their reviews will be dreadful. I wonder where Mike's threat to sue us comes into all of this. I make a quick decision.

'Leave it with me,' I say.

BACK IN THE HOUSE, I dig out my guest file and find the phone number for Mr and Mrs Andrew Carter from Bristol. Mr Carter answers the phone. I explain the situation whilst he listens to me in silence. When I finish talking, he doesn't say anything, and I wonder if he's still on the line.

'Hello?' I say.

'I'm here. I'm thinking.' He pauses and I wait. It seems like the silence goes on for minutes, but I suppose it's only long seconds. 'In a nutshell, we have booked your property, and you have decided you don't want us to come. You are giving us the option of taking another week. The problem, Mrs Pieters, is that we are coming to the Peak District for my sister and brother-in-law's golden wedding anniversary. As you will appreciate, that is not an event that can be postponed to fit in with your plans. The way I see it is your only option is to find us alternative accommodation within a ten-mile radius of Macclesfield of a similar or better standard than your property. Needless to say, you will have to pay the difference.'

'I am so sorry about this, Mr Carter. Yes, of course I shall do that. Please leave it with me, and I will get back to you.'

I put the phone down, relieved that he was so rational and

unthreatening. Now all I need to do is find somewhere else they can stay for the week. I ring around everywhere. There isn't a single holiday cottage available next week; hardly surprising for this time of year. That means I need to find a hotel. By the time I have rung fifteen hotels, I am near to despair. All that is left on my list is a five-star hotel near Alderley Edge, with an eye-watering daily price.

'Yes, we have one double room remaining,' the receptionist tells me.

'Could you hold it for me for a few hours, please?'

'I'm sorry, but that won't be–'

I cut her off. 'Just for one hour, please. Or at least give me first refusal. If someone else wants it, give me a call. I would be extremely grateful.'

Eventually she agrees, so I leave my name and phone number. I pace the kitchen for a while, trying to consider if there's any other option available to me. I even debate offering for the Carters to stay with us in our house, free of charge, but I know that Daniel would go apoplectic at the idea. Either I chuck the Joneses out and accept the terrible reviews they'll leave, or I agree to let them remain in the barn and pay for the Carters to stay in the expensive hotel. I call a couple of the other cheaper hotels in the area and ask them to put my name on their cancellation lists; then I call the expensive one.

'I'll take the double room for the week, please.'

I give her my credit card details, and when I put the phone down, I want to weep. I have just wiped out all my potential profits for the next few months. Have I done the right thing? Should I tell Mike and Nadia that they have to go, but then will they sue us for damages, as Mike unsubtly suggested? For a moment, I wonder if his ankle is really broken, but then I wipe aside my cynical thoughts. It was evident he was in pain, and he has a cast on his leg. I groan. I consider discussing it with Daniel. He knows all about negligence and every year moans about his huge insurance premiums to protect him from being sued for medical negligence. But I can just imagine his reaction, and I don't want to be made to feel any worse than I already do. I lay my head down on the table. When Daniel sees the bill for the five-star hotel on our joint credit card statement, he is going to go apoplectic. I wonder how I can hide it from him.

8

It seems that everyone is happy except me. Mr Carter was lost for words when I told him I had booked him and his wife into one of the best hotels in Cheshire. I sent Nadia a text message telling her that they could remain in the barn for a few more days, and received a message back crammed with emojis. Daniel rang at 9 p.m. He sounded exhausted, so I didn't tell him about Mike's accident. Unsurprisingly, I didn't sleep well.

And now it's late morning, and once again, Nadia appears on my doorstep. She thrusts a bunch of carnations and gypsophila wrapped with cellophane into my hands. I recognise the pale yellow and white bouquet; they're sold on the garage forecourt of the local petrol station for £3.99.

'Just to say thank you for letting us stay on.'

I accept the flowers and force a smile so as not to appear churlish. 'How is Mike today?' I ask.

'He's feeling very sorry for himself and expects me and Kayleigh to wait on him hand and foot. Mike's never a good patient.' She laughs, as if we're sharing an inside joke. 'But it's a relief not to be going home and navigating our staircase. Here, have a look at our house.' She takes her mobile phone out of her pocket and clicks on her photos. She turns the device around so I can look at the screen.

'That's our house in Sussex.' The photograph shows a quaint country cottage constructed from pale bricks with a slate tiled roof and beautifully tended flower beds either side of a garden path. 'It's small but pretty,' she says.

As I'm staring at the house, I realise what is odd. This style of property is found in Oxfordshire, not Sussex. I should know, because my paternal grandparents lived just outside Oxford, and when I was a kid, we used to have family holidays in Sussex.

'How long have you lived there?' I ask.

'Not long. We were in Northumberland for five years before that.'

I am confused. I remember distinctly how Kayleigh told Rosa that they lived in Wales – a foreign country, as she described it. But perhaps Kayleigh was wrong. I can't see any reason for Nadia to lie about where they used to live.

She quickly flicks through to the next photograph. 'And this is my horse.' A fine-looking dark-brown horse with a neatly brushed mane stands underneath a tree in a field. She puts the phone back into her trouser pocket. 'You could have horses in the field next to the barn.'

'I don't think so,' I say.

'Shame. When will your cleaner be coming into the barn?'

It's a bit of a non-sequitur, and I have to think. In the panic of the past twenty-four hours, I have forgotten that they will need clean sheets and towels, now they're staying a further week. My terms and conditions say that guests staying longer than a week are entitled to have the premises cleaned once a week. Having said that, no mention has been made of payment. I think I'll need to let the dust settle for a couple of days before bringing it up.

'I'll do the cleaning myself,' I say. 'When would it be convenient for me to come over?'

'Oh goodness, we don't expect you to clean. If you could just give me some fresh linen, I'll strip and make up the beds and do a quick tidy up.' Nadia steps closer to me, so close that I feel her breath on my cheek, and the scent of her almost pungent perfume is overwhelming. I am uncomfortable and want to step backwards. She lowers her voice to a whisper. 'The spirits were talking to me earlier. I know that I warned you about what the cards said, but I'd love to do a free Ouija board session with you so we can get further clarity. I can tell you're a good person, Hannah, and knowledge is power, don't you think? The spirits will speak through the board, and we can find out exactly what it is that you need to be aware of.'

I take two steps backwards. Nadia is so earnest, and all I want to do is giggle nervously and run away. 'Thank you,' I say hurriedly. 'I don't want to offend you, but I'm not really into the occult.'

'Oh goodness! This isn't the occult. The spirits are all around us. Some lucky people like me are able to hear them or see them. I feel very blessed to have that gift. You've no reason to worry; I don't allow evil spirits to come through. It is my job to protect my clients.' Her blonde bob shimmers as she tilts her head to the side, a look of concerned pity on her face.

I try to smile. 'Perhaps another time,' I say hurriedly. 'I've left something on the stove, so I must hurry. I'll drop the linen off later.'

Nadia's shoulders slump and the corners of her lips turn down. It's obvious I've upset her by not taking her up on her offer, but it's the last thing I need – some phony, ridiculous scaremongering. She waits for a moment, and as I step back inside and make to close the door, she eventually turns and leaves. I have never felt so relieved to close the door on someone.

. . .

DANIEL RETURNS home at 6 p.m., and after the children have thrown themselves at him, it's my turn. I squeeze him tightly.

'I'm dirty, Hannah. I've been on the train.' He places a quick kiss on my forehead and pulls away from me. 'Can you make me a gin and tonic?'

'Okay,' I say through gritted teeth, thinking, *Why the hell can't you make it yourself?* I then chastise myself; he's been working all week away from home; he's tired. Of course I can make him a drink.

I tell Alexa to play a coffee house jazz selection, and twenty minutes later, I have laid the table and am busily chopping up vegetables. Daniel saunters into the kitchen, his hair up on end from being towel-dried. He looks handsome in a button-down pale blue shirt and chinos. I pop out a few ice cubes from the mould in the freezer and hand him his gin and tonic. He sits down at the kitchen table in his normal place, stretching his legs out in front of him.

'What's been happening?' he asks, doing little to stifle a yawn.

I know I need to tell him about Mike's accident, but I'm worried about his reaction. I throw him a tight smile. 'We've had a bit of a nightmare with the barn guests. Mike tripped over a loose paving stone on the patio and has broken his ankle. They've asked to stay on another week.'

Daniel sits up straight. 'Shit, Hannah. Have you notified the insurers?'

'Um, no. Should I have done?'

'Is he saying it's our fault?'

'He said there was a loose paving stone.'

'And was there?'

'Yes.'

Now I feel angry with myself. Why didn't I think about

calling our insurance company? I'm on the back foot with the Joneses and my husband.

Daniel jumps up and starts pacing the kitchen. 'For God's sake, Hannah. Do you realise what this means? They could hold us liable for his injuries.'

'I'm sure it'll be fine. Mike seemed a bit grouchy, but Nadia has been really nice. She creeps me out a bit though. She wanted to give me a Ouija board reading.'

Daniel rolls his eyes. 'I hope you said no.' He picks up his gin and tonic and takes a large swig.

'Of course I did.'

'What a load of nonsense. I suppose I'd better have a word with Mike. Make sure that he's not thinking about suing us; smooth things over.'

'I think it's all ok,' I say, gritting my teeth. Why does Daniel have to interfere? The holiday cottage is my domain.

He swigs back his remaining G & T. 'What time will supper be ready?'

'7.30 p.m., as normal.'

'Right. I'll go and have a word with them now.'

'Daniel!' I call after him, but he is already out of the door.

DANIEL SAUNTERS BACK into the house on the dot of 7.30 p.m.

'You were with them for ages. What were you talking about?' I ask.

'This and that.'

'You don't think they're weird?'

'Mike's a tad rough, and Nadia is a bit hippyish for my taste, but there's nothing wrong with them. No mention of suing us, thank goodness. I asked about his ankle, and he said he's on painkillers and that he's returning to the hospital for a follow-up consultation next week. I suspect it's not as bad an injury as he made out to you.'

I turn the gas down on the hob. 'I'm just concerned that they're going to leave a lousy review.'

'And I think you're taking this all much too seriously. Renting out the barn is a hobby business, Hannah. It's not like we need the money. But you need to be damned careful that no one tries to sue us.'

I am bristling. I don't want to argue with Daniel, but I have to speak my mind.

'It might be a hobby business to you, but it's important to me. You've got your career; I had to give mine up.'

'Had to? Come on, Hannah. You were a music teacher. What's more important? Being a mother to our children or teaching stranger's children how to sing "Baa, Baa, Black Sheep" or teach a bunch of talentless kids how to thump the piano?'

I turn my back to Daniel and grip the smooth edge of the granite work surface. He does this from time to time, puts me down, belittles me. I don't think he means to be so hurtful, but it cuts me every time. I may not be saving lives as he does, but I loved my job, and I hope that one day I will be able to go back to it.

He hasn't always been like this, putting me down. I remember how proud he was of me, introducing me as his breath of fresh air, someone who has a vocation 'like me', he used to say. He would text me his music requests, broad-ranging from classical to the latest chart hits, and I played them for him when he got home, or I recorded and sent them to him. The changes have been gradual, since he got the new consultant cardiothoracic surgeon position and spends more time away from home.

I hear his footsteps as he walks over to me. He puts his arm around my shoulders and squeezes me. 'I don't mean to upset you, love. It's been a long week. Let's eat and have a nice chat.'

He lets go and walks over to his wine fridge, where he selects a bottle of white wine and uncorks it.

I sigh as I take the plates out of the heated drawer and ladle up buttery new potatoes, pieces of salmon and a medley of vegetables. When Rosa and Joel come and join us at the table, they are a welcome distraction.

AFTER SUPPER, Daniel retires to his study, as he does most Friday evenings after work. He pays bills, deals with anything related to the house and letters that have arrived here at home during his absence. I am drying up the dishes when he comes storming into the kitchen.

'What's this?' he asks, waving a piece of paper in front of my face.

'What?'

'This, Hannah, is our credit card statement.'

I curse under my breath. The statement hasn't arrived in the post yet; I've been keeping an eye out for it and was going to hide it. He must have gone online and checked our spending. He's never questioned anything before, and I didn't realise he studied it mid-month.

'You've bought bedding from John Lewis, and there's a pending hotel bill at the most extortionate rate. What the hell is it for?' Daniel stares at me.

I swivel around and glare at him. 'I had no choice. I had to buy the bedding for Mike. He didn't like the down pillows.'

'One always has a choice in life. Can you explain why you spent a bloody fortune on putting the highest quality furnishings in there only a couple of months ago!' He takes a step towards me, standing so close it's threatening.

'It seems that our current guests don't like quality things. And the hotel bill is for the guests who should have been staying in the barn this coming week. I had to bump them so that Nadia and Mike could stay on.'

Daniel sighs, takes a step backwards, and runs his fingers through his hair. 'Running a holiday cottage isn't a charity, Hannah! It's a bloody business, and it looks like you're screwing it up before you've even got going. What the hell were you thinking, spending so much money?'

My heart is battering inside my chest. I feel as if I'm going to erupt with fury that Daniel doesn't understand. I speak through gritted teeth. 'You've only just told me that we need to be careful that Mike doesn't sue us. That's why I had to spend the money, to make sure that I don't upset them.'

He shakes his head. 'They saw you coming, didn't they? You've been totally screwed over by them and the other guests. I've let you set up a holiday cottage, but there is no way that we will be continuing with it if it's going to cost us so much. It doesn't make any financial sense.'

'I'll pay for it out of my own money,' I say.

'What, the thirty quid an hour you make from teaching the piano? You'll be at if for the next ten years.'

I blink rapidly to stop the tears of frustration spilling onto my cheeks. My immediate reaction is to articulate my frustration, but I know that Daniel won't respond well to that. I need to apply quiet reason. 'I know it hasn't worked out the way I'd hoped, but I want this business to work, Daniel. It means a lot to me. Besides, all businesses run at a loss for the first year or so.'

'It may mean a lot to you, but not throwing good money after bad means more to me. It's my money that you're chucking away. And I want to be sure that my wife is caring properly for our children, not being distracted by bloody guests.'

At that, I throw the tea towel onto the kitchen counter. I turn to Daniel, my eyes narrowed, my arms crossed over my chest. There has been that unspoken undercurrent for years that he is the principal breadwinner, but he has never blatantly chucked the fact in my face before. It's one of the many reasons I wanted to carry on working. I don't like being financially dependent on anyone, even my husband.

'Are you saying that I'm a bad mother? Because how the hell would you know? You're never here. It's as if your patients are more important than your own children.'

'You know that's not the case.'

'Mummy!'

Daniel and I turn towards the doorway. Rosa is standing there in her nightdress, her eyes wide and her bottom lip quivering. I rush towards her and scoop her into my arms. How long has she been standing there? What did she hear?

'Mummy and Daddy were just having a silly argument,' I say, stroking her hair.

'Are you going to get divorced?' she asks.

'Mummy loves Daddy and Daddy loves Mummy, but sometimes we disagree about things.' I look up to catch Daniel's eye, but he has his back to me and is staring out of the window.

9

Joel jumps onto our bed at 7.30 a.m. Daniel tickles him until Joel is breathless, and then they have a raucous pillow fight. I leave them to it, get dressed and pad downstairs. I think about last night, how Daniel apologised for shouting at me, and how, for the first time in weeks, he made love to me. It was perfunctory, but at least he made an effort.

Even so, I feel a disconnect. He's resentful about the holiday cottage, and it makes me feel guilty that it's costing us rather than generating money. But then again, we promised each other that we would share everything, and it was Daniel who insisted I give up work. It's not as if we have any immediate money worries. I have access to our joint online banking, and the balances are more than healthy.

I rustle up a cooked breakfast of pancakes, maple syrup and blueberries. As we sit around the table, I look at my husband and two children and remind myself that I am blessed. We are all healthy, we have no real worries; life is good.

'I'm going on a bike ride this morning,' Daniel says, looking at me over the rim of his coffee cup.

'Can I come?' Joel asks.

'No. You'll have to wait until your legs have grown a bit longer. I'm going over the hills.'

Joel blows a raspberry. I would normally tell him off, but this morning I simply want an easy life.

'Hey, monster. Do you want me to tickle you again?' Daniel threatens. It's such a relief that he is in a good mood. Joel jumps down from his chair and tries to tickle Daniel. Rosa joins in, but I know they won't be successful. Unlike me, Daniel isn't ticklish.

'How about we all go for a walk this afternoon? Peanut will be happy,' Daniel suggests as the children give up trying to attack him. He gets up from the table, picks up his plate, rinses it under the tap, and places it in the dishwasher. Then he takes a kitchen wipe and a bottle of spray detergent from the cupboard under the sink and sprays the kitchen table. I've learned not to say anything. Daniel is a clean freak. Most of my girlfriends complain that their partners do nothing around the house, so I don't complain. I am grateful. Really, I am.

'MUMMY! LOOK OUTSIDE!' Rosa grabs my hand and pulls me to the window. Before I can say a word, she has darted off, and I see her running down the steps towards Kayleigh and Nadia, who are standing outside the barn. Kayleigh is gripping a narrow red lead. At her feet is a tiny, fluffy, adorable puppy.

I watch as Kayleigh and Rosa bend down and start playing with the little ball of fluff. And then Nadia says something, and she picks up the puppy. The three of them walk towards the barn and disappear inside.

'No!' I speak out loud. They cannot have a puppy inside the barn. It is immaculate inside there – or at least it was – and my terms and conditions are very clear: no pets without written permission. The puppy may be cute, but I have to stop this.

'Joel!' I say. 'Can you come with me, now. We need to go to the barn. Kayleigh has got a puppy.' He dumps his tractor and trots alongside me as I walk quickly to the barn's door. I rap on it.

Kayleigh appears with Rosa by her side. Kayleigh is cradling the puppy. It has a mottled white and brown shaggy coat and the sweetest coal-black eyes.

'Mum and Dad have bought me a puppy! She's called Snoopy and she's all mine!' Kayleigh has the widest smile on her face, and she's hopping from one foot to the other in excitement.

'That's lovely, Kayleigh, but can you get your mummy for me. I need to have a word.'

Nadia must be standing just behind the door because she appears immediately. 'Hannah, how are you this morning?' Her voice is saccharine. Kayleigh and Rosa edge past me, with Joel following behind them. They disappear around the side of the barn.

'I see you've got a puppy.'

'Yes.' She tilts her head to one side.

'Unfortunately, we don't allow pets in the barn. Would you mind playing with the dog outside, please.'

Nadia frowns. 'We can't keep Snoopy outside all the time. She needs to sleep.' Nadia puts her hands on her hips.

'Is she staying with you permanently?' My heart sinks. I suppose I was hoping that they were borrowing the dog for the day.

'Of course. A dog is for life, not for Christmas! Or in this case, an early birthday present for our daughter.'

'I'm thrilled for you, but I'm afraid it's strictly against our rules. Perhaps the dog could stay with a friend whilst you're staying here?'

'Oh, come on, Hannah. It's like saying we need to take a

newborn baby back to the hospital. You can't possibly deny us the joy of our new arrival.'

'I'm afraid it contravenes my insurance policy.' I have no idea if it does, but I do not want an untrained, chewing puppy in my perfect property. I love dogs, but there is a time and a place. I hear heavy shuffling footsteps, and the door opens behind Nadia. Mike is standing there leaning heavily on his crutches.

'What's going on?' he asks.

'Hannah says we can't have Snoopy in the barn. It's against some rules apparently.'

'You can shove your rules where the sun doesn't shine. We're stuck in this bloody place because *you* didn't maintain your property properly. This is all your fault, so you don't get to tell us what we can and can't do. All right?'

I take a step backwards as Mike's spittle flies through the air and lands next to my shoe.

'Don't get worked up, love,' Nadia says, putting her hand on Mike's. 'It's not good for your blood pressure.'

'She's not bloody well—'

Nadia interrupts him. 'The thing is, Hannah, we promised our Kayleigh that we would go to Alton Towers, but because of Mike's leg we had to cancel, so we're just trying to do something nice for her. We said we'd get her a puppy for her birthday, but as she's having a tough time right now, we've brought that forwards. Kayleigh doesn't make friends easily, but look how well she and Rosa are getting along. They're besties. It's going to break Kayleigh's heart when we leave here to go home and she won't be around Rosa anymore, so we thought that Snoopy would be perfect for her. I'm sure you wouldn't want to upset Kayleigh, would you?'

'I don't want to upset anyone, it's just—'

I hear a screech of bicycle brakes, and Daniel comes to a halt right next to me. Dressed in his Lycra, he looks fit and younger than his years, a contrast to Mike, who is overweight and unshaven, yet probably Daniel's junior by a decade.

'Hello, everyone. What's up?'

'Your wife is telling us that we can't have our new puppy in the barn. Bloody outrageous!' Mike puffs out his chest.

Daniel puts an arm around me. 'I'm afraid she's right. We have a no-pets policy in the holiday cottage.'

'So what are we meant to do? Send the dog back? Put her out on the street?' Mike is growing increasingly red in the face.

'I'm sure you can see it from our perspective,' Daniel says. 'We need to keep the property in top-notch condition, and a puppy is inevitably going to cause damage.'

I am pleased that my husband is staying calm and reasonable and backing me up.

'Who said anything about damage?' Mike leans his shoulder against the wall and starts waving one of his crutches in the air. 'We'll bloody do what we like so long as we're staying here. If you'd maintained this place properly, I wouldn't be in agony, and we'd be gone home. Instead, we're stuck here. You're damned lucky I haven't instructed my solicitor yet. Is that what you want?'

Daniel steps off his bike, leans it against the stone wall of the barn, and takes a step forward. 'I don't appreciate threats,' he says in a low, controlled voice. 'We are doing everything we can to accommodate you, but it is unreasonable to bring a puppy into the barn without checking it with us first.'

'Who said we didn't check with you first? Did your pathetic little wife forget to tell you?'

Daniel inhales deeply and takes another step forward so he is just inches from Mike. A nerve pulses in his jawline. Mike has gone too far, and I can tell that Daniel is about to explode. He doesn't lose his cool often, but when he does, he goes from calm to fury in an instant. I should be pleased that he's standing up for me, but when Daniel gets angry, it can be terrifying. I grasp his wrist and pull him backwards.

'Don't rise to it,' I say in an urgent whisper. Daniel's breathing is fast and his face has paled. I need to get him out of here, now. Fortunately, it's Nadia who comes to the rescue. She holds both hands up in the air in a gesture of pacification.

'I'm sorry if we've caused any upset. It's not what we intended. All we wanted to do was give our daughter a present, but I totally understand that you're worried about the damage Snoopy might cause. How about we promise to pay any damages? I think that's only fair. And she'll sleep in a cage, and we'll keep an eye on her all the time.'

'Thank you, Nadia. I'm sure that will be fine. Come on, Daniel, we need to get lunch sorted.' I turn and edge Daniel backwards. He grabs his bike and wheels it back towards the house, but I can see the tension, the way that his muscles tighten his jawline and the hunching of his shoulders.

When he comes into the kitchen, I am not sure what to expect, but he turns towards me with an apologetic look.

'You're right and I'm wrong. That Mike is a total jerk.'

I let out a loud sigh, relieved that at last Daniel shares my view.

ON THE SUNDAYS that I'm not cooking a roast for my parents, we tend to go out for lunch at the Three Skeins, a country inn with a fabulous carvery. Set high on a hill in the Peak District between Macclesfield and Buxton, the pub has spectacular views across a verdant valley. It is always packed, especially on a Sunday, as they offer the best roasts in the area. When we pull into the car park, I recognise a few of the cars belonging to neighbours and families that attend the same school as my two.

Joel tugs excitedly on my hand as we walk in through the front door. Daniel has to duck to stop himself from knocking his head on an ancient wooden beam. Only Rosa is subdued because she asked if Kayleigh could join us, and Daniel replied with a swift and resounding no. One of the young waitresses takes us to our table. We are seated next to Jamie and Rachel Mole and their three kids. Jamie manages the family farm, which includes all the fields around our house. Immediately Rosa perks up, chatting noisily with Olivia, who is in her class.

'How are things going with your holiday cottage?' Jamie asks.

'Fine,' I say breezily.

Daniel frowns at me and then turns to Jamie. 'I wouldn't describe our current guests as fine!' he says, laughing. 'Not exactly the sort of people you'd readily invite into your home.'

'Daniel!' I say in a reproaching tone.

'Come on, Hannah! Jamie and Rachel are hardly going to say anything to them, are you?'

'That's not the point,' I say hurriedly. I can't believe Daniel has said that.

Rachel throws me a quizzical glance. She is one of those uber-efficient women who manages to juggle businesses, children, in-laws and charity commitments and still produce a home-baked cake every afternoon and ensure that her children always win fancy dress competitions wearing her elaborate home-sewn costumes. She sits on the local parish council and is a governor of the children's school. I've always felt she looks down on me, the newcomer townie who will never quite fit in. But she's only ever been polite, so perhaps I'm drawing unfair conclusions.

'It must be hard for you, Hannah, having Daniel away so much. We all think you're very brave running a holiday cottage alone,' Rachel says.

'I'm hardly alone,' I say.

'You know you can call us any time, night or day. We're used to getting up in the middle of the night to deal with birthing animals, so don't hesitate.'

'Thanks, Rachel,' I say, but then our waitress arrives with drinks, and the Mole family turn around and finish eating their roasts.

'I can't believe you said that about the Joneses, but to be truthful, I am uneasy about Mike,' I say to Daniel in a low voice. 'He's gone off the deep end with me and now with you. Any chance you could cancel your three nights away this week?'

'Sorry, Hannah, out of the question. You don't need to worry about Mike. He's not going to do anything to you. He's just angry with himself because he hurt his leg. And with a broken ankle, I doubt he's going to come running after you!'

'I suppose you're right.' But I don't feel comfortable having Nadia and Mike in the barn. I find Mike rude and uncouth, and Nadia is just a little strange.

When we're tucking into our roast beef, Daniel gets a slap on the back from Elliott, another of the dads from school.

'How are you doing, mate? Haven't seen much of you recently.' Elliott places a hand on Daniel's shoulder and squeezes. There is black grease underneath his fingernails. 'How are things with the Pieters family?' He grins at me in a leering manner.

Daniel swallows a mouthful hurriedly. 'Good. How are you?'

'Hunky-dory with me. Word on the street is you're doing well with your new holiday cottage.'

I suppose I shouldn't be surprised that it's the talk of the town. After all, the local newspaper ran an article about me and the business.

'Let me know if you need any help.' Elliott gives Daniel's shoulder another squeeze, using his left hand, the hand with the missing little finger. He then strides away.

'Creep,' I murmur under my breath.

Elliott is a mechanic and part of a group of local men who meet in the pub for a beer every Thursday evening, not that Daniel has attended in months. Elliott has split up from his wife, and he has custody of their son every Wednesday night and every other weekend. Sakura is Japanese, and the unlikely gossip around school was that Elliott joined the Yakuza – that is, the Japanese mafia – to impress her. When Elliott did something the Yakuza didn't approve of, the story then goes, they forced him to chop off his own little finger.

I expect that the truth of the matter is much more prosaic. He probably lopped it off by mistake when he was working under the bonnet of a car.

He walks with a swagger and is always jovial and overly tactile, standing too close to people. It's obvious that he thinks his classic good looks entitle him to any woman he wants. He tried it on with me when I first took Rosa to school, offering to fix my car at a special rate any time I wanted. I smiled tightly and strode away. I've never understood why Daniel is friendly with him.

'It's nice how everyone is offering to help,' Daniel says.

'Yes, but I'm still worried. If Mike and Nadia give me a bad review–'

'For heaven's sake, Hannah. Stop worrying about reviews. It really isn't important, is it? The way you're acting, it's like the income from the holiday cottage will make or break us.'

'It's not about the money, Daniel, it's about the fact I want this to be a success.'

'Of course you do, but you need to keep it in perspective. If it continues to cause us problems and costs more than you're making, it's not a sustainable project.'

'I know that, which is why I'm trying so hard to make it successful.'

And then I notice Rosa. Her eyes are watery, and she's clutching something in her right hand.

'What's up, darling?' I ask quietly. The waitress is putting our drinks on the table.

'Nothing.' Rosa doesn't meet my eyes.

'You don't look very happy.'

'Not,' she says, turning her head away from me. Her fingers are rubbing whatever it is she has in her palm.

'What are you holding?'

'Kayleigh's mum gave it to her,' Joel pipes up.

'Shut up!' Rosa says.

'Rosa,' I say, choosing to ignore her rudeness towards her brother. I rub her arm. 'What is it that Nadia gave you?'

Rosa speaks in a whisper. 'She said something bad is going to happen.' She opens her fingers to reveal a cheap plastic charm in the shape of an evil eye.

Daniel surprises me by laughing. I thought he might be angry. 'Rosa, do you really think that this little bit of plastic trash is going to change what's going to happen?'

Rosa shrugs.

In his typically rational way, he explains to Rosa how people have used their belief in religion and spirituality as a crutch to make sense of the world. Rosa listens and asks some surprisingly mature questions, but I don't think she truly buys Daniel's simplistic explanation.

'What do you think, Mum?' Rosa asks, her evil eye now lying on the table next to her glass of water.

'I think that people can believe in whatever they like. If it brings someone comfort to believe in God or spirits, then that's fine. But I don't believe in Nadia's supposed powers of predicting the future, and I think she's just trying to scare you by saying something bad will happen.'

'But why would she do that?' Rosa asks, her eyes wide.

'I really don't know, darling.'

10

It's Monday morning and I am putting a load of washing in the machine when Nadia appears at the door. Kayleigh is standing next to her, the puppy in her arms.

'I need to take Mike to the hospital for another X-ray. Can you look after Kayleigh and Snoopy today?'

Kayleigh looks at me with big pleading eyes. Nadia glances at her watch and shifts from foot to foot. The woman has me cornered yet again. I can hardly say no, yet the fact she doesn't even say *please* makes me want to slam the door in her face.

'Come in, Kayleigh,' I say, standing back to let the little girl inside. 'Don't put Snoopy down yet, as we'll need to shut some doors so she doesn't go into the rooms with carpet.'

'See you, Kales!' Nadia says. 'Thanks, Hannah.'

And then she's gone.

I DON'T MIND HAVING Kayleigh over, even with her impressive vocabulary of swear words, but I am annoyed that I'm being used as a babysitter. As Nadia is clearly a negative influence on Rosa, feeding an irrational fear, it's certainly preferable having

Kayleigh here rather than Rosa in the barn. The other advantage is, when the children have friends over, they entertain each other. With the puppy around, the three kids are fully engrossed for hours. It's only Peanut who seems less than impressed.

I'm in the kitchen preparing lunch when the girls screech. There's a thud. I turn around and see Kayleigh on her bottom on the kitchen floor. The children are convulsed with laughter.

'What's happened?' I say, rushing over to help Kayleigh up.

'Kayleigh slipped in Snoopy's pee!' Joel is jumping up and down, his eyes watery with laughter. 'It's gross!'

'That's why you have to take puppies outside regularly. This little thing isn't house-trained yet.' I hate to think what damage the dog has done in the barn. 'Rosa, take Kayleigh upstairs to get changed, and have a shower if you need one.'

'Can I get my clothes out of the barn?' Kayleigh asks. 'I'm bigger than Rosa.'

'Yes, of course. How wet are you?' I inspect her and she's barely wet. I grab some detergent and paper towels and wipe up the dog's mess.

'Right, let's go and get your things.' I select the spare key for the barn from the pegs of keys behind the door in the utility room, and Kayleigh and I walk over to the barn. I'm quite pleased that I have a legitimate reason for going inside, as I'll get the chance to see what state Mike and Nadia have left it in. I put the key into the lock, but it doesn't turn. I take it out and try again. Nothing happens. I bend down to peer into the lock, but I can't see anything jamming the keyhole. I try for the third time.

'That's weird,' I mutter more to myself than to Kayleigh. 'Did your mum say anything about a problem with the lock?'

Kayleigh shakes her head. I walk along the outside of the long barn and peer in a window. Most of the curtains have been pulled, but there is a slither of a gap in one of the living room windows. The place is a tip; even worse than when I last looked. Clothes are draped over the sofas, dirty glasses left on the coffee table, and empty pizza boxes on the floor. I turn away. It's not fair to take out my annoyance on Kayleigh, so I take a couple of deep breaths.

'Perhaps my spare key isn't working properly. You'll have to borrow some clothes from Rosa or me until your parents get back.'

I can't recall whether I've used the spare key before, so perhaps it wasn't cut as an identical replica of the original. Frustrated, I stride back to the house.

IN THE AFTERNOON, I give a piano lesson, and then it's teatime, yet Mike and Nadia still haven't appeared. I try calling Nadia's phone, but it goes straight to voicemail. I'm worried now. I've got no suitable food for the puppy.

'Did your mum say how long they expected to be?' I ask Kayleigh. She shrugs. I'm surprised how little she cares as to where her parents might be. If it were Rosa, I know without a shadow of doubt she would be calling me to double-check when I was coming to get her.

At 6 p.m. I call Amber. I take the phone into our bedroom so I'm as far away from little eavesdroppers as possible.

'The weirdos in the barn have dumped their daughter and a puppy on me. They've been gone since first thing this morning, and their phone is switched off.'

'Do you think something bad has happened to them?' Amber asks. I can hear running water in the background.

'I don't know. It's crossed my mind that they've done a runner.'

'What? Leaving their child with a semi-stranger? If you really think that, you need to call the police.'

'Probably too premature for that. It's just they're so

presumptuous and horrible. And Daniel doesn't care. He calls the holiday let my hobby business.'

'Oh, hun, that's miserable. I'm sure he'll come around when he knows what a success you're making of it.' I don't tell Amber how much the barn is costing us. 'I'd give it another couple of hours if I were you.'

'I suppose I should ring the hospital. Perhaps they had to take Mike in for an operation.'

'Let me know if you need any help. I can always pop over.'

'Can we chat properly when we meet tomorrow? I'm about to give Billy his bath.'

'Of course. I'm here any time.'

'And call me later if your guests don't show up.'

Just before 7 p.m. I get a text message from Nadia. 'Sorry we haven't been in touch. We got sent to a hospital in Manchester for an MRI and have had to wait for hours with no phones allowed. Hope Kayleigh and Snoopy are ok. Can you hang onto them both? Not sure what time we'll be home.'

I take a deep breath and reply with a single word: 'Ok.'

Kayleigh and Rosa are delighted that Kayleigh is to stay with us until her parents return. I suggest that they both get ready for bed, and if her parents aren't back by 9 p.m., then she will stay the night. I boil up some rice, take some mince from the deep freeze, and fry up a little. I feed it to Snoopy and hope that it won't do her any harm.

WHEN THE CHILDREN are tucked up in bed, I decide to try the key in the lock of the barn again. It doesn't make sense to me that the key doesn't work. Perhaps I need to pull the door towards me or push it back slightly. It's nearly dark now, and the shadows are long. The outside light flickers on as I walk up to the barn's front door. I ease the key into the lock and pull the handle towards me, then away from me, but still the door doesn't open. And then I see headlights jumping up and down as a car eases its way down the hill. I pull the key from the lock and hurry back into the house.

Standing in my piano room with the lights off, I watch as Mike and Nadia get out of their car. Nadia supports Mike as he hobbles to the barn. She puts her bag on the ground and rummages inside it, eventually bringing out what I assume is the key. The door opens immediately. I'm relieved there's nothing wrong with the lock and assume my spare key must be a dud. I wait for Nadia to come back out, expecting her to come over to collect the puppy, but she doesn't appear.

Eventually I go into the living room and turn on the television with the sound down low so I will hear her when she knocks on the door. I wait and I wait. At 10 p.m., I decide to take the dog back to them. I lift up the sleeping puppy and, with a torch in one hand and clutching the puppy to my chest with the other hand, walk over to the barn. The curtains are pulled, but there are still lights on inside. I knock on the door. There is no answer. I knock again. I debate whether to rap on the window, but perhaps they are in the bedroom or the bathroom. Sighing, I give up and turn back to our house. I try calling Nadia's mobile, but as before, it goes straight to voicemail.

Resigned to having to clear up a mess in the morning, I find a couple of towels and fashion Snoopy a little bed, shutting her inside the utility room. She gives out a few yelps and then falls silent. When I glance in five minutes later, the puppy is fast asleep.

I am astounded that Nadia is so disinterested in her daughter and puppy that she hasn't bothered to come and collect them.

I cannot wait for them to leave.

11

I try not to be judgemental, but I find it very difficult not to put myself in someone else's shoes, and I simply can't fathom how a mother could leave her young daughter and new puppy with strangers and not even call to ask how they are. The more I think about it, the more appalled I am.

When the girls have got dressed and finished their breakfast, I walk over to the barn with Kayleigh, who has Snoopy in her arms. It's gone 9 a.m., but the curtains are still pulled. I'm glad; it gives me the chance to try my key in the lock for the third time. Just as I'm easing it in, the door swings open, and Nadia is standing there dressed in a grey tracksuit and bare feet. Her hair is tied back, exposing a wide forehead, and her face is make-up-free. Her eyes look puffy, and I wonder if she's been crying.

'My babies!' she says, flinging her arms around Kayleigh and kissing her repeatedly on the top of her head. 'Did you have a good day? Did you sleep well?'

'Yes. Snoopy pooed all over the floor.'

'Oh dear. That's what puppies do.'

Nadia stands to one side to let Kayleigh past, and I can see that she has made some attempt at clearing up. Even so, I get a whiff of stale alcohol and the faint sickly-sweet smell of cannabis. I really hope they haven't been smoking weed in the barn.

'How are things with Mike?' I ask curtly.

'Yesterday was one of those nightmare days. We were kept waiting for hours, and then the MRI machine broke, and I lost my mobile phone, so I couldn't even call you to let you know. Eventually, I found it under the seat in the car. Thanks so much for having Kayleigh and Snoopy overnight.'

My fury towards her mellows. 'Kayleigh wanted to get some of her belongings, but I couldn't get my key to work in the door. Have you had any problems with it?'

Nadia rubs her forehead with her fingers and lets out a loud groan. 'I'm sorry. With everything that's been going on, I totally forgot to tell you that we changed the locks.'

'You what!' I exclaim, but Nadia talks over me.

'Your locks were so basic and pretty useless, so we've done some home improvements for you. Mike put some proper security locks into the door, and they're much harder to break. You might want to do the same for your house if you have the cheap locks you installed in the barn. Mike's great at all sorts of DIY, even with the broken ankle. It's our way of saying thank you for looking after Kayleigh and Snoopy and for letting us stay on.'

I am sure that I am opening and closing my mouth like a fish, but I am totally stumped for words. What on earth were they thinking? They don't have the right to change the locks or make structural changes to the property. I can't remember what my terms and conditions say, but surely they must have breached them.

'You look quite shocked,' Nadia says, putting a hand on my shoulder.

'I am. Have you got a spare key for me?' I take a step backwards, and her hand falls to her side.

'We were going to organise that yesterday, but with all the delays at the hospital, the locksmith was shut by the time we got there. Don't worry, I'll get a duplicate key when we next go into Macclesfield. I hope you don't mind. We put our thinking caps on as to how we might do something for you, and although you probably don't get many burglars stuck out here in the middle of nowhere, everyone should have the best security they can afford.'

I am relieved when I hear Mike shouting, 'Nadia!' She turns around, and I take the opportunity to slip away.

I hurry back towards the house, my brain working overtime. I cannot believe that Nadia is being genuine; she must be messing with me. Before setting up the holiday cottage, I devoured information on chat rooms about nightmare guests and things to look out for when renting your home, but no one ever mentioned guests changing the locks. It's as if Mike and Nadia are trying to take possession, and it reminds me of a sitting tenant that Dad had years ago when he rented out Gran's flat after she died. But Nadia didn't seem shifty when she was talking to me, and if she gets me a duplicate key in the next couple of days, then I have nothing to worry about. I want to think the best of them, I really do. But it's so hard. They are shifty, weird and unlike anyone I've ever met before. I pace around the kitchen for a while and then decide to ring Daniel. If I'm lucky, he will be in between seeing patients. I call the direct line to Coleen, Daniel's secretary of the past twenty years.

'Hello, how are you, Hannah? And how are those gorgeous children?'

We exchange pleasantries, as we always do, and then I ask to speak to Daniel.

'Sorry, but he's still on the wards, and then he's got back-to-back appointments. I can ask him to call you at lunchtime.'

'Thanks, Coleen. If you could get him to call me on my mobile, that would be great.'

'You take care, Hannah, and hope to see you one of these days.'

Daniel is lucky to have Coleen, and so am I. She is in her late fifties, a grandmother several times over, and is the most organised and efficient woman I have ever met. She manages to treat Daniel with a combination of deference, forcefulness, no-nonsense, and humour. I think she views my husband like a rather brilliant but errant child, and she reads him better than I do. I was in her office shortly after Daniel and I got married, and Daniel had received a letter from the husband of a patient threatening to sue Daniel for medical negligence. Daniel was getting paler and paler in the face, the muscles in his jaw were tensed, and his breathing shallow. Unlike many people, anger seems to physically manifest itself in my husband by drawing the blood away from his extremities.

'You have nothing to worry about, Daniel,' Coleen reassured him in a calm and level voice. 'Your patient is alive and well, and I have checked with the secretaries of a few other consultants whom this litigious gentleman has visited. He has form. He's trying it on. Leave it with me and go and look after the hearts of the people who need your skills.'

Daniel exhaled, smiled and left the office. Yes, I've learned a lot from Coleen. Daniel may be a brilliant surgeon, but he is surprisingly quick to anger; Coleen manages to keep him calm. I am also grateful that Coleen has a triple chin, a penchant for below-the-knee tweed skirts, and hair that has never been touched by a hairdresser. I know too many consultants and surgeons who have fallen for their extremely attractive and fawning secretaries. In the early days of our relationship, I was worried that Coleen might view me as the usurper, the younger second wife pursuing Daniel for his money and status. I was pregnant with Rosa when Coleen told me that she never understood what Daniel saw in Alison, his first wife, and that I was so

much better for him. It felt like I had received the ultimate seal
of approval.

'HURRY UP, CHILDREN!' I shout up the stairs. The kids have an
appointment at the dentist this morning, and then we're
meeting Amber and Billy for a late lunch at Pizza Express. Joel
comes hurtling down the stairs, but it takes a little more
cajoling to get Rosa out of the house. For the first time, I feel a
deep sense of relief as we drive away from our home, and away
from the Jones family. At the same time, I am concerned. What
will they do next? It really beggars belief that they have
changed the locks.

Rosa is unusually quiet in the car. When I glance at her in
my rear mirror, I notice that she's scratching her head.

'Are you all right, darling?'

'My hair is itchy,' she says in a quiet voice.

My heart sinks. To date, we have avoided getting head lice.
Even when it was doing its rounds at school last year, neither
Rosa nor Joel caught them.

'Kayleigh says that only clean people get nits, that they like
clean hair. I think she gave them to me.' Rosa sighs.

'Has she got them?' I ask, my fingers clenching the steering
wheel.

'Maybe. She says she has them several times a year, and that
it means she's clean.'

'What a load of nonsense,' I mutter. But when I glance in
the mirror again, I see that Rosa is crying.

'It's all right, darling, it's not a big deal. We'll buy some
special shampoo and a comb from Boots, and I think it would
be a good idea if you keep your distance from Kayleigh when
we get home.'

When we're at the dentist, I mention that Rosa might have
nits. The receptionist is lovely about it, reassuring us that their

chairs are plastic coated and wiped down vigorously between patients. Afterwards, we nip into Boots and buy the treatment along with a hair bobble so Rosa can tie her hair up. Lunch is a welcome relief and a chance to forget about my unpleasant barn guests.

It isn't until we're in the car on the way home that I remember that Daniel hasn't returned my call. I expect he's crazily busy. I'll discuss the changing of the locks with him when we speak tonight.

The moment I put my key in the lock of our back door and step inside, something feels different. The children bound in behind me and get covered in licks from Peanut, but I stand stock-still in the middle of the kitchen, and I sense it. Someone has been in here. I glance around. Everything is exactly as I left it; the chairs are neatly wedged under the kitchen table, which has been wiped clean. There is an empty glass standing in the sink, and the fridge is covered in the children's artworks.

And then it strikes me. That scent. The faintest whiff of florals mixed with something heavier, incense-like. Frankincense perhaps. Has Nadia been in here? How could that even be possible?

'Stay in the kitchen,' I instruct the children. I stride through the kitchen and along the corridor, gingerly opening the doors that are closed, and peeking into each room. I hurry upstairs and check every room. There is no one here.

Taking several deep breaths, I force myself to calm down. It is absolutely absurd to think that Nadia has gained entry to the house. She hasn't got a key, no windows or doors are broken, and nothing appears to be missing. Even so, I wish Peanut could talk. The dog would be able to tell me the truth.

12

The next day, I am hanging the laundry on the washing line at the side of the house, and my timing couldn't be worse. Nadia shimmies out of the door to the barn.

'Good morning, Hannah. We're off to the supermarket. Is there anything you need?'

'No, thanks,' I say curtly. I have no desire to talk to Nadia. It's windy and one of Daniel's shirts flaps in my face.

She frowns. 'You seem a bit tense.'

I clench my jaw. We're a good ten metres apart, so I don't know how she can make that judgement.

'I hope I haven't done anything to upset you,' Nadia says, her face furrowed with concern.

I would like to tell her that my daughter is devastated because her child gave her nits; that they are nightmare tenants and I want them out of my beautiful barn right now. Instead, I hold my tongue and simply say, 'No.' I bend down to take a pair of my navy cotton trousers from the laundry basket. 'Can you remember to get a key to the barn cut for me,' I say, without looking at her.

'Of course. Would you like Rosa to come with us to the supermarket? Kayleigh would love it.'

'No, it's not convenient.' I carry on hanging up the laundry.

'Hannah, I'm only trying to help.'

I sigh. I suppose I am being rude. I glance up at Nadia. Her head is tilted to one side, and she has crossed her arms in front of her chest. 'I just want to be your friend. We're living in close quarters.'

'And you are temporary guests here and this is my home. It's not an easy situation for any of us.' I pick up the empty laundry basket and stride towards the house. 'Have a good day.'

A minute later, I position myself to the left of the patio door where I can see Nadia, but she can't see me. She is still standing there, her eyes narrowed, staring at the house. It's as if she's been frozen. I feel a bit guilty now. It's not as if Nadia has done anything particularly wrong; it's Mike who is so vile. But Nadia makes me feel uneasy. I have that spooked feeling around her, as if she can read my inner thoughts, and although when I first met her, I thought she was pretty, now I feel slightly repulsed by her. Perhaps it's the heavy, cloying scent she wears or those icy blue eyes, or perhaps it's simply because she claims to be a psychic and I'm bestowing her with powers that she doesn't have. Or perhaps I shouldn't be so rigid in my thinking. Maybe she does know something that I don't. Maybe she is genuinely looking out for me. I shiver. I shouldn't have been so offhand towards her; undoubtedly I've made a difficult situation even worse.

MUM AND DAD arrive at 10 a.m. to collect Rosa and Joel. Rosa was desperate for me not to tell Mum about her nits, but my parents need to know that she's only had one treatment. I send Mum a text message and hope that she reads it. When they're gone, I get ready for Cameron's piano lesson at 11.30 a.m. But

11.30 a.m. comes and goes. I have never known Ellen Snow to be late, so I grab my diary and double-check that I have the day and time written down correctly. Then the phone rings.

'There's a car blocking your road,' Ellen says curtly.

'Is it the farmer's?'

'Does the farmer drive a battered silver Mercedes?'

'No. I'm sorry, Ellen, it belongs to the holiday guests staying in our barn.'

'Well, you'd better get them to move it. It's totally blocking the road, and I'm not wearing the right shoes to tackle the walk.'

'I'll come and collect Cameron. I'm very sorry for the inconvenience.'

I grab my mobile phone and feel relieved that Mum has taken the kids for the afternoon. What were Nadia and Mike thinking leaving their car in the road? I lock the house and run over to the barn, knocking on the door. It's patently obvious they're not at home. As I walk as quickly as I can up the hill – which is incredibly steep and makes the fittest of people breathless – I wonder if their car has broken down. Perhaps they're waiting for it to be towed. I try Nadia's mobile, and this time it fails to connect. I wonder if she keeps it permanently off, or perhaps it's a dud number. Ten minutes later, I am by the Mercedes, panting and red-faced. Ellen is correct. No one can get in or out. I put my hand on the bonnet of the car, but it feels cold. The car must have been here a while, perhaps dumped shortly after Mum and Dad left.

Cameron jumps out of Ellen's white Skoda estate, clutching his music bag, a brown leather bag with his initials emblazoned on the front.

I bend down to speak to Ellen, who lowers the window.

'Really sorry about this. Would you like to get a coffee somewhere, and I'll call you when I'm ready to bring Cameron back up the hill?'

'No, I'll stay here. I want to talk to you about the Georgia Bosconi Tchaikovsky competition. I would like Cameron to enter it.'

I glance at the young boy, who shakes his head desperately at me. I have let him down. I promised to speak to Ellen last week and totally forgot.

'I'm afraid I don't think it's in Cameron's best interests to enter a competition at the moment,' I say.

'What, you don't think he's good enough?'

'Oh, he's good enough, but he is too young. Pressure at such a young age can be so detrimental in the longer term. There's a good reason why the music schools don't like entering their pupils into competitions.'

'Well, I disagree. I think Cameron deserves the opportunity to get widespread recognition.'

'He will get that in due course, Ellen, but I beg of you: please don't push him too hard.'

She screws up her eyes at me and raises the window.

'Come on, young man,' I say, gesturing at Cameron. 'I'll race you down the hill.'

I let Cameron beat me, and we both collapse giggling in the kitchen. I pour him a glass of juice, and when we have regained our breath, we walk into the piano room.

'Don't worry about the competition. I'll have another word with your mum about it.'

His shoulders relax, and when his fingers touch the keyboard, he plays with such exquisite sensitivity, I have to stop myself from crying. It's as if he is touching a raw nerve deep inside my solar plexus that makes me think about my life and in particular my marriage; makes me realise that despite everything I have, true happiness is elusive. I squeeze my fingers into fists so tightly that it hurts. I can't think about that. Not now. Not in front of my young pupil.

. . .

BY THE TIME Cameron's lesson has finished, it's drizzling, so I take my navy Toyota Rav to drive him back up to Ellen. The Joneses' car is still there, and I have to reverse down the extremely steep and narrow hill. I grit my teeth with frustration.

I call my parents, because I don't want them getting stuck when they bring the children home, and Mum suggests that Rosa and Joel stay the night with her. I agree.

A little after 8 p.m., I see bouncing lights, and the Joneses' old Mercedes pulls up in front of the barn. I consider going over and asking them why they dumped their car in the middle of the road, and where they went all day without it, but I don't have the energy for confrontation. But it does make me realise how very vulnerable the children and I are out here. It's easy to block the road, and then no one would be able to get in or out to rescue us. Not a happy thought.

After a lengthy telephone conversation with Rosa, Joel and Mum, I pour myself a large glass of wine and relax in front of the television. I try calling Daniel but get his voicemail. I leave him a message, but don't tell him about the changed locks. Sometimes it irks me that my husband isn't around to talk to when I need him. Other times, I feel sorry for him, working such long days. I have a long bath and an early night, switching my bedside light off shortly after 10 p.m.

A crash.

I sit bolt upright in bed, my heart pounding as I strain my ears to listen. I can't hear anything. But then Peanut barks. I switch on my bedside light. It's 1.29 a.m. Grabbing my dressing gown, I tiptoe through the house. My breathing is coming in short bursts, and it feels as if my heart is about to pump straight out of my chest. I creep downstairs and into the kitchen. The house is in darkness. And then I see it.

A large, semi-human-shaped shadow is inching around the side of the house. Peanut lets out another yelp. Trembling, I turn on all of the lights outside, bathing the terrace in light. I can't hear or see anything or anyone. Was it a person, or did I get it wrong and could it have been that manky old fox I saw skulking around a couple of weeks ago? I need to look at the video footage from the wildlife camera in the morning. I open the patio doors that face the barn.

'Who's there?' I shout. I hope that I scare off whoever or whatever is skulking around the house. Peanut returns to his bed.

'What's going on?'

I jump when I see Nadia standing in the doorway of the barn, dressed in white pyjamas that make her look ethereal due to the exterior floodlights.

'Sorry if I woke you,' I say, thinking that there is no way that Nadia could have been awoken and come to the door so quickly. 'I saw someone creeping around the house and got scared. There was a crash; then Peanut barked and woke me up.'

Nadia rolls her eyes at me. 'It was probably Mike out for a smoke, having a little wander around.'

'Ok,' I say lamely. 'Goodnight.' I close the door and wish that I had blinds on the kitchen windows and doors facing the barn. Is Mike still out there? Is he peering into the rooms of our house, and why? Why creep around our house at night when he can stand on the terrace of the barn to smoke a cigarette? The thought of him out prowling around the exterior gives me the shivers. I double-check the bolts on all of the doors and walk upstairs to bed.

When I dream, I am being chased around the house by a large beast of a man, my terror so overwhelming I wake up with cramp in my leg, a dry throat and a film of sweat over my body.

13

L ast night's scare and my uneasy dream leaves me with a steely resolve. Mike and Nadia need to leave. I cannot have Mike creeping around the exterior of our house in the middle of the night. My friend Maya is a solicitor, and I telephone her to seek her advice.

'They've changed the locks in the barn and claim they've done it as a form of house improvement and a thank you to me. I think it's nonsense.'

'I've heard a lot of things in my years as a solicitor, but I've never come across that. It's brazen,' Maya says.

'Is it illegal?' I ask. 'Can I call the police?'

'No. A holiday let doesn't constitute a lease or an assured shorthold tenancy. The only circumstances under which you can ask the police to evict them is if they do criminal damage. Have they done any damage?'

'Other than the place looking like a tip, probably not. They've promised to give me a spare key for the new lock, but it hasn't been forthcoming yet.'

'In which case your only option is to apply for a court order because this is a civil matter. The courts can force an eviction.'

'How long does that take?'

'Anywhere from five weeks to three months. When are they planning to leave?'

'Hopefully at the end of this week, maybe tomorrow, even.'

'In which case, the best course of action is to talk to them. Get a decisive leave date. At the moment you have no reason to think that they plan on staying longer. Hopefully you're worrying about nothing.'

'Ok,' I say quietly, feeling chastened. Perhaps Maya is right. Daniel will be home tonight, and I will discuss it with him.

'ANYONE HOME?' Daniel is standing in the kitchen, his overnight bag at his feet. The children come careering into the room, throwing themselves at him.

'You're back early,' I say, leaning over Rosa and Joel to give Daniel a kiss on the lips.

'Surgery was cancelled, so I caught an earlier train. It's been a hell of a week.'

'Snoopy peed all over our kitchen floor,' Joel says.

Daniel scowls at me.

'Later,' I say quietly.

He nods.

'Right, you two monsters, Daddy needs to have a shower and a few words with Mummy first, but how about we go for a quick bike ride before tea?'

They both dance around with excitement.

'It's my birthday tomorrow!' Joel beams.

'I haven't forgotten, young man,' Daniel says, picking Joel up and swinging him around the kitchen. Joel has been counting down the sleeps until his birthday for the last month.

I follow Daniel upstairs and perch on the edge of the bed as he strips off.

'How are our delightful guests?' he asks sarcastically.

I am about to tell him about them changing the locks, but just as the words are about to slide off my tongue, I change my mind. Daniel will be furious, and I don't want to sour his mood.

'I want them gone. I think Mike was creeping around the house at one o'clock in the morning. They're freaking me out.'

Wearing just his boxer shorts, Daniel puts his hands on his hips, one eyebrow raised. He is standing barely one foot away from me.

'I rang Maya,' I say, 'and she says in order to evict them, we'll have to take civil action, but it's best just to ask them to leave nicely.'

A brief and rare smile crosses his lips. 'I agree. We have to tread very carefully. The last thing we want is for them to sue us. Has Mike said anything more about us being liable for his accident?'

I shake my head. He lays his hand on my shoulder. I don't want to think about Mike and Nadia now; I need to grasp this moment of potential reconciliation with my husband. But he doesn't leave his hand there; he steps backwards and turns away.

'I need to have a shower.'

TEN MINUTES LATER, Daniel is back downstairs. I'm rifling in the fridge.

'I'm going to talk to Mike,' Daniel says, easing his bare feet into a pair of loafers. 'Man to man.'

I'm about to make a snide comment about his chauvinism, but I bite my tongue. There is no point in antagonising Daniel when he's trying to help out. I watch as he walks over to the barn and knocks on the door. Both Mike and Nadia come out and stand on the doorstep. I can't hear what they're saying, but Nadia is smiling, and Mike gives Daniel a mock punch on the arm.

What the hell? It looks like they're best mates. And then Daniel is laughing, and I can't stand this any longer. I march out of our house, down the steps and across the road.

'Hannah!' Nadia exclaims, a broad smile on her face. 'Mike and Daniel were going to go to the pub for a pint, but I suggested to Daniel that we all go. We can have supper together.'

'What?' I exclaim.

'We'll go in two cars,' Daniel says. 'See you there at 6.30 p.m.'

Nadia's smile is so wide it looks as if her face will split in two. I feel like I'm in an alternative universe. A few minutes ago, Daniel and I were discussing how to get rid of Mike and Nadia, and now we're all going out for supper together. It doesn't make sense.

As soon as Daniel and I are back in the kitchen, I turn to him.

'What the hell? I don't want to socialise with those creeps!'

'Come on, Hannah. Surely it's better to have an amicable conversation? If you chuck them out, they'll have every right to sue for negligence. I would if I were in their shoes. Let's be friends and appeal to their better nature.'

'They don't have a better nature, and since when have you been the voice of reason?' I can't keep the bitterness from my voice.

'Look, I'm only trying to help extricate us from the mess that you've got us into!'

'Me! All I'm trying to do is run a business.'

'A business that is proving more trouble than it's worth. I've got enough problems of my own at work without having to deal with this crap when I come home. We will go to the Three Skeins and have a nice evening.'

I grit my teeth.

. . .

DANIEL KEEPS his promise to the kids and takes them out for a short bike ride. With the house to myself, I sit down at the piano and play for a while, losing myself in the music and letting the tension release from my body. By the time they return, my anger towards Daniel has dissipated, and I accept that he's only trying to appease a difficult situation.

'I'll drive to the pub, and you can drive home,' Daniel says. I don't know why he bothers telling me this, as it's what we always do. It's just as well I'm not bothered about drinking alcohol.

We are in the car when Joel says, 'Rosa's got nits.'

Rosa elbows her brother, but it's Daniel's reaction that I'm concerned about. His fingers whiten as he increases his grip on the steering wheel.

'Why didn't you tell me?' he whispers to me, his jaw jutting forwards.

'Because I gave her the first treatment, and it's just one of those things. Nothing to get worked up about.'

'I hugged her earlier and you didn't tell me!'

I glance over my shoulder and am relieved that Rosa has earphones on.

'You are meant to keep our children clean and safe. It's your only job!' Daniel says.

'And they are clean and safe. She got nits from Kayleigh. You're a doctor, so you know it's no big deal.'

Daniel keeps his eyes firmly on the road, but I can tell from the tightness of his jaw that he is furious. I sigh and look out of the passenger window. Rosa having nits is the least of our problems.

DANIEL PARKS THE CAR, and we climb out. Daniel strides in ahead of us as we walk into the Three Skeins.

'Twice in one week!' Rory, the landlord, jokes as he leads us to a table for seven. Elliott, Daniel's friend with the missing little finger, is seated at the adjacent table with two men I don't recognise. He raises his pint glass in the air towards Daniel.

'Hello, mate!'

Daniel nods at him. I position myself so my back is towards Elliott. And a moment later, Nadia, Mike and Kayleigh arrive. Kayleigh flings her arms around Rosa, but I notice that Rosa keeps her head well away. Nadia leans towards me in an attempt to give me a kiss on the cheek. I also lean backwards so she misses and almost falls into me. Her heavy scent assaults my nostrils. Why is she pretending that we're best buddies?

'This is very lovely,' she says as she regains her balance and sits down opposite me. 'You're lucky to have this as your local.'

'Bit posh for us, don't you think, Nads?' Mike says. I notice that he's put on a pair of trousers this evening, but his checker short-sleeve shirt is too small, and the buttons strain over his belly.

'We can do posh when we need to,' she says, directing her response towards Daniel. I wish the woman would stop fluttering her eyelash extensions at my husband.

A young waitress comes over to take our drinks order.

'I'll have a pint of Stella, the wife will have a glass of the house white, and our Kayleigh will have a Coke,' Mike says, without bothering to ask either Nadia or Kayleigh what they would like to drink.

'Please, can I have a Coke too?' Rosa asks.

'Yes, as a special treat,' Daniel says. Neither of us like to give the children sugar-laden fizzy drinks, but Daniel wisely decides this evening isn't the time to rock the boat. 'Two half pints of Coca-Cola, I'll have a glass of Malbec, and what would you like, Hannah?'

'Just a sparkling water for me, please,' I say.

'Aren't you drinking?' Nadia asks.

'Perhaps she's preggers!' Mike says and roars with laughter. I catch Daniel's eye, and we both squirm.

'What's preggers?' Joel asks.

'I never drink when I'm driving,' I say, realising I sound totally stuck up.

'Quite right too,' Nadia says.

'How is your ankle?' Daniel asks Mike.

'Bloody painful.'

'But it's a simple fracture?'

'There's nothing simple about it!' Mike reddens and puffs out his cheeks.

'It's a medical term,' Daniel explains. 'You either have a simple fracture or a compound fracture, the latter being when the bone breaks through the skin.'

'Gross,' Mike says. 'Anyway, I can't put any weight on it for six weeks.'

'Thank goodness we're able to stay at yours,' Nadia adds. 'He'd never get up the stairs at our place.'

'But you can't stay here for six weeks!' I exclaim.

Mike leans his elbows heavily on the table. 'Chucking us out, are you?'

Fortunately, the waitress returns with our drinks and takes our food order. As soon as she leaves our table, I turn back to Nadia.

'I've got other guests coming. I'm afraid you will have to leave tomorrow.'

'Not now, Hannah,' Daniel hisses.

'Just as well your hubby has his head screwed on right.' Mike sniggers.

I clench my fingers into fists and am about to start talking to the children, when Nadia says, 'I'm sure we'll come to some compromise, Hannah. Let's just have a nice evening.'

'Hear, hear!' Mike raises his empty beer glass. He waves at

the waitress, who hurries over to our table. 'Another Stella, please. Anyone else?'

'I'll have another glass of the Malbec,' Daniel says. I'm surprised how quickly he's drunk his wine.

'You working tomorrow?' Mike asks Daniel.

'Yes. I split my time between hospitals in Cheshire, Manchester and London. I have a clinic here in the north-west tomorrow.'

'You're quite fond of the old vino, aren't you?'

Daniel tenses and removes his hand from the stem of the wine glass. 'What is that supposed to mean?'

'Onto your second already and the food hasn't even come yet. It's just I wouldn't fancy having a heart bypass carried out by a doctor who has been out drinking the night before.'

I reach for Daniel's hand under the table and squeeze it. My husband takes great pride in his professionalism, and I know exactly how he will react to a comment like that. Not well.

'Holding a clinic isn't the same as surgery though, is it?' Nadia asks. It's obvious she's trying to break the tension.

That telltale nerve flickers in Daniel's jaw, and his eyes are narrowed, so I answer for him. 'A clinic is when he examines patients, so no, it's not the same as surgery.'

'So it's okey-dokey to drink when you're diagnosing, but not okay when you're cutting, is that it, mate?'

'I'm not your mate,' Daniel says through gritted teeth.

'Calm down, Danny boy!' Mike grins. His gold tooth catches the light. I glance at the children and am relieved that the three of them are concentrating on colouring on their place mats.

'I thought that doctors were a bit like pilots. You know, can't drink the night before and all that. What happens if you get a tremor of the knife? You could cut off the wrong vein.'

'I'm sure the lovely Daniel here wouldn't do anything like that!' Nadia says, laying her hand on Daniel's. I'm relieved that he instantly shakes it off.

'Still, must make you so powerful playing God, choosing who will live or die.'

Daniel pushes back his chair and stands up. He hesitates, and I hope that he is going to turn away and take himself off to the gents' to calm down. I can tell how hard Daniel is trying to keep himself under control, to not lose his cool.

My husband turns and I let out a sigh of relief.

'What I want to know is, if you walk away when the going gets tough, how do you manage when someone's ticker stops? Does one of your lovely nurses stroke you to keep you calm?'

I gasp as Daniel takes one large stride towards Mike and grabs the collar of his shirt.

'You're an ignorant piece of shit!' Daniel hisses at Mike.

The children drop their crayons and stare at the men, looks of horror on their faces. Joel jumps off his chair and runs around the table to me, burying his head in my lap.

'Daniel!' I say, ready to pick up Joel and grab my husband. But Rory, the pub landlord, is quicker than me.

'What's going on here, gentlemen?' he asks, putting a hand on Daniel's shoulder. Daniel steps away. Silence falls in the small pub as everyone turns around to look at us. My cheeks are burning. These people are our neighbours; Daniel is a highly respected member of the community. What will people think now? I glance around the pub and see Elliott grinning as he ogles the spectacle at our table. I feel like slapping him, telling him to mind his own business. I'm sure this little debacle will be all around the neighbourhood tomorrow morning. Rory puts his arm around Daniel's shoulders and leads him to the bar. Mike tips his chair backwards onto its rear legs, and I hope it topples over.

'Well, that was quite a little show, wasn't it!' Mike smirks. 'God help any patient who speaks out of turn to Dr Pieters.'

'That's enough, Mike!' Nadia says.

Rosa slips off her chair and comes to stand next to me. I put my arm around her. 'I want to go home, Mummy,' she whispers. Kayleigh is still colouring, totally nonplussed about the scene that has played out between her father and Daniel.

'I think that's a good idea.' I kiss Rosa on her forehead. 'Come on, little monster,' I say quietly to Joel. 'Let's go home and dig out some fish fingers. Would you like that?'

He nods.

'We're going to leave,' I say to Nadia. She looks everywhere except at me. For the first time, I feel sorry for her. It must be awful being married to Mike.

'That's a shame,' Mike leers. 'The fun was just beginning. Oh well, more food for us. Tell your old man to leave his credit card at the bar, and we'll put our dinner on his tab.'

I am so gobsmacked I simply shake my head and turn my back to him. I grab my handbag and hold my children's hands.

'I'm sorry, Hannah,' Nadia says.

'I'm sorry for you,' I reply.

I WALK TOWARDS THE BAR, where Daniel is in deep discussion with Rory and our neighbour, elderly Marty Burt. 'We're going home,' I say, interrupting him.

'Good idea.'

'I'm sorry, Rory,' I say. 'We'll eat double next time.'

'No worries, Hannah. You take care.'

We drive home in silence, me at the wheel, Daniel staring resolutely out of the passenger window.

'Why did you argue with Kayleigh's daddy?' Rosa asks.

'He's not a very nice person,' Daniel says. 'I think it's better if you don't play with Kayleigh anymore.'

If I had said that, Rosa would have thrown a hissy fit. With Daniel, she says nothing, but when I glance in the rear mirror, I can see tears sliding down her cheeks.

It isn't until much later, when the children are fed,

appeased and in bed, that I get the chance to talk to Daniel. By this point, he has consumed the best part of a bottle of red wine all by himself, and it crosses my mind that Mike may have a point. Is Daniel drinking too much? I decide this evening is not the time to mention it.

'That was quite a reaction,' I say as we sit in the living room. I love this space, with its calming pale blue curtains and large fireplace and views through the oversized windows. It's dark now, so I pull the curtains and sit on the cream-coloured sofa, tucking my legs up under myself.

'He's a total arsehole, and if I could have beaten him up, I would have done.'

I would like to tell him that he should control his temper in public and in front of the children, but I don't want to risk him raging at me. Instead, all I say is, 'I'm sorry he got to you.'

'Of course he bloody got to me! What the hell did you want me to do, Hannah? Sit there and take all his bullshit? I'm not a wet flannel that he can walk all over. No one has the right to talk like that.'

'I know,' I say. But Daniel could have walked away and refused to take the bait. I need to defuse the tension. 'Is everything else ok?'

'You don't get it, do you, Hannah? I'm working a super high-stress job, away from home, with life-changing responsibilities, and when I get home, I want an easy life. I don't want idiots living on my property. I don't want to be worried that they're going to sue us. This little venture of yours was meant to be uncomplicated and keep you busy. It's a bloody nightmare and it isn't working. Once the Joneses are gone, I want you to shut it down.'

'No, Daniel. That's not fair! We've been unlucky with this set of guests, but it doesn't mean we'll have problems in the future.' I jump up and start pacing around the living room.

'I've made my decision and enough is enough. Invite

friends and family to come and stay in the barn. Get an au pair if you want; I'm not having strangers staying there anymore.'

'This is my house as much as yours.'

Although. of course. it isn't. It's Daniel's house; he bought it with Alison, and I'm just the second wife who has slotted in. I very much doubt my name is on the deeds, and I've never dared to ask. On the other hand, I've lived here far longer than Alison ever did, and I've changed the interior decor and brought up our children in this house. I need to calm this situation down.

'I'm sorry things haven't worked out the way we wanted with this set of guests, and I'm doing everything I can to make things better. Running a holiday cottage is my life-long dream.'

'And that's exactly what it should remain. A dream.'

I open my mouth, but Daniel speaks first. 'You're being fundamentally selfish here, Hannah. You need to think about what's best for our family.' He stands up and lets the newspaper drop to the floor. 'I'm going to bed.'

'Remember, it's Joel's birthday tomorrow. His party starts at 3 p.m.'

Daniel ignores me.

14

I stay downstairs to blow up balloons and hang up some bunting so that the kitchen will be dressed up when Joel bounces in tomorrow morning. I don't put out his pile of presents because the chances are he'll be up before us, and he might not be able to restrain himself from having a peek. Decorating the room also gives me a few minutes to decompress. The tension between Daniel and me is unsettling. I don't understand why the holiday cottage is making him so irate. There must be more going on than that.

Shortly before 11 p.m., I lock up, say goodnight to Peanut, and tiptoe upstairs, hopeful that Daniel will still be awake and that we can make up. I'm surprised that the door to our bedroom is ajar, and as I peer into the darkness, expecting to see the shape of my husband huddled under the duvet, the bed is as neat as it was after I made it this morning.

I swear under my breath and switch on the light. Daniel isn't there. His favourite memory-foam pillow is also gone, and it doesn't take much deduction to work out that he's moved to the spare room. I tiptoe along the corridor and knock gently on the closed door. There is no answer. Holding my breath, I ease the door open. Daniel is lying with his back towards the door.

'Daniel,' I say quietly.

I wait in the darkness for a moment, but there is no reply. Sighing, I close the door behind me.

UNSURPRISINGLY, I sleep badly. I know Daniel was angry, but our disagreement hardly warranted moving to the spare room. When I wake in the morning, it's 6.30 a.m. I fling on my dressing gown and hurry downstairs. But I'm too late. I hear the engine of Daniel's Range Rover start up and watch with dismay as he drives away. The huge happy birthday banner is unmissable, so there is no way that he can have forgotten it is Joel's birthday. Surely he isn't punishing our son for his anger towards me? We should be giving Joel his birthday presents together in exactly the same way we have for every one of Rosa's and Joel's birthdays. It is unreasonable to expect our little six-year-old to wait for his presents until Daniel gets home. I'm livid that he's taking out his anger with me on our innocent son. I try calling Daniel's mobile, but unsurprisingly, it goes straight to voicemail. He won't get any reception until he's on the fringes of Macclesfield. I send him a text.

Why did you leave before giving Joel his presents? I'll have to give them without you. Please be home around 2 p.m. for Joel's party.

And then I send Nadia a text.

Just to remind you that checkout is 10 a.m. so we have time to clean before the next guests arrive later this afternoon.

The latter part of that statement isn't true. The next set of guests are due to arrive tomorrow, and I've booked in my lovely cleaner, Hazel, to help out this afternoon. With Joel's party today, there is no way that I can get everything done alone.

A moment later, Joel comes bouncing down the stairs, excitement swirling around him like dancing flames.

'Daddy said happy birthday to me, and he gave me a present!' Joel says.

'He did?' I'm surprised. Daniel tends to leave all the present buying to me.

Joel produces a bone and a stethoscope. 'Daddy says I can listen to Peanut's heart with this, and this is a bone from a real dinosaur!'

I very much doubt that, but I'm pleased that Daniel gave Joel something before leaving for work. It's just a shame he didn't wake me for our normal present-opening ritual. I push down the disappointment and concentrate on my son. The next couple of hours are a whirlwind of present opening, filling party bags, showing the men where to erect the bouncy castle, blowing up balloons, and containing Joel's excitement. Mum and Dad arrive shortly after 10 a.m., and it's a relief to be able to palm off some of the tasks to them.

It's nearly 11 a.m. when I realise that I haven't heard from Nadia, and there has been no movement in the barn. This is just what I don't need, today of all days.

'Mum, can you hold the fort? I'm going to the barn to talk to our nightmare guests.'

'Of course, love.'

For a moment, I feel an overwhelming sense of relief. The Joneses' car is gone. With all the activities this morning, I hadn't seen them leave. I turn the handle in the front door, but my relief is short-lived. The door is locked. I peer in the window to the living room, and the place is a total tip – exactly as it was every day this week. Belongings are scattered all over the floor and furniture, all the lights are on despite it being a lovely, bright day, and the television is also on, but for a change, the sound is turned down low.

I knock on the door. No answer. I walk around the outside of the barn and, standing on tiptoes, peer into the master bedroom. Mike is lying on the unmade bed, fully clothed, doing something on a phone. I rap on the window. He looks up and then sticks a middle finger up in the air at me.

'You need to leave,' I shout through the glass. But he just shrugs and returns to looking at his phone.

I let out a long groan. What the hell am I going to do? It's obvious that they're going nowhere soon. I hurry back to the house and cancel Hazel. There is no point in her coming over if she can't get in. Hopefully I can talk some sense into Nadia when she returns and encourage them to leave this afternoon, and then I'll clean the place myself tonight.

By 2.45 P.M., we're just about ready for the party, although I feel so exhausted, I could sleep for a week. Daniel still isn't home, and Joel is beside himself with excitement. The magician has arrived and is setting up his table in front of the sprawling elderflower bush. I have filled a couple of large jugs of elderflower cordial that I made from the flowers a few weeks ago, along with an array of juices and nibbles on a trestle table on the edge of the lawn. Mum is in the kitchen, keeping an eye on the sausages in the oven, finishing off making copious mini sandwiches, and filling up bowls with crisps. When I hear the first car, I turn quickly, expecting it to be Daniel. It isn't.

By ten past three, Daniel still hasn't arrived, and I'm feeling sick with worry. In the excitement of his friends arriving laden with wrapped birthday presents, Joel hasn't even noticed his dad is missing. Daniel is a good dad; there is no way that he would be knowingly late.

'Everything all right?' Amber asks as she saunters into the kitchen, looking beautiful in a white embroidered summer dress. She puts an arm around me.

'Yes, all fine,' I say brightly. 'Just need to bring out the birthday cake.'

By twenty past three, I am pacing the kitchen. Everyone else is outside: parents chatting to each other with glasses of wine or elderflower in their hands, children jumping and screeching on the bouncy castle, overseen by Dad, who looks totally bewildered by the cacophony. The weather couldn't be more perfect for an outdoor party. I send one more text message to Daniel and then fling my mobile phone down on the kitchen table. There's nothing more I can do. I must concentrate on making this a wonderful afternoon for my little boy.

And then I see her. Nadia is chatting with Rachel Mole and Sara Burrows, her head thrown back with laughter, her fingers clutched around the stem of a glass of wine, her diamante nails sparkling. Rachel and Sara look utterly captivated, as if they're bewitched by an exotic bird who has deigned to pop into our run-of-the-mill party and has instantly become the star attraction. I walk a few steps onto the terrace and watch Kayleigh and Rosa laughing as Kayleigh does somersaults on the bouncy castle. I feel as if I'm going to explode with fury. How dare the Jones family attend Joel's party!

'Hey. Everyone's having a great time. No need to look so glum,' Amber says as she hands me a glass of wine.

'The dreadful guests in the barn who refuse to leave have gate-crashed the party. And Daniel hasn't turned up.'

'Okay,' Amber says, drawing out the word as if she's thinking hard. 'Daniel first. Have you rung him?'

'Yes, repeatedly.'

'Perhaps he's been held up in surgery,' Amber suggests. I don't mention that Daniel didn't have any surgery today.

'Which are the barn guests?'

I point out Nadia, who is now holding court in the centre of a larger group of women. A couple of dads, including creepy Elliott and good-looking Ben, are standing to one side.

'She seems okay,' Amber says.

'Until you get to know her.'

'Try to enjoy yourself.' Amber plants a kiss on my cheek.

'Hello, Amber!'

We both jump and turn around. Daniel is standing there, his jacket slung over his shoulder, a glass of red wine in his right hand, as if it's totally normal to turn up late for your own event.

'Where have you been?' I ask.

'And hello to you too,' he says, giving me a perfunctory kiss. 'I got held up. Glad to see the party is in full swing.'

'Looks like you're just in time to see the magic show,' Amber says. Amber and I walk silently across the patio and stand behind the parents gathered to watch the magician. He is wearing an oversized black hat, a black cape with a bright red lining and matching waistcoat, and is ringing a high-pitched bell and encouraging all twenty children to sit cross-legged on the grass in front of him. I look on in admiration at how successful he is, instantly captivating their attention. Rosa and Kayleigh are seated to the edge of the group, their arms flung around each other's shoulders. So much for discouraging their friendship.

After five minutes of watching the magician produce a white rabbit from a hat and threaten to turn Joel into a frog, much to the hysterical shrieks of his friends, I turn and walk quietly along the edge of the grass, up the couple of steps onto the stone terrace and move towards the kitchen. I need to put another batch of sausages in the oven, along with the sausage rolls and mini quiches.

I pause outside the kitchen as I hear Daniel's voice.

'What are you drinking?' my husband asks.

'Red wine.'

'I can see that.'

There is a pause, and my heart sinks as I realise Daniel is talking to Mike.

'For fuck's sake, you've helped yourself to a bottle of

Chateau le Moulin 2011 Pomerol. That's a seventy-quid bottle I was keeping for a special occasion.'

'Isn't your son's birthday a special occasion?'

'You have no right to be here in *my* kitchen drinking *my* wine. Didn't you listen to what my wife told you? You need to leave.'

'Your wife told me it was perfectly ok,' Mike says. I am shaking as I walk into the kitchen. I cannot believe the audacity of this vile man.

'I did not!' I exclaim, but Mike is in the doorway, and he appears to have mastered the skill of walking on the surgical cast, and he successfully pushes past me, a crutch in one hand and a full glass of wine in another.

'You bastard!' Daniel shouts.

'Ssh, please, darling,' I say. 'Let's deal with this after the party.'

But Daniel isn't listening to me. He also pushes past me. Now the two men are standing together on the terrace.

'You need to leave,' Daniel hisses.

Mike steps towards Daniel so they are practically nose to nose. My heart sinks.

'You see this foot?' Mike points to the cast on his foot. 'It's giving me so much grief we're going to have to stay another fortnight at least.'

'No,' Daniel says much too loudly. A couple of mums turn around to look at them.

'Be quiet,' I hiss.

'Look, Dan my man, we won't sue you for negligence, but you'd better watch your steps around me and Nads. We know the law. We know our rights.'

Mike eases past Daniel and hobbles towards the group of other parents watching the magic show. But Daniel moves faster. I try to grab his sleeve as he passes me, but he's too quick.

'Are you threatening me?' he spits at Mike.

'Ergh, no mate. You're threatening me!' Mike guffaws, and some of the red wine slurps over the edge of his glass onto the stone patio. Mike's voice carries across the stillness of the afternoon. I can tell that Daniel is about to explode, and I need to stop this right now; but how, without drawing any further attention to us? It looks like the magician is about to finish his act as he places a green dinosaur-shaped balloon on top of Joel's head. Mum bustles past us, into the kitchen. A moment later she walks back outside, holding Joel's birthday cake, shaped like a dinosaur and bought from a Wilmslow bakery at an obscene price.

Mike steps down onto the grass and then swings back to face Daniel, and this time some of the wine splashes onto Daniel's shining brown brogue shoe. 'Forgot to tell you that I've got an appointment with Professor Eugene Entwhistle. He's the head of cardiology at your hospital, isn't he? I'm a bit worried about me old ticker.' Mike lets the crutch swing from his wrist as he clasps his hand over his chest. 'Thought I'd tell him that I'm a mate of yours, staying over in your grand residence. I'll ask him how much wine it's safe to drink the night before surgery.'

My heart sinks as time stands still. Professor Entwhistle is Daniel's *bête noir* and one of the reasons that Daniel took up the consultant's position in London. Close to retirement age, Entwhistle is still head of the cardiothoracic department at the hospital where Daniel works here in Cheshire, and, as Daniel says, the man is stuck in the twentieth century, unwilling to embrace modern systems and technologies. There is no love lost between the two of them. How does Mike know that, or perhaps he doesn't? It only requires a quick look at the hospital's website to see who the head of the department is and who are the associate consultants.

Blood drains from Daniel's face. He inhales audibly, steps towards Mike, and gives him a shove in the chest. But with the crutch still dangling from his wrist, Mike isn't well balanced, and he topples backwards, letting out a loud yell as he lands on his fleshy backside, the remaining wine tipping over his beige shorts, creating a deep red stain across his crotch. It would be comical if it weren't so awful.

'You bastard!' Mike yells.

Everyone turns around. The children, the magician, the parents. Nadia. She rushes towards her husband, her navy cotton dress billowing out around her. There is silence, with only the birds chirruping, unaware of the humiliating scene in our garden.

Daniel takes a step towards Mike and pulls back his arm as if he's about to hit the man whilst he's down.

'No!' I say, grabbing Daniel's arm, pulling him backwards with all my might. He freezes and mutters, 'Shit,' under his breath, aware suddenly of all the eyes upon him. 'Sorry,' he mumbles, and he turns, rushing back into the house.

'Children, what have I got in here!' The magician rings his little bell and holds his top hat aloft. 'Whoever guesses wins a present!'

And instantly, the children's attention is back with the magician, little arms reaching into the air, high-pitched shouts breaking the tense atmosphere. He places his white-gloved hand into the hat and produces a white dove. The children gasp.

Meanwhile, Nadia helps Mike haul himself up from the ground. There is clearly no further physical damage done, as he mutters under his breath, promising to sue us, uttering a litany of swear words. He lets Nadia guide him away from the party back towards the barn. While the children may be otherwise engaged, all the parents' eyes are on Mike's and Nadia's retreating backs. And I want the ground to open up and swallow me whole.

· · ·

IT SEEMS to me that the party is all over in minutes after the fight between Daniel and Mike. The other mums and dads, whom I have tried so hard to befriend over the years, are in a hurry to leave, barely allowing their children time to eat the massive tea Mum and I have prepared. And as soon as the cake is cut and happy birthday is sung out of tune, one after the other parent is clutching the sticky hand of their child, tugging them away from the bouncy castle, muttering thanks and curtly accepting the going-away bags I have carefully put together. Joel's party will be the talk of Cheshire and for all the wrong reasons.

Amber is the last to leave. 'I've told everyone that Mike is a jerk and was threatening Daniel,' she says in a chirpy voice.

'Pretty obvious that Daniel shoved him, though,' I say.

'With good reason. People have short memories, Hannah. They'll gossip for a few days, and then it'll all be forgotten. Everyone likes you and Daniel. You don't need to worry.'

'Thanks,' I mutter, but I don't believe Amber. She wishes me goodbye, and I watch her huddle Billy into the car, get behind the wheel, and drive away.

The only children left are Joel, Rosa and Kayleigh, the three of them jumping and screeching on the bouncy castle, high on too much sugar. Kayleigh has done nothing wrong, but I wish the child would leave.

Mum and Dad are in the kitchen, starting to clear up.

'Would you mind keeping an eye on the kids?' I ask Dad.

'Of course, love,' he says, dropping the tea towel onto the work surface.

'Any excuse to get out of clearing up!' Mum jokes.

'Did you see what happened?' I can't remember where my parents were during the altercation.

'Yes, love. And I am sure that Daniel had every justification to shove that horrible man.'

I let a smile briefly pass my lips. Daniel can do no wrong in my parents' eyes. 'I don't think physical violence is ever justified.'

'You make sure you stand by your man,' Mum says, planting a kiss on my cheek.

I sigh deeply as I walk through the house. Mum has such an old-fashioned attitude. I was adamant that I would never morph into her, not because I don't love her, but because I didn't want her life. My dream was to be independent, to change the lives of children through music. I had it all plotted out. What I hadn't factored into my life plan was meeting Daniel.

We should never have met. I can't imagine how under normal circumstances our lives could have collided. We didn't live in the same area; we didn't have any mutual friends; we worked in totally different sectors; and he is nearly ten years older than me. And yet we did meet. And against all odds, we fell in love.

A couple of months earlier I had been through a miserable break-up. Mark and I had been together since college, and I genuinely thought we would buy a flat together, get married, and start a family. Evidently, he had other ideas. In the sixth and final year of our relationship, he gave me a new kettle for Christmas and forgot my birthday altogether. My girlfriends rallied around, all indignant, and suggested I call time on the relationship. But I couldn't bear the thought of having wasted the best part of my twenties on a man who wouldn't be with me for the rest of my life. Stupid.

I found the little stud pearl earring, minus its back, under my pillow. When I confronted Mark, he readily admitted he was seeing someone else, that he hadn't wanted to tell me because he knew it would break my heart, and he hated hurting me. If he thought a clumsily discarded earring would be easier to bear, he was wrong. In fact, we were both wrong.

After the initial tears and sense of betrayal, I felt liberated. My life was my own to do whatever I wished.

It was coming up for the long summer holidays, and I booked to visit a girlfriend who works as a translator for the United Nations in Geneva. I was in the aisle seat on the EasyJet flight, and an older woman was in the window seat. I settled myself in for the short flight, relieved that the middle seat was empty, so I could clasp the armrest without disturbing anyone next to me. I hated flying. I still do. Just before they shut the plane's doors, a man hurried in: late thirties, I guessed, dark hair, a nose a little too big for his face and mesmerising hazel eyes. But what I noticed most were his fingers. They were long and elegant with neatly clipped nails. I thought they might be a musician's fingers; they were, in fact, a surgeon's.

Deeply apologetic, he sat in the seat next to me and spent the flight reading *The Lancet*. We had just begun our descent into Geneva when the turbulence began. It was the worst I have ever experienced. The whole plane was jolted upwards and back down again; lightning flashed outside the windows. We were in the midst of an Alpine summer storm. The seat belt signs pinged on, and the air hostesses took their seats. My heartbeat soared and I grabbed the armrests. For the first and only time in my life, I had a panic attack. I was alone on a plane that was about to slam into a mountain.

'My name is Daniel and I'm a doctor,' he said in a quiet, calm voice. 'I'm a cardiothoracic surgeon. You're not dying, we're not going to crash, but you need to breathe slowly. Close your eyes and breathe in and out as I tell you.' He put his cool, strong fingers around my clammy left hand, and it was if he took control of my brain and my body. Ten minutes later, we landed smoothly at Geneva airport, and I felt like a total idiot.

'I'm so sorry,' I said, embarrassment searing my cheeks. 'That's never happened before.'

'No need to apologise. Panic attacks happen to the best of us.'

I smiled coyly at the debonair man next to me, thinking how I doubted he ever lost control. It just goes to show that first impressions can be very wrong. I thanked him profusely, and we parted ways as we went through customs and on to the baggage reclaim area. Even though there were crowds of people, I was acutely aware of the handsome stranger in the bright blue shirt and neatly pressed jeans.

When I switched my phone on, I was dismayed to get a message from my friend telling me that she had been called away to a conference in New York at the last minute; it was the offer of a lifetime, stepping into the shoes of someone who was sick. She was deeply apologetic. She'd leave her flat keys with the concierge, and I was welcome to stay there in her absence.

On a whim, I decided I didn't want to stay in Geneva. I would rent the cheapest car I could find and take myself off on an exploration of the mountains. Trying to muster up confidence that I didn't have, I followed the signs to the car-rental booths. The handsome stranger was pacing up and down, talking rapidly into his phone, a nerve pinging on the side of his square jaw. I pretended not to look and was quickly at the desk.

'I'd like to rent your cheapest car,' I said.

The car-rental clerk threw me a snooty look as he handed me a leaflet with the tariffs on it. 'We don't have any cars available in the lower categories.' The cheapest car available to rent was going to cost me over a thousand pounds for the week, money I certainly didn't have.

'But I can't afford that!' I said, horrified at the prices. I felt thwarted and was about to walk away, when my saviour from the plane interrupted.

'Excuse me,' he said. I glanced up at him, flushed. 'I couldn't help but overhear. Where were you planning on driving to?'

'Um, I haven't actually decided, but at these prices I won't be renting a car.'

The rental clerk tapped his fingers on the counter and rolled his eyes at us.

'I have managed to leave my driving licence at home, and I have to get to Verbier. This is a bit of a long shot, but if I pay for the car rental, any chance we could team up? I'm afraid you'll have to do the driving.' He looked really coy, and for the first time, I wondered if the attraction was mutual. 'I don't know if you like classical music, but I have a spare ticket to hear Lang Lang play at the Verbier Festival tomorrow night.'

I suppose my lower jaw must have dropped open, because Daniel laughed. He paid; I rented the car and pretended not to be the slightest bit scared of driving on the wrong side of the road. I got us there.

There were no games, no conventional dates. We fell into each other's arms that first night in the dark-wood chalet-style hotel, where he had rented a room for four nights. It was as if it was meant to be. He told me about the messy divorce he had been through with Alison; I told him about my recent break-up with Mark. A year to the day we met, we got married and we honeymooned in the Canadian Rockies. It was all so romantic... but a lifetime ago.

I WALK into Daniel's study. He has polished off the best part of a bottle of red wine and is holding a wine glass.

Daniel talks before I even open my mouth. 'Don't, Hannah.'

'Don't what?'

'Have a go at me. He was lucky I didn't slam his brains out.'

I gasp. I have seen Daniel lose his temper, but I've never thought he was capable of physical violence. He shouts, he swears, and a few years ago he broke a plate in anger, but he's never hurt anyone.

'It was all a show,' he says.

'Are you telling me that I imagined you pushing him over?'

'The shove I gave him was insufficient to make him fall. He was playing to the crowd.'

'It's your son's birthday!' I exclaim. 'You left before we could give him our presents together this morning, and you were late for his party.'

'For God's sake, Hannah. Leave me alone!'

And so I do. I turn around and storm out of his study.

After my parents have left, Daniel reappears and sits with Joel whilst he opens the rest of his presents. It isn't until much later, when darkness is falling, that I have time to sit and think. I pour myself a glass of white wine and perch on the bench outside. Although he is in the house, I feel the most estranged from Daniel that I ever have, yet I don't fully understand why. Of course, Mike and Nadia have caused tension, but it's not as if all was rosy before they arrived. We have been spending less and less time together, just coasting along with our separate lives that converge from time to time, normally regarding decisions about, or activities with, the children. We need to talk. Really talk. But tonight isn't the night. And then my thoughts are interrupted by deafening, thumping, heavy music coming from the barn.

'Shit,' I murmur to myself. Not only are they still here, but they're doing everything they can to wind us up. A moment later, Daniel comes storming out.

'The bastards!' he says.

'Hey.' I try to grab his hand, but he pulls it away.

Daniel stands on the edge of the terrace and shouts, 'Shut the fuck up!' His voice carries, and I imagine it echoing across the hills and winding along the rivers until it dissipates above the sea one hundred miles away. 'I'm going over there!' he says, his chin pushed forwards and hands on his hips.

'No, please don't, Daniel. It'll only make a terrible situation worse. Remember that they are threatening to sue us for his broken ankle, and now he'll claim you pushed him. If you go over there and end up in a fight, you'll be playing into their hands.'

'You always twist things so that it's my fault, Hannah. If you hadn't invited them into our home, then we wouldn't be in this untenable situation.'

'I didn't...' But I let my words fade away. There is no point in getting into another argument with my husband. He has drunk well over a bottle of wine and is in no mood to be rational. 'Shall we watch television?' I ask in a desperate attempt to change the subject. Daniel ignores me. He stands with his hands on his hips and screams again, 'Shut the fuck up; otherwise I'll call the police!'

'You'll wake the children!' I say.

He edges past me and stomps back inside the house. There is no point in trying to engage with him whilst he's in this state of mind.

I stay out a little longer, but the music is incessant, and the beat jars through me as if it's vibrating my bones. It's time for bed, although it's unlikely sleep will come.

When I'm in the kitchen, pouring myself a glass of water, Daniel comes in and opens yet another bottle of wine.

'Are you coming to bed?' I ask.

'What does it look like?' He holds up the corkscrew.

'I was wondering if you'll be sleeping in our room tonight,' I ask.

He shrugs and turns away from me. He doesn't see the tear drip down my cheek.

Unsurprisingly, I can't sleep. I don't understand why our relationship has deteriorated so much. It's as if Mike and Nadia have been a catalyst for the unravelling of our marriage. Or am I being melodramatic after a stressful day? I find it so hard not to listen to the incessant thump, thump of the music, and I marvel at how the children have slept through everything. But I suppose I do drift off to sleep eventually.

But then I'm jolted awake. I glance at my clock. It's 1 a.m. and Daniel isn't next to me. Then I hear his voice and Mike's voice. They're shouting at each other. I open the bedroom window. Daniel is standing on the patio, the loud music still thumping away. I can't see Mike, but he yells back, a litany of profanities.

'Daniel!' I speak urgently, but as quietly as I can. He turns to look at me.

'Go back to bed.' He jabs his finger at me as he slurs his words.

'You'll wake the children.'

'Just go back to bed and shut the fuck up.'

His words lurch me backwards, and I shut the bedroom window and fumble my way back to bed. I cannot believe that Daniel has spoken to me like that. He rarely swears and has never sworn at me. Why is he so very drunk and angry? Surely Mike can't have caused all of this rage? I turn my head into my pillow and cry silent, gut-wrenching sobs, wondering how on earth we can put our marriage back together.

15

When I next awake, my heart is racing, and I jolt upright in bed, trying to catch my breath. What the hell was that?

The noise comes again. A hammering on the door and the screaming voice of a woman. I flick on my bedside lamp, and my heart lurches once more as I see that Daniel isn't lying next to me. My clock says it's 3.07 a.m. The banging comes again.

I rush out of the bedroom, running downstairs, fumbling to switch lights on so I can see where I'm going. Where is Daniel? Is he sleeping through this racket, upstairs in the spare room, or is he passed out on the couch in the living room? I haven't got time to look. I career through the hallway into the kitchen, where Peanut is letting out half-hearted barks from his bed.

Nadia is at the patio doors in the kitchen, lit up by the sensor lights that come on at the front of the house. She is bashing her hands against the glass panes of the doors, totally hysterical. I fumble for the keys and eventually unlock the door.

'What's happened?' I ask, shivering more from the shock of being awakened than by the cool night air.

'I can't... It's... You need... Come...' Nadia is trembling all over, her face white, her teeth chattering, her eyes wide and darting from side to side. She is wearing thin jersey pyjamas in dark grey that cling to her slender body. She grasps my forearm and pulls me outside. I'm barefoot and in a cotton nightdress, but I let her tug me, and then we're stumbling down the steps to the drive between the house and the barn, eyes straining to see where we're going. All the lights are on in the barn, and it throws strange, distorted shadows across the drive and the lawn, making me disoriented. And then Nadia falls to her knees on the ground and lets out a horrific guttural sound, and as my eyes adjust to the low light, I see what she sees.

I don't know if it's her or me who lets out the scream.

There's a body lying on the gravel drive. Arms and legs are at contorted angles, a viscous puddle of darkness pooled underneath the head.

'Daniel!' I howl, and my legs give way as I crumple onto the ground next to the body.

Nadia grabs my shoulder, her fingernails digging into my flesh. She yanks me backwards as she stands up.

'No!' she screeches.

'What's going on?' It's a male voice coming from behind us.

The voice I know and love.

I stand up, slowly, my jaw slack. I was sure it was Daniel lying here on the ground, but no. Daniel is walking out of the house, wearing his navy pyjamas, his hair up on end, rubbing his eyes. I glance back at the body on the ground, swiping away the tears, my eyes better adjusted now to the low light.

'Shit,' I murmur as I realise that the body lying here looks nothing like my husband.

'It's Mike,' I whisper to myself as I take in the cast on his foot, the distended belly, the blood oozing from his head, and the jagged, bloodied, broken wine bottle lying next to his face.

Nadia lets out a moan and collapses to the ground. I fling

my arms around her. And then Daniel is there, his drunkenness dissipated, straight into the no-nonsense, let's-save-his-life doctor mode.

'Hannah, get a torch and my doctor's bag from my study. Switch on every light in the house and call for an ambulance,' he says.

I hesitate.

'Go!' he yells, and it spurs me into action. I run up to the house and grab the torch we keep above the coat stand in the utility room. Then I skid into his study and grasp his large black leather doctor's case and hurry back through the house, down the steps to where Daniel is kneeling on the ground, next to Mike's prone body. I put the case down and hand Daniel the torch.

'Is he alive?' I ask. Nadia lets out a yelp.

'Have you called an ambulance?' Daniel asks.

I don't wait to answer and rush back into the house to call 999. 'There's a dying man,' I say breathlessly, my eyes fixed on the door to the hall, praying that the children are still asleep and stay asleep. After the emergency controller has taken down all of our details, I grab my anorak from a hook in the utility room and walk outside again, reticent this time, as I don't want to see. I really don't. Nadia is holding the torch, but her hand is shaking too much to keep the light still. Daniel stands up slowly. I stare in horror as I see the blood all over Daniel's pyjamas, on his hands, even a smear across his face.

He turns towards Nadia.

'I'm sorry,' he says. 'There's nothing more I can do.'

And then Nadia turns into a wild animal. She is screaming and punching Daniel. 'No!' she yells.

'You need to try harder, Daniel,' I shout, almost tripping as I hurtle down the steps. 'You can't give up.' It's Daniel's duty as a doctor to try to bring him back to life.

'He's dead,' Daniel says quietly.

Nadia turns on him again. 'You're a murderer! How could you kill my husband? What have you done, you bastard?' She kicks and punches him, and Daniel just stands there, his face gaunt with dark shadows, and he lets Nadia hit him. He doesn't move a muscle.

I stare at my husband.

What has he done?

Eventually, Nadia falls back onto the ground next to Mike, her cries becoming more like hiccups, as if all the energy from her body has been siphoned out.

'Oh my God!' I say. It feels as if my legs are about to give way. I grab the side of the building. Has Daniel done this? Has he killed Mike? They were arguing last night. But no, it wasn't last night, it was just two hours ago. Did Daniel smash a bottle over Mike's head in a fury? A surge of nausea pushes up through my throat, and I have to swallow hard to stop it.

'Daniel!' I lurch towards him and pull him backwards, out of the light and into the shadow of the doorway. 'What did you do?' I am shaking violently now, but Daniel just stares at me, his eyes empty and his mouth open. 'You need to tell me,' I urge. I slap him on the cheek, but I'm not getting through to him. He doesn't move, his arms hanging loosely, his eyes barely blinking, Mike's blood smeared all over him.

And then the sirens get louder and louder, and the dark night is lit up by blue lights. Kayleigh appears in the doorway to the barn, her face white, her eyes wide and uncomprehending. Nadia rushes to her and buries her daughter's head in her chest, moving her backwards into the barn.

Vehicles come to a screech behind us, and men and women in uniform pace forwards and take control. In seconds, our property morphs from being our home and a place of refuge into a crime scene, and everything I thought I knew disintegrates.

There are two police cars and an ambulance. Daniel snaps

out of his stupor and talks to the paramedics. There is a lot of nodding and low voices, and I stand, my back to the barn, shivering uncontrollably.

'Mummy.' Hearing Rosa's voice, I rush up to the house, putting my arm around Rosa and leading her back towards the staircase. And then Joel is there, too.

'What's happening, Mummy?' Rosa asks.

'There's been an accident, darling.'

'Where's Daddy?'

'He's outside helping the paramedics and the police.'

'Police? Why are there police here?'

I fumble for an explanation. 'Because when there's an accident, the police have to check it out.' I think of that barbed, bloodied, broken wine bottle with its shards of protruding glass dumped next to Mike's head. This was no accident.

'I want to see the policemen,' Joel says.

'No, sweetie. They can't be disturbed. You both need to go back to bed and sleep. It's the middle of the night, and if you don't sleep, you are going to feel horrible in the morning.'

It's a relief that both the children's bedrooms face the back of the house, so they can't see what's happening, but Rosa is too curious. I'm worried she will tiptoe into our bedroom, where she will have a full view of Mike's body. I have to gulp in large breaths of air to stop my stomach from heaving. How will I ever dispel that horrific, vivid image of Mike with his head bashed open and all of that blood, not just on him, but on Daniel, too.

Daniel. Oh, Daniel, what did you do?

When I have settled both the children, I slip on some old clothes and walk slowly back downstairs, first to Daniel's study. It is spotless, as it always is: nothing lying on his desk, his chair slipped neatly under his desk, books neatly arranged on the bookshelves, no hint of a heavy drinking spree. I go into the living room and back into the kitchen, and it's the same in there. I have no idea how much Daniel drank, but it must have been at least two bottles. Yet there is no empty glass in the sink or bottles on the table. Even when he is close to a drunken stupor, Daniel clears up after himself, putting empty glasses in the dishwasher and empty bottles or cans in the recycling bin at the back of the house. But the police will surely smell the wine on his breath. And then what conclusions will they draw? The same one as I have come to? That my husband, my brilliant, handsome, life-saving Daniel became so enraged tonight that he took a life.

I sink into a kitchen chair and put my face in my hands. What will become of Nadia and poor little Kayleigh? However disagreeable Mike was, he didn't deserve to die. And our home, it will be tainted forever. But the palpable fear is all around Daniel. Did he take his empty bottle and smash it over Mike's head? Did the incessant music and relentless provocation become all too much? Was Daniel's efforts to revive Mike a charade for Nadia, me and the police?

Is my husband a killer?

'Mrs Pieters?'

I jump as the kitchen door is opened and a policeman walks in. My eyes are drawn to the horrific scene outside, where the emergency services have turned night into day with bright white lights illuminating everything. I watch as they erect a white tent over Mike's body, and he transforms from a person into a corpse and a piece of evidence in a crime scene. I see Daniel standing to one side, talking to two uniformed police officers. He is gesticulating and looks nothing like the calm, controlled man that I thought was his default mode. I search for Nadia, but she isn't there. I suppose she is inside the barn, being comforted by strangers. Poor Nadia.

'Mrs Pieters?' he asks again.

'I'm sorry, it's just... it's such a shock.'

'Of course. May I ask you some questions?'

'Yes,' I say, wondering if I should offer this man and the rest of the team a cup of tea, but it's the middle of the night; is it even appropriate? My thoughts are racing, unfurling in different directions. The policeman takes a step nearer to me, and his small grey eyes peer over a pug-like nose. But I can't look at him; my eyes are fixed on the scene outside. A policewoman opens the rear passenger door of a police car, and a policeman standing to its side gestures at Daniel. No, surely not! My Daniel, who is still wearing his pyjamas stained with blood, with his leather moccasin slippers on his feet, is getting into the back seat of the car. A policeman slips in beside Daniel, and the policewoman gets into the driver's seat. The car starts up and begins reversing up the drive.

They are taking my husband away.

What did Daniel say to them? What has he done?

'Daniel!' I say, my hand over my mouth. 'Where are they taking him?'

'Mrs Pieters, I understand that this is a very distressing time for you, but I need to ask you some questions. May I sit?'

I nod and sink further into the kitchen chair. 'Where have they taken Daniel?'

'Mr Pieters is attending an interview at the police station.'

'But he just wanted to help. He's a doctor. He hasn't done anything!'

'I would like to ask you a few questions.' He pulls the chair away from the table, the legs scraping on the flagstone floor, and sits in it heavily.

'My name is DS Jason Murphy. Am I right in thinking that you and your husband own this property and that the building over there' – he points at the barn – 'is run as a holiday cottage?'

I nod.

'How long have you lived here, Mrs Pieters?'

'Ten years. My name is Hannah.'

'Thank you, Hannah. And how long have you been running the holiday cottage?'

'Only a month. They are our second guests.'

'You mean the deceased Mike Jones; his wife, Nadia; and daughter, Kayleigh.'

I nod. *Deceased.* It's such a soft word for something so finite.

DS Murphy places an A4 notebook on the table, along with a black biro. He leans towards me, and I can smell garlic on his breath. 'Hannah, can you talk me through what happened tonight?'

I fumble for coherent thoughts. 'I went to bed about 11 p.m. Nadia and Mike were playing music really loudly. I fell asleep, but got woken again by the music around 1 a.m. And then Nadia was banging on the door and screaming at just after 3 a.m. That's when I went downstairs and followed her outside, and I saw...' I let out a little whimper. 'I'm sorry,' I whisper.

'What time did Mr Pieters come to bed?'

I freeze. I can't look at this policeman. What will it sound like if I say Daniel didn't come to our bed? But I can't lie. I don't know what Daniel has already told them.

'Daniel and I had a bit of an argument, and he didn't sleep with me.'

'Where did your husband sleep?'

'In the spare room, I think. He slept there last night, too.'

'Is this a common occurrence, for your husband to sleep in another bedroom?'

'No.' I blush as I hang my head. 'It's only happened once before. But Daniel is a doctor. He would never hurt anyone.'

DS Murphy's face is impassive.

'And how much did you have to drink last night?'

'Just a glass of white wine.'

'And your husband?'

'I don't know.' My voice is almost inaudible to me. 'Maybe two bottles.'

'Is that normal for him, to consume so much?'

I hear the judgement in the question, and I want to scream at this man. My Daniel is a good person; he may drink a bit too much from time to time, but you only have to look at him to see he's in great shape. He's a carer. He spends his life making people better.

'He drinks at the weekends. Everyone does, don't they? But he's not an aggressive drunk if he consumes too much. He's more likely to fall asleep.'

'You mentioned that there was loud music playing from the barn. Did either you or your husband ask your guests to turn the music down.'

I think of Daniel standing on our patio, screaming profanities into the night air. I remember how I needed to restrain him and beg him not to go over there, not to make a bad situation any worse.

Did he? Did Daniel and Mike come to blows? Did my husband take his empty wine bottle and smash it over Mike's head?

'Daniel shouted at them to be quiet, but he didn't go over there. I doubt they would have heard him, their music was playing so loudly.' My voice is barely audible, even to me.

'What was your relationship like with the Jones family?'

'We didn't really have a relationship. They are paying guests, not friends.'

'Had you met them before they arrived to stay at your cottage?'

'No.'

'And how have they been whilst they've been staying here?'

'Okay. Their daughter, Kayleigh, gets on very well with our daughter, Rosa.'

'Your children, Hannah. Where are they?'

'Upstairs, asleep.'

'I'm afraid you are going to have to wake them, and you will all need to leave the property.'

'What!' I exclaim, jumping up from my chair. 'This is our home.'

'Unfortunately, this property is now a crime scene. We will need you to leave whilst our team carries out a search.'

'What are you looking for? There was a broken bottle with blood on it on the ground next to Mike. Was that used to kill him? You need to be looking for burglars or talking to the friends that Nadia and Mike had over the other night. And what about Nadia? Perhaps she hit her husband?'

DS Murphy tilts his head to one side and throws me a pitying look.

'I realise how very hard this must be for you, Hannah, but I'm afraid you will have to leave. One of our team can drive you to a neighbour or a member of your family.'

'How long will we have to stay away?' My voice cracks.

'Probably twenty-four to forty-eight hours. We will keep in constant contact, and rest assured, everything here will be kept safe. Incidentally, do you have any CCTV or security cameras?'

I shake my head. 'No. We don't even have an alarm.'

16

It's already gone 5 a.m.; the sky is light and the birds are singing, oblivious to the horrors that have unfolded at our home. I ask if I can make coffee before waking the children. DS Murphy gets one of his colleagues to make it for me.

I have no choice but to go to Mum and Dad's. I consider contacting Amber, but I don't want to put her in an awkward position. I'm all too aware that people get tainted by terrible events, and she has enough problems of her own without taking on mine. And so I go upstairs to wake up the children, a plain-clothed policewoman who introduced herself as Lizzie Hargreaves on my heels.

'You can't come in with me. The children will be terrified seeing a stranger here.'

'Don't worry, Mrs Pieters. I'll wait for you in the corridor, but please leave the door ajar.'

I consider making some sarcastic comment, asking what evidence she thinks I'll be tampering with in my little girl's pink room, but I'm too tired and too worried about what I'm going to say to Rosa, knowing that she will be the most affected, that never again will she feel totally safe. I ease the door open and walk inside. She's facing away from me, her dark hair splayed out on her pillow. I open the curtains to let in the daylight and sit gently on the edge of her bed.

'Rosa, you need to wake up, sweetheart.' She doesn't stir. Rosa has always been a good sleeper and difficult to rouse. Gently, I shake her at the same time as stroking her forehead. 'Darling, wake up, please.'

She gives a little cry, and then her eyes flicker open.

'What is it?' she asks, rolling over to face me.

'Darling, you need to get up.'

She frowns as her eyes glance at her large red alarm clock.

'I know it's very early, but something sad has happened.'

'What?' She sits bolt upright.

I hold her small warm hand in mine. 'Kayleigh's Daddy has died.'

She blinks several times. 'How?' Her eyes are wide.

'We don't know yet. That is why the police are here. They are investigating.'

Rosa tugs her hand away from mine and pushes back the duvet. She jumps out of bed and reaches for the clothes that she dumped on her small daisy-patterned armchair last night.

'I need to go and see Kayleigh. She'll need a friend as well as her mum.'

'Sweetie, you won't be allowed to see Kayleigh.'

Rosa stands stock-still. 'Why?'

'Because...' I struggle to come up with a decent answer. 'The police want to keep everyone separate for now.'

'I don't understand,' she says in a whisper.

'None of us do,' I say, pulling her towards me for a hug.

'We're going to stay with Grandma and Grandpa for a couple of days. Can you put the clothes and toys you want to take with you in your big bag? I need to go and wake Joel.'

.   .   .

HALF AN HOUR LATER, the children have each had a bowl of cereal and a glass of orange juice. Lizzie Hargreaves is an older woman, dressed in a pair of navy trousers and a white blouse, with straight mousey-brown hair and a forgettable face. She tries to be discreet as she shadows us.

'Where's Daddy?' Rosa asks me.

'He's gone to help the police find the baddie.'

'Can I go too?' Joel bounces off his chair.

'No, darling. We have to spend the day with Grandma and Grandpa.'

'But I want to stay here.'

I sigh as I stand up and look outside. The drive where Mike lay has been cordoned off with police tape, just as one sees on television. Our property is officially a crime scene. And although no one has explicitly said anything, it appears they have just one suspect. My husband.

I give Lizzie Hargreaves my parents' telephone number and address. 'We will need your phone too,' she says.

'But why?' I ask.

'I know it's an inconvenience, but we need the phones of everyone who was here last night.'

Reluctantly, I hand it over.

'What's happened to Daniel?' I ask.

'He's being interviewed at the station.'

'When will he come home? Will he be brought to my parents' house?'

She shrugs. 'Sorry, I don't know.'

I DRIVE AS SLOWLY as I can to my parents' house, but I really can't make the journey last more than twenty minutes. It's just before 6 a.m. when we arrive. And then I realise I can't even call them to let them know we're outside; the police have got my phone.

Holding Joel's hand in my left hand and Rosa's in my right, and with Peanut waiting patiently by our feet, I get Joel to ring their doorbell. We have to wait for a long time before the hall light goes on and I hear shuffling in the corridor.

'Who is it?' Dad asks.

'It's me, Hannah. I've got the kids and the dog with me.'

The door swings open, and Joel rushes into Dad's arms. He looks every one of his seventy-three years as he frowns over the top of Joel's head.

'Sorry to wake you,' I say. 'I'll explain all.'

'We've got lots of police in our house,' Joel says excitedly. 'They're searching for the baddie.'

Dad's face furrows. 'Why don't you two monsters go into the kitchen, and I'll switch on the telly.'

Morning television is something that never happens in our household, so they both skedaddle through the house.

'What's going on, love?' Dad asks, his hand on my shoulder. I notice how skinny he appears in his burgundy pyjamas.

'Mike Jones, the holiday guest, has been found dead on our drive. He was bashed with a bottle.'

'Bloody hell. Do they know who did it?'

I shake my head.

It isn't until we're walking down the corridor towards the blaring noise of children's television that Dad asks, 'Where is Daniel?'

'Nothing to be worried about,' I say, without looking at him. 'He's just helping the police with stuff.'

Dad stiffens. I know he's seen right through my words. 'I'll go upstairs and tell your mother that you're here.'

Two hours later, the front doorbell rings.

'It's for you, Hannah,' Dad says.

I walk slowly to the door. My limbs feel leaden and my head

pounds, the result of no sleep and three cups of coffee. My heart sinks when I see DS Murphy.

'Hello, Hannah. We would like you to attend an interview at the police station.'

'Why? You've already interviewed me.'

'We can't force you to attend, and of course this is a voluntary interview, but it would definitely be in your and your husband's best interests if you do. You're allowed a solicitor if you would like one.'

'But I haven't done anything wrong!'

'No one is suggesting you have. We just need to get a clearer understanding as to what happened last night.'

'Are you interviewing Nadia?'

'Yes, she is helping us with our enquiries.'

I feel a warm arm wrapping around my shoulders. It's Dad. 'You should go, love. Always best to help the police.' Dad has always had the greatest of respect for anyone in a position of authority. 'We'll keep the children entertained whilst you're gone.'

And so, just like Daniel a few hours ago, I find myself seated in the back of a police car; fortunately for me, an unmarked, ordinary saloon.

I HAVE NEVER BEEN inside a police station before, but I don't get much chance to look at my surroundings as I'm whisked straight through the reception lobby into a small room with a mock-wooden table and wooden chairs and a thin industrial grey carpet. I shiver from the strong air-conditioning and try not to inhale the unpleasant scent of disinfectant and stale sweat.

'Have a seat,' DS Murphy says, pulling out a chair for me.

He takes a seat opposite me, and a moment later, another policeman enters the room and sits next to Murphy.

'Good morning. I am DC Miles Buchanon, and as you know, we are investigating the death of Mike Jones at your property last night. You are not under arrest and you are free to leave at any time. You have agreed to be here to give a voluntary interview, and you are entitled to legal advice,' he says. He places a notebook on the table and removes a biro from his jacket pocket.

'Do I need a solicitor?'

'You don't need one, but you have the right to have a solicitor present should you so wish.'

I think of the only solicitor I know. Maya. But does she even do criminal law? I have only heard her talk about contracts and conveyancing. And do I really want her knowing what's happened? I can't think straight. It's not as if I have anything to hide.

'Did Daniel have a solicitor?'

'I'm afraid we're not able to comment on any other witnesses.'

'Can I speak to my husband?'

'Regrettably, no,' DC Buchanon says.

'Why?'

'Dr Pieters–'

'It's Mr Pieters,' I say. 'My husband is a surgeon.'

'Quite. Mr Pieters is still helping us with our enquiries.'

I try to count how many hours Daniel has been here. Why are they still talking to him? Does that mean... I can't go there. I sit on my hands to stop them from shaking, and gaze at the blank wall.

'Mrs Pieters, may we continue?'

I turn to face the policemen and nod.

'Can you please talk us through the events of yesterday evening and early this morning.'

'Again?' I direct the question to DS Murphy.

'Yes.'

And so I repeat what I have already told them, how I went to bed and then was awakened by Nadia.

'How would you describe your relationship with Nadia and Mike Jones?'

'Cordial. They were our guests, but they have caused us some aggravation.' As soon as I say that, both policemen stare at me, and I instantly regret my words.

'They insisted on staying on another week because Mike Jones hurt himself, and they are rather messy and noisy.'

'Nadia Jones mentioned an argument between your husband and the deceased that took place in the early hours of this morning. What did you hear?'

'They were shouting at each other, but Daniel would never do anything to hurt Mike. He's a gentle person. And he tried so hard to resuscitate Mike when we found him on the drive.'

'Where was your husband between that argument at 1 a.m. and 3 a.m., when Nadia Jones found her husband dead?'

'Asleep in the spare room.'

'But you have already said he wasn't in your bedroom; therefore you cannot know for sure where he was.'

There is silence. 'I suppose not,' I say eventually, in a small voice.

'Can you explain how your husband's prints were found all over the broken bottle that was used to kill Mike Jones?'

I tremble and blink quickly. 'My husband drinks wine. I suppose it was his bottle. Mike Jones preferred to drink beer. So obviously it would have had Daniel's prints on it, because he handled it. That doesn't mean he hit Mike over the head with it. My husband is a good person. He's a doctor. He would never knowingly hurt anyone.'

The two men are impassive.

'Tell us about the various arguments your husband had with Mike Jones.'

Everything I say will make Daniel appear guilty. He has

been aggressive towards Mike, but only because he was needled and provoked to such a degree that he snapped. Besides, arguing with someone doesn't lead to murder. But what should I say?

'Mrs Pieters?' DS Murphy prompts me.

'It was because Mike Jones was threatening to sue us for negligence. He slipped on a paving stone and broke his ankle. He was incredibly rude to Daniel and provoked him. Yes, Daniel shouted at him, but I know my husband. He would never resort to physical violence.'

'But that isn't true, is it, Mrs Pieters?' DI Buchanon glances at his notebook. I try to read it upside down, but he closes it before I can decipher any words. 'Your husband pushed Mike Jones over at a children's party. There were numerous witnesses.'

Oh God! Everything suggests that Daniel is guilty.

'Mike was exaggerating. He wasn't hurt.'

'You see our problem: All the evidence points to your husband losing his temper and smashing a wine bottle over Mike Jones' head.'

'Nadia could have done it.' I speak in a small voice.

'You say you were asleep, but perhaps you crept out of bed and in the dark smashed the wine bottle into Mike Jones' skull yourself,' DI Buchanon suggests, his head tilted to one side.

'No!' I am horrified. 'I could never do anything like that, nor could Daniel. Please, when can I see him?'

DS Murphy taps his fingers on the table. It makes me feel even more nervous, and I am having to bite my lip to stop the tears from coming. I don't think I have ever felt more helpless and anxious.

'Unfortunately, you can't see your husband. We will be holding him for the maximum twenty-four hours whilst we question him on suspicion of murder, and we'll probably seek an extension. We are awaiting some forensics to be analysed, but you need to prepare yourself for the fact that it is extremely likely your husband will be charged with murder.'

'No!' I exclaim, my hand over my mouth. And then I burst into tears.

ANOTHER YOUNG POLICE officer takes me back to Mum and Dad's house. We sit in silence during the journey, and this time I'm in the front passenger seat, gazing out of the window, but unseeing. Are the police right? Could Daniel have killed Mike? He was very drunk last night and angry. The two make a terrifying cocktail.

I think back, and not once during the past decade has Daniel been physically violent towards me or the children. I keep on thinking about that plate he broke about four years ago, hurling it across the kitchen like a Frisbee. It hit the wall, leaving an indent, before shattering into a thousand pieces on the floor. Peanut bolted out of the room. But Daniel was full of remorse and he was under such pressure. His father was dying, Professor Entwhistle was blocking any chance of promotion, and he'd lost a high-profile retired football player on the operating table. The papers didn't go so far as to name Daniel as responsible, but it didn't make for comfortable reading.

What was it that pushed Daniel over the edge and provoked him to chuck the plate? As the car speeds towards Macclesfield, I remember. He received a letter from Alison, demanding more alimony.

I met Alison a few weeks before our wedding. She appeared at the house, ostensibly to collect some horse equipment she had left in the barn. Daniel was out, and it was obvious that she chose her moment to find me alone. Although I had seen a photograph of her online (it goes without saying that I was going to check out my predecessor), she was nothing like I had imagined. Austere, with a long face and hair chopped into a severe, spikey style – masculine even – she helped herself to a cup of tea and sat down at the kitchen table.

'You need to know what you're getting into,' she said, slurping her hot drink. 'It's no fun being married to him. He's a selfish bastard with a temper. If that's the sort of thing that takes your fancy, then you're welcome to him. Just remember that his work will always come first. Always.'

I don't know how she managed to consume the hot tea as quickly as she did, but she was gone within five minutes, any pretence of collecting items from the barn forgotten. Daniel laughed when I told him that she had visited me. He pulled me towards him and said he hoped that I now understood why he and Alison were so incompatible. That I was the love of his life and the only person who truly understood him.

But do I really understand him? Now I'm not so sure.

BACK AT MY PARENTS' house, Mum makes a late lunch, a quiche and salad, but I'm not hungry. Afterwards, I ask if they would mind if I lie down for an hour. I swipe Dad's iPad from next to his bed and take it to the guest room, where I lie down on the unmade bed to think. Although I am bone-weary, my mind can't stop racing. There are three possibilities. Daniel killed Mike in a rage; Nadia killed her husband, or a stranger took him out and disappeared after the deed was done. Could Mike have slipped and hurt himself and been lying there bleeding to death? The police must have discounted that. Could Nadia have had the strength to bash her husband over the head with a bottle? She must be half his size and is so very slender. I don't see how she could have reached his head.

I do a search for the Joneses, but all I find are a few glowing reviews they've left on TripAdvisor. And I'm not even sure it's actually them. There are no photos, no social media accounts that I can find. Basically, Nadia and Mike Jones are invisible.

17

I feel like a caged animal at Mum and Dad's. For nearly seventy-two hours, I pace their house, watch inane daytime television, and play board games with the kids. Rosa thinks I'm losing on purpose, being kind to her and Joel. I'm not. I can't concentrate. And then DS Jason Murphy calls on my parents' landline.

'Just to let you know that you can return home.'

'Thank you,' I say. 'And Daniel. When can I see my husband?'

'Sorry, I'm not sure about that.' He doesn't sound sorry.

'The barn. Are Nadia's things still there?'

'No. Nadia and her daughter returned this morning to collect their belongings.'

I let out a quiet sigh of relief. It may be cowardly, but I don't want to see Nadia. I don't want to have to pick up the Joneses' belongings and inhale her scent and clear away their dirty glasses.

Yet now we are allowed to go home, I'm not sure I want to.

I need to be strong for the kids, and for Daniel, so I force myself to say goodbye to Mum and Dad and bundle the kids and dog into the car for our homeward journey. I think of Nadia and her desire to know what the future holds. She must have got the tarot reading totally wrong: it was her who was being warned, not me. And then I chastise myself. I'm not superstitious in the way she is, but I don't look at hearses when they're driving past me, and I get the shivers when I see those little shrines that are left at the side of roads to commemorate the person who has died there. So perhaps I am more like her than I pretend. Maybe she does have a gift. As I steer the car slowly down our steep hill and approach the house, I glance over to where Mike lay. I wonder if I will ever be able to walk on the section of driveway where Mike died. It fills me with horror.

The children bound into the house as if they have never been away, seemingly unaware that strangers have been combing through our things. But Peanut and I sense it. He stands in the middle of the kitchen, his nose in the air, sniffing. It does smell differently in here. There is a chemical odour that I can't place, and although the counters are spotless and the chairs neatly pushed in under the kitchen table, there are things that are in the wrong place. The telephone that is normally wedged into the corner, underneath the window, is in the middle of the counter, its lead stretched along the wall. My yellow rubber gloves that I use for washing up aren't hidden in the cupboard under the sink but have been left neatly to the left of the kitchen taps. My mobile phone is lying on the kitchen table. I suppose the police have kept Daniel's.

I carry our little suitcases through the house and upstairs. Here it looks just as we left it. Our beds are unmade, stale glasses of water on bedside tables. But when I go into the spare room, hoping to pick up the pillow that Daniel last slept on, the bed has been stripped bare and the sheets are gone. I walk back into our bedroom and open the sliding door to Daniel's wardrobe. His shirts that are sent away to be ironed, because I never get out all the creases, are normally lined up with an inch between each shirt, starting with the lightest colours on the left and morphing to the darkest colours on the right. But someone has rifled through here, and now the shirts are all wedged up together. I swallow a sob as I slide the door closed. Daniel will be gutted. He must be terrified, holed up in a cell, not knowing if he will ever get his liberty again.

A few hours later, DS Murphy telephones me again, this time on our landline. 'Just to let you know that Daniel has been formally charged with the murder of Mike Jones. I'm sorry to be the bearer of bad news. He will be attending a bail hearing at the magistrate's court tomorrow.'

DS Murphy carries on talking, but I don't hear him. I drop the phone onto the mattress as I collapse onto the bed. This cannot be happening. This is a total travesty of justice. Daniel is not a murderer. I go into the bathroom and turn the taps on at full blast. I allow myself to sob for a minute or two, and then I throw cold water over my face and wipe my eyes.

I have to pull myself together for the children.

Rosa and Joel are in the kitchen, sitting on the floor next to Peanut. 'Mum, can I go and see Kayleigh?' Rosa asks.

I stare through the patio doors at the barn. There are no cars outside it, and the lights are off.

'She's gone,' I say, my voice flat.

'She can't have gone!' Rosa exclaims, jumping up from the floor. 'We're blood sisters. We're best friends for ever. She wouldn't have gone away without saying goodbye!' She runs towards the doors and puts her nose up against the glass.

'Her daddy died. She can't be here anymore.'

'That's so unfair!' Rosa says. 'Poor Kayleigh.'

I glance at her, and her bottom lip is quivering. I pull her towards me. 'Sometimes life isn't very fair. You'll find another best friend soon.'

But Rosa shakes her head and tugs away from me. I listen to her footsteps as she runs upstairs. I hurry after her, into her bedroom, and sit on the edge of the bed, where she lies in a huddle.

'Don't be sad, darling. You'll make new friends when you go back to school in a couple of weeks.'

'You don't understand,' she says and shifts further away from me.

BUT PERHAPS I'M like one of those rubberneckers drawn to the scene of a fatal accident, the type of person I thought I abhorred, because later in the afternoon, when Peanut is restless for a walk, I follow him towards the barn. I stay far away from the patch of ground where Mike died, averting my eyes in case there are still any telltale traces of red-brown blood. The front door is unlocked, and I hold my breath as I walk inside. The key is on the inside of the door, and the place is a total tip. I wonder how the police managed to go through all of this mess, because I assume they must have given it as careful a search as they did in our house. The Joneses' belongings are gone, but cushions from the sofas are scattered on the floor; old pizza boxes and filthy glasses of wine and cups of coffee have been left on every surface. The kitchen is marginally cleaner, as if someone has made a half-hearted attempt to wash up the dirty dishes. The legs of two of the chairs are gnawed where the puppy must have chewed them, and the long curtains either side of the patio doors are stained yellow. A large dried-up puddle of urine has seeped out from under the sofa. The scent of rotting food, stale beer and urine makes me want to gag.

The place disgusts me. My beautiful, carefully curated holiday cottage has been decimated. I can't look at it anymore, so I hurry back to the front door and lock it behind me. I will deal with the barn at a later date.

. . .

THE BAIL HEARING is set for 11 a.m. Mum and Dad arrive at 9.30 a.m., and Mum takes over the care of the kids and Peanut. Dad insists on coming with me to the court. I have put on a straight navy skirt and a cream blouse and look like I'm going for a job interview. I have no idea what to expect, but I can't wait to see Daniel and tell him how much I love him. I refuse to let any doubts cloud my head. I believe in my husband's innocence.

Dad takes control, and it's exactly what I need. He knows much more about the justice system than I do. About twenty years ago, he decided to apply to be a magistrate, working on his application and learning as much about the legal system as he could. But then his number two in the business became seriously ill, and Dad's workload increased. The opportunity to carry out his public duty passed him by. Although Dad is the most law-abiding person I know, he isn't intimidated by it, and if the circumstances were any different, I know that he would relish the opportunity to have a session in court.

He gives my hand a quick squeeze as we walk into the courthouse building. There are lots of people milling around the lobby, and we have to weave through them. Dad finds the notice that lists which hearing is being held in which court. My heart sinks as I see Daniel's name. R v Daniel Pieters, Court 3.

The room is panelled all the way around in a light wood. There are three magistrates seated on a high podium at the back of the court, a woman seated in the centre, and a man either side of her. A man wearing a black suit sits at a desk in front of them, facing the same direction. Seated opposite at two separate tables are another two men, the solicitors for the defence and prosecution. I wonder why there is a lot of muttering and people shifting around in the public gallery. We take seats at the end of a row in the public gallery, and then silence falls as a door to the right of the magistrates opens and Daniel is led in, handcuffed to a court guard. I have to stuff my fist into my mouth to stop myself from calling out. Dad grabs my hand and, once again, squeezes it tightly. Daniel looks exhausted, with grey rings under his eyes; his hair is greasy and sticking up at the back. His lips are firmly closed in a straight line, and those eyes that I love are staring at the ground. Where is his confidence? He is wearing a white, creased shirt and a pair of black trousers, clothes I don't recognise. I will him to look up at the public gallery, to seek me out so that I can give him reassurance. But he doesn't raise his eyes.

The man in the black suit seated below the magistrates starts speaking.

'Please state your name.'

'Daniel Pieters.'

'Mr Pieters, you have been charged with the murder of Mr Michael Kevin Jones. Do you plead guilty or not guilty?'

'Not guilty.' Daniel's voice rings out clearly through the court. A few people inhale audibly, and I glance to the right to try to work out who is here.

The chair of the court, the middle-aged woman in the centre wearing a navy-blue cardigan with little gold buttons, speaks. 'As this is an indictable offence, Mr Pieters, you will be committed into the court system and remanded in custody, and your application for bail will be heard at the crown court. A date will be set for a plea and case management hearing at the crown court. Dismissed.'

And then the policeman leads Daniel away, through the door that he came out of only moments earlier.

'What?' I gasp. 'What does that mean?' I turn to Dad.

'His bail hearing can't be heard here in the magistrates court. It's got to be referred upwards,' Dad says.

I grab my handbag and hurry out of the courtroom. Dad scrambles to stay with me.

'Wait, Hannah!' he says.

'I need to speak to Daniel,' I say, weaving in and out of people in my desperation to find Daniel. But when I get into the lobby, Daniel is nowhere to be seen. I accost a young man with a lanyard around his neck.

'Excuse me. Can you tell me where I should go to talk to someone who has been remanded in custody?'

He throws me a strange look and shrugs. And then I see Daniel's solicitor. He's talking to someone, but I rush over and grab his sleeve. He looks up at me, startled.

'I'm sorry to interrupt. I'm Hannah Pieters, Daniel's wife.'

'How do you do? Matthew Stocksdale.' He puts his hand out to shake mine.

'Where is Daniel? Can I talk to him?'

'Sorry, Mrs Pieters. Your husband will be taken to jail until his PCMH in the crown court.'

'He's going to jail?' I ask, in a whisper. Dad puts his arm around my shoulders.

'Yes, he'll be held on remand until his bail hearing. Hopefully, we can persuade the court to let him out on bail at that hearing.'

'When will it be?'

'The courts are running so behind at the moment, I would expect four to six weeks.'

'You mean he's going to be kept in prison for a crime he didn't commit for that long?' My voice is high-pitched and strident. 'How can that be fair?'

'Indeed,' Dad chips in. 'I thought there was a presumption of innocence in this country.'

'As much as I would like to change the system, unfortunately, it is what it is. You should be able to visit your husband in the prison in approximately a week's time.' He hands me a business card, with embossed writing on a thick white stock. 'We'll stay in touch, Mrs Pieters. Please excuse me. I have another case to attend to.'

And then he's gone.

'This isn't justice,' I whisper to Dad as I wipe tears from my eyes.

'It's a system,' he says. 'Come on, let's get you home.'

As we walk out of the court building, I hear the click of a photo lens. I look up and see two photographers pointing their oversized cameras in my direction. There is a cluster of people, several with microphones. And then I see her.

Nadia is speaking to a journalist, her diamante nails catching the light as she waves her hands around. One of the journalists looks up and spots me.

'Mrs Pieters!' he exclaims. Nadia glances in my direction, her eyes narrowed, but as several of the journalists move towards me, like a flock of crows descending on their prey, Nadia disappears. How do these people know who I am? I feel as if I can't breathe, as if something is gripping my throat.

'What do you have to say about your husband, one of this country's most eminent heart surgeons, being accused of murder?'

A microphone is thrust into my face.

'Why did your husband do it?'

'No comment!' Dad says firmly, elbowing a couple of them out of the way. He grabs my hand and pulls me through the melee. My eyes are darting from left to right, desperately trying to spot Nadia. Where has she gone? And then we are walking briskly along the pavement towards the car park, and I discover that my cheeks are wet with tears I hadn't realised I had shed.

'I wanted to speak to Nadia,' I say to Dad as I slip into the passenger seat.

'Good heavens! Why would you want to speak to her?'

'I don't know. It's a travesty of justice, and I want to look her in the eyes and ask her if she killed her husband.'

'Just as well the two of you didn't come face-to-face.'

Dad drives the car out of town, slowly heading back towards Macclesfield. I lay my forehead against the cool glass of the window and shut my eyes. And then I remember that the fridge is bare and the children must be fed.

'I need to do some shopping, Dad. Can we stop off at Tesco's?'

'Of course, love.'

A few minutes later, we're driving into the large car park.

'I'll stay here and listen to the cricket on the radio,' Dad says.

'Okay. I won't be long.'

I hurry into the store. Newspapers are displayed on a stand to the left of the entrance, the local paper taking pride of place. I stop in my tracks.

'Watch out, love,' a man says as he misses my legs with his trolley by a whisker.

It feels as if my insides have been ripped out whilst someone is gripping tightly around my neck. I can't breathe. There is a picture of Daniel on the front page of the newspaper. *Leading Surgeon Charged With Murder of Holiday Guest.*' I turn around and run back to Dad's car.

18

I have to wait a whole week before I'm allowed to visit Daniel. We speak on the phone once, but the call is hasty and unsatisfactory. I try to hold it together, but my voice is high-pitched and my tone ridiculously upbeat. Daniel sounds close to tears, constantly asking me if I believe him. He repeatedly promises that he didn't do anything wrong. Hearing his voice, I feel shame that I ever doubted him.

And now, I am booked in for a visit.

As I step out of the car and walk up to the security gate, I am terrified. I have never set foot in a prison and never expected that I would. I hold my bag close to my chest and walk with what I hope suggests confidence, towards the entrance. It's much like going through airport security, other than I have to put my bag in a locker and they double-check that I have nothing in my pockets.

I am so relieved to see Daniel. For some reason, I thought that we wouldn't be allowed to touch, that we might be seated with a transparent screen between us, but no. Daniel is standing up, and he holds open his arms. I rush into them, my tears soaking through his white shirt. Although the fabric

smells of harsh chemicals and not the non-bio laundry detergent I use at home, it's as if I've come home.

We sit down opposite each other. Daniel leans forwards and
takes my hands, holding them tightly on the small table in
front of us. He looks me straight in the eyes.

'I didn't do it, Hannah. I'm innocent.'

'I know, darling.'

'But do you really know?' He is peering at me. A nerve
flickers uncontrollably underneath his left eye and he blinks
rapidly, as if to make it go away.

'Of course I know you didn't do it.' I glance away for a
second and then speak as quietly as I can. 'The problem is, I
heard you shouting at Mike. What happened?'

Daniel sighs and releases my hands. 'We shouted at each
other, but I stayed on the patio. Mike was standing in front of
the barn's door, smoking a cigarette. I hurled some insults at
him, then went back into the kitchen, tidied up, locked the
doors, shut the windows, and went upstairs to the spare room. I
was exhausted and more pissed than I've been in a long time. I
fell asleep. The next thing I knew was hearing you and Nadia
screaming. When I left Mike, he was alive. I promise.'

'So what happened?'

'Nadia must have killed him or hired someone to do the
deed.'

I bite my lip. Could Nadia really have the strength to kill
a man?

'The children send their love. I haven't told them where you
are. They think you're in London, working.'

Daniel nods, but I wonder if he's heard me. He leans across
the table and speaks in a whisper. 'Have the police searched
our house?'

'Yes.'

'Did they find the SD card in the bird camera?'

'What?'

'The hidden bird camera under the drainpipe by the bins.'

'I know where the camera is. Why are you asking?'

'If they haven't, don't mention it. I need you to look at the footage and double-check to see if it shows anything. I'm pretty sure I tidied away all the bottles before I went to bed, but I was plastered, and I can't remember exactly.'

'The kitchen was tidy,' I say flatly.

'Just double-check the camera for me, darling. If we're lucky, the footage will show Nadia or some accomplice going through the recycling bin. But I need to be sure it doesn't incriminate me in any way.'

'Incriminate you how?' I frown.

'I don't know,' he says in an urgent whisper. 'There may be some holes in my memory from that night.'

'Why didn't you say anything about the bird camera to the police or your solicitor?'

'Because I don't know what it shows. You are the only person I can trust.'

'I don't understand, Daniel. If you didn't do anything wrong, then why are you worried about it?'

'Because I remember shouting at Mike. I remember locking up. I remember waking up when I heard your screams, but I don't remember clearing up or getting into bed.'

'So you might have hit Mike?' I sit back in my chair, staring blankly at Daniel.

'Of course I bloody didn't!' he hisses at me. 'I'm a doctor. I save lives. I'm not violent. For God's sake, Hannah, if *you* don't believe me, then I'm truly doomed.'

I let out a sigh. 'Sorry, darling. Of course I believe you.' But now Daniel has planted a little nugget of doubt. I shake my head. I need to be strong for him, to be one hundred percent committed to believing justice will be done and that he will be exonerated.

The bird camera is facing ninety degrees away from where

Mike was found, so it won't show who struck the fatal blow. Of course, it might reveal a stranger coming down the drive or snooping around the property, and it might show someone rifling in our recycling bins and taking out the empty bottle of wine that had Daniel's fingerprints all over it. Or it might show Daniel doing something... I'm not sure what.

'Are you okay, Hannah? And the children? Are they all right?'

His words jolt me from my reverie. 'We're coping. Mum and Dad are lifesavers. We just need to get you home and clear your name.'

'I miss you,' Daniel says. He hangs his head, and for the first time since that first moment I set eyes on him, he looks vulnerable. Worse than that, pathetic. 'Hannah, please. You must believe in me. I need you.'

'Time's up. All visitors to leave,' the guard shouts.

It is almost a relief.

I DRIVE HOME on autopilot and find myself parked behind our house, climbing out of the car, having just visited my husband in prison. Prison. We are law-abiding, good, middle-class people. These sorts of things don't happen to people like us.

I stomp into the kitchen and open the fridge. I feel like drinking a glass of wine, but it's barely 3.30 p.m., and Mum and Dad will be bringing the kids home in a couple of hours. I don't give in to the temptation and instead close the fridge and put the kettle on. Whilst it's heating up, I walk back outside and around to the gable end of the house. I stand back on the approach road and look up at the drainpipe. It's impossible to make out the bird camera. Even when I walk right up to it, I can't tell it's there, neatly tucked underneath the eaves just above the black plastic drainpipe.

Inelegantly, I clamber on top of the bins and reach up for it.

And then it hits me. The small black bracket that Daniel screwed to the wall is there, but the camera itself is gone. No wonder I couldn't see it.

'Shit,' I say out loud. When was the last time I looked? It must have been when I played back the footage of the newly hatched chicks to Rosa and Kayleigh. I removed the card and then replaced it afterwards. It was the night that Nadia and Mike had their raucous guests over. It was nearly dark, and I recall thinking it wasn't very clever climbing on top of the bins as the light was fading. I definitely put the card back in the camera and haven't touched it since.

I jump down from the bins. The police must have found the camera and taken it along with the SD card to check for any relevant evidence. It was so well hidden, they must have scoured every centimetre of our property, in and out, to spot it. Obviously they wouldn't have seen Nadia collecting an empty bottle; otherwise Daniel wouldn't be locked up in prison. At best, perhaps it showed nothing. At least Daniel has nothing to worry about regarding that.

I am pouring hot water into my mug when I hear the crunch of car tyres outside. My immediate thought is that Mum and Dad must have brought the kids home early; perhaps one of them isn't feeling well. But when I stride over to the window, I see a white van parked outside. We don't get many unwanted visitors here, as we're so off the beaten track, and when a strange vehicle turns up, it makes me nervous. Peanut barks and I stride towards the patio doors.

I don't like what I see.

Elliott is strolling up towards the house, his hands in his jeans pockets, whistling to himself as if he doesn't have a care in the world. What the hell is he doing here?

I open the door and walk onto the patio.

'Hello.'

'Hannah! Dear Hannah!' he says, grinning at me. His teeth

are very white, as if they have been artificially brightened, but the effect is somewhat lost, as one of his front teeth is chipped. He carries on walking up the steps until he's standing so close, I can feel his breath on my face. I take a step backwards but catch my foot on the doorstep.

'Careful, pretty lady,' he says, reaching out to grab my arm.

'Hello, Elliott. Why are you here?'

'Come to check you're all right now your old man is in the slammer.'

'Thanks. I'm fine,' I say curtly.

'Me and you need to discuss something.'

'To do with the children?'

'Nope,' he says, his head cocked to one side, a look of infuriating amusement on his face.

'I don't need any help with my car.'

'I'm not here to tout for work. It's something a bit more personal than that.'

'I don't think we have anything to say to each other,' I say. I have no reason to dislike this man, other than he sends shivers up my spine for no obvious reason.

'You're gonna have to get comfortable with me, darling. Are we going to sit down over a nice cuppa, because I'm not sure you'll be wanting to have this conversation out here.'

'I'd like you to leave.' I cross my arms in front of my chest. I don't care if I'm rude. I don't care if Elliott slights me to the other parents. Besides, what could be worse than your husband being accused of murder?

He tightens his lips. 'No can do. You and me got things to discuss. Let's sit down and do it the nice, polite way, shall we?'

He eases past me through the open door and into the kitchen and stands by the table, his head cocked to one side. His mid-brown hair is slightly too long and curls at the neckline of his khaki T-shirt, which is stretched tightly over his chest, his pecs and muscles all too evident. He has a square jaw and green eyes that flicker with amusement. At what, I don't know. There is no doubt that Elliott is conventionally handsome, but there is something about him that makes me want to run a mile. I have no choice but to follow him inside my own house. Peanut barks once or twice and then lies down again.

Elliott pulls out a kitchen chair and sits down, his legs stretched out in front of him. My eyes are drawn to that missing finger.

'So, Mrs Pieters, wife of the doctor. I know something about your husband that you don't know.'

19

I stare at Elliott, who is looking at me with amusement.

'Spit it out, then,' I say. I lean my backside against the island unit, my arms crossed. I will not let this creep dictate to me in my own home.

'Has Daniel told you about a rather violent road-rage incident that occurred just under two years ago?'

I look at him blankly.

Elliott nods his head slowly. 'Thought not. You see your hubby, Dr Daniel Pieters, has a temper on him. He was driving home one evening in that souped-up black Range Rover of his, and he came along the A54 much too fast. I'd been minding my own business and had been up to the Burts' place to mend the old man's tractor. Anyway, I was just tootling along at a steady pace and had to pull into the middle of the road a bit to miss a pothole. Your Daniel came hurtling round the corner too fast, slammed on the brakes, and missed me by a whisker. He stopped the car, put his hand on his horn, and was making all sorts of rude gestures at me. Not my fault that he was driving too fast. I stopped the van, and he reversed the fancy motor. All I wanted to do was tell him to slow down, but oh no.

Daniel got out of his car and walked over to mine. He was all fired up. He yanked open the van's door, grabbed hold of my T-shirt, dragged me out the driver's seat, and walloped me. One big punch to the nose. See this?' Elliott points to the bump on the bridge of his nose. 'Your hubby did that. Blood every-where. Anyway, he quickly came to his senses. All apologetic, he was, begging me not to report him, saying that he had had a bad day. Well, there I was, bleeding out all over the van, in agony, and I wasn't too happy. But I'm not the violent type, so I didn't throw a punch back at him, even though he deserved it. I was ready to call the cops, and your Daniel must have realised that, because he made me a deal right there and then. If you keep quiet, he said, and don't report this, I'll pay you. Two grand, five grand, what do you want? If I hadn't just had my brains bashed, I might have asked for more. But I'm not a greedy man. So we settled on eight grand cash. Eight big ones for me to keep my lovely lips sealed. Did he tell you that, Hannah?'

I realise I am gawping, my mouth open, unable to believe what I'm hearing.

'Don't believe me? Why don't you ask him? Or check his outgoing payments. Fourth September it was, two years ago. He paid me cash, so the dosh must have come from somewhere.'

'Daniel wouldn't do something like that!' I say.

Elliott throws his head back and guffaws. 'Shame you don't know your hubby very well, and now he's locked up in the slammer, it might be too late.'

'Why are you telling me this?' I ask in a whisper.

'Because information is knowledge. Information is power. Information is money. What do you think the police might have to say about my little story? I don't think they'd be very impressed that their number-one suspect for murder had done a round of GBH a couple of years back and then begged me to keep quiet in exchange for eight grand. Wouldn't make him look like the good upstanding doctor, would it? But don't worry, pretty lady. I've got a solution.'

I am gripping the edge of the marble island unit and can feel my teeth grinding against each other.

'You don't need to look so worried!' He laughs at me. 'Here's the deal. You give me twenty-five thousand in cash and I won't say a word. Not a single word. The secret remains between you, me and the fine doctor.' Elliott stands up and stretches, the T-shirt lifting up to show a taut, muscley stomach. 'I'll collect the dosh tomorrow at 6 p.m.'

'No! No, I can't do that. I can't do anything until I've checked with Daniel. I'll tell the police that you're threatening me!'

He takes a step towards me and slowly licks his lips with a bumpy, pointed tongue.

'Feel free, love. But if you do that, it won't look very good for your hubby, will it? Grievous bodily harm, concealing an offence, paying me off. I don't think the police will look too kindly on it. Anyways, you have a little think, and I'll be back here tomorrow to collect the twenty-five grand.' He swivels around and strides towards the door. In the doorway, he looks back over his shoulder at me, tilts his head to one side, and winks.

As I watch Elliott's van climb slowly up the hill, I realise I am shaking. My first instinct is to call the police and tell them that he's threatening me, but something stops me from picking up the phone. Why would he invent a story like that? Did Daniel really beat him up and pay him off? Elliott will know that I will check with Daniel. I pace around the house as I think. I need to speak to Daniel – ideally, to see him – but I was at the prison just this morning. I grab my phone and go online to book another visit, but the next available slot is in the three days. That will be too late.

If I can't see him, I will need to speak to him. The prison has a voicemail service where I can leave a message and Daniel can call me back. That will have to do.

I call the number. My voice is hesitant, because I know the message will be monitored. 'Daniel, it was great to see you today. I had a visit from Elliott. His son is having a birthday party. He told me about the meeting you had in the car. Can you confirm it?' I hang up without saying goodbye. I hope Daniel will know what I mean.

My head is in turmoil, and I need to clear my thoughts before Mum and Dad arrive with the kids, pouncing on me for information on Daniel as soon as the children are out of earshot. Frankly, I have no idea what I'm going to say.

Joel has accepted that Daddy is away on a work trip for a couple of weeks, but I'm not sure that Rosa is buying the story. She asks me too many questions that I can't answer, but I can't bear to tell her the truth. They need to believe that their daddy is invincible, that he's a good man, and that justice is always served. As it's the school summer holidays, we can just about get away with the lie. The children aren't exposed to any news, and other than Amber and Billy, they haven't seen anyone since Mike died. I've cancelled all of my piano pupils but have little doubt that I would have lost them anyway. Who wants to be tarnished with murder? What sane parent would allow their child to be taught by the wife of someone accused of such a heinous crime? I just pray that Daniel gets released before the children go back to school. I can't bear the thought of having to tell them the truth.

'Come on, Peanut. Let's go for a walk.'

The clouds have descended and the air is damp and cool. I can't tell if it's the drizzle causing wetness on my cheeks or my tears. Could Daniel really have beaten up a man? We have never discussed physical violence; it's just a topic that hasn't arisen, a presumption that neither of us have a propensity towards it. We talked about previous relationships, old friendships, some that have faded away, others that remain strong, but I have never asked him if he got into a fight when he was younger, whether his perfectly straight nose was once upon a time broken, or whether it has been surgically enhanced. If Daniel has kept such a big secret from me, what else has he hidden? I think of other times when Daniel lost his temper. It's not a common occurrence, but when he flips, it does tend to be spectacular. But other than that broken plate, he has never been violent. I wonder if he has ever lost his temper at work. Somehow, I doubt it.

I stomp along a narrow track pocked with craters and large rocks, gorse bushes to my right and a dry-stone wall to my left, beyond which there is a wide field of ragged grass and weeds ready to be grazed by the hundreds of sheep higher up on the hill. The clouds are low, blocking the spectacular views. I was right to take a dislike to Elliott. Now it makes sense, that mock swagger and ill-placed bravado. He knew something that I didn't. If what he's saying is true, he most definitely had the upper hand on us. No wonder Elliott boasted in the schoolyard about his trips to Costa del Sol and Gran Canaria. I suppose they were courtesy of our money.

As the rain gets heavier and my trainers become covered in mud, Peanut and I turn back homewards. I have clarity now. Daniel is innocent, and it is up to me to prove it.

THE NEXT FEW HOURS, I am busy with the children. Despite Mum's offer to help cook supper, to take the children for a walk and hang around so I don't feel too lonely, I persuade them to leave. I need to be alone in the house. I am on tenterhooks for the phone to ring, for Daniel to tell me that Elliott is a liar and that he has never hit anyone.

Once the children are in bed, I grab my laptop and sign into our online banking. Daniel and I have two joint accounts. One is a savings account and the other is our everyday current account. I do a double take. We have £18,465.86 in our savings account and just under two thousand pounds in our current account. That can't be right? We had over one hundred thousand pounds in the savings account the last time I looked. A huge amount of money. How long ago was that? I simply can't remember. Weeks, months? I only ever look at our current account. So what's happened to all of our savings? What has Daniel done with the money? Even if Elliott was telling the truth and I agreed to pay him twenty-five thousand pounds, we don't have enough cash. I need those sums to pay the bills, to cover us should Daniel not be able to go back to work for a while. I chastise myself. Of course, I won't be paying Elliott a penny. It's bribery. My fingers are slippery on the keyboard, and it takes me a couple of attempts to bring up the statements that covered 4 September two years ago. I study each entry. We had well over one hundred thousand in our savings account back then. No large sums were taken from either account during that period. That doesn't surprise me. I would have noticed. The bastard must have been lying.

And then the phone rings.

'Hello,' I say breathlessly.

'It's me,' Daniel says, his voice is flat.

'Thank God!' But as Daniel carries on talking, I realise that this is a message he has left me and not a live call.

'It's true what our friend said. Spend whatever you need to on the present. He's a good kid, so give him whatever he wants. Nothing's too much for him. I'll explain when I next see you. I miss you, Hannah.'

My brain seems muddled, as if it can't process Daniel's words. I listen to the recording again, and then for the third time. I let the phone drop to the table.

It's true. What Elliott said is true. Surely Daniel can't mean anything else. Daniel wants me to give Elliott whatever he asks for. Twenty-five thousand pounds in exchange for silence.

I WANT TO WEEP. I have never felt so alone and so confused. Can it really be true that Daniel beat up Elliott and paid him off? If Daniel kept that from me, what else could he have been hiding? And that gap that Daniel says he has in his memory, is he doubting himself? Could he have smashed the bottle over Mike's head and just not remembered doing it? He has shown that he has a propensity for violence. My husband, who I thought was a good human being, has a side to him that I have never seen. I go through the statements again and see that Daniel took out eighty thousand pounds just before Christmas. He wrote out a cheque. To himself. So where did the money go? Did the transfer of funds have anything to do with Elliott?

I run upstairs and find Daniel's iPad, which I put in the top drawer of his bedside table. I wonder if the police have looked through Daniel's phone yet. Did they find an exchange of messages between Daniel and Elliott? I turn the iPad on. There is still thirty percent battery. I type in his code of 130981, my birthday, and I'm in. I flick through to his contacts and glance down the long list. Most are names that I have heard him mention, people he works with, but there are some names that mean nothing. I suppose that isn't surprising. Elliott's name and mobile phone number is listed. I click through Daniel's text messages, but there is nothing from or to Elliott. I suppose he deleted any incriminating messages, or perhaps there were none. Perhaps during their roadside altercation, Daniel agreed to drop off the cash at Elliott's home.

I catch a glimpse of myself in the mirror as I walk back downstairs. My hair is lanky and dull, and my face grey and lined. It's as if I've aged a decade in a week. In the kitchen, I pour myself a glass of white wine and drink it in two swigs. I never drink alone, not when I'm responsible for the children, but I need something in my veins to fortify myself. I stare at the chair that Elliott sat in. I feel like rubbing it down with bleach.

What should I do? Daniel says I have to give Elliott whatever he's demanding, but we simply don't have that amount of cash in our bank account. If Daniel gave him eight thousand two years ago, I could give him ten thousand now. That's a huge amount of money and hopefully will be enough to make him go away.

I copy Elliott's phone number from Daniel's iPad into my phone and stare at it. I take a few deep breaths and type a text to Elliott's number.

We don't have enough money to pay you £25k. I can pay you £10k. Send me your bank details, and I'll do an online payment.

Almost immediately, the phone rings. The number is withheld.

I hesitate before answering. 'Hello,' I say cautiously.

'It's Elliott.' He starts laughing, hiccupping, hysterical laughter. I sink down onto a kitchen chair, and the fingers of my left hand grab the edge of the table.

'What's so funny?' I spit.

'You are. You can't do an online transfer!' He says the latter two words in a false, hoity-toity voice. 'Cash. I want it in cash. Ten grand isn't enough. I want twenty-five. I'll collect it from yours at 6 p.m., as we agreed.'

I didn't agree to anything, and I do not want this hideous man in my home ever again. 'I'll meet you in the coffee shop at Tesco, or in the car park.'

'No can do. I'm coming to yours. Tomorrow 6 p.m. Make sure you've got the dosh. All of it. You need me on side more than ever.' He hangs up on me.

. . .

UNSURPRISINGLY, I toss and turn all night. What choice do I have but to give Elliott money? Who in their right minds would believe Daniel to be innocent if he's capable of beating someone up and offering them hush money? And for that matter, what the hell do I believe? Even if Daniel hit Elliott, it doesn't mean that Daniel subsequently killed Mike. But then I imagine Elliott visiting the police and sharing what happened, and how they would tell the judge, and there wouldn't be a hope in hell of Daniel getting bail. And what about at his trial? The jurors might be told that he had a propensity for violence, and then Daniel would be convicted of murder, and our lives as we have known them will be over. I will have to sell up, move away, and what would I tell Rosa and Joel? How will their lives be affected knowing that their father is a murderer? The more I think about it, the more I realise that Elliott has backed me into a corner. I have to pay him. But I won't pay him twenty-five thousand. I can't pay him that amount, as we don't have enough cash. I'll pay him ten. That is a good compromise.

THE NEXT MORNING, I take the children with me, and we go into town. 'Mummy needs to go to the bank,' I say. 'When we're home, we can make a picnic and go for a walk with Peanut.' Usually the kids like to do this, but today they seem subdued. I wait in the queue at the bank, feeling increasingly nervous. There is a woman standing in front of a podium-like desk.

'Good morning, how can I help you!' she says cheerfully.

'I need to take some money out.'

'Would you like some help using the cash machine?'

'It's too large a sum for the machine,' I say quietly.

'How much do you wish to take out?' Her voice booms, and I glance around, hoping that no one is listening. I remember not that long ago when privacy was the norm in a bank.

I lower my voice as much as possible and whisper, 'Ten thousand in cash.'

'Have you booked this?'

'No.'

'In which case, I will need to talk to my branch manager, because normally you need to book in advance if you wish to take out such a large sum.'

I feel chastened.

'Please come with me, and I'll get one of my colleagues to talk to you.' She leads us to a small room, a cubicle really, with a narrow glass desk, a computer monitor and three chairs. The air smells stale and stuffy. Joel jumps onto the chair behind the desk.

'You'll need to stand up, Joel. That's for the bank staff.'

He juts out his lower lip, then steps towards Rosa, trying to shift her off the chair.

'Mum!' she moans.

'Stop it, Joel!' I say, too harshly. I need to keep a lid on my nerves, but it's so hard. After ten long minutes, the door opens, and a tall, wiry man comes in, wearing a short-sleeved white shirt and dark trousers.

'Good morning. My name is Angus Scaraman, and I'm the deputy branch manager. My colleague says you wish to take out ten thousand pounds in cash. Is that right?'

'Yes.'

He sits down and types on the keyboard. Rosa is seated on the chair next to me, but Joel is bouncing around the small space, playing with an imaginary train and making tooting noises.

'Can I ask why you need the money?' Angus Scaraman asks.

'Um. No. Do... do you need to know that?' I stutter.

'Yes. Money-laundering regulations. We need to be able to trace all funds.' He frowns at me, and I wonder if he can see the guilt all over my face.

'Um. Ok. I'm buying a car off a friend,' I lie.

'But we've already got a car!' Rosa says.

'Shush,' I say. I can feel Rosa's querying eyes on me.

'That's fine,' Angus Scaraman says. 'Do you have an invoice?'

'No. Sorry. It's quite casual.'

'What's the make and model of the car and its registration number?'

'Um... I can't remember exactly. I don't understand why you need all of this information!'

'I know it's not an easy time for you, Mrs Pieters, but we have procedures in place to protect our clients.'

I squirm and feel my cheeks reddening. I suppose I shouldn't be surprised that this stranger knows all about our situation.

'I hadn't realised you need all this information,' I say hurriedly. 'I'll have to come back when I have the paperwork together.'

'Absolutely.' He stands up and puts out his hand to shake mine. 'I look forward to seeing you again soon, and perhaps it would be best to telephone in advance so we have the money ready to give to you.'

I nod and usher the children out of the room. That was a disaster. I had no idea it was so difficult to take out one's own money in cash. It was humiliating that the bank manager knew who I am and that Daniel is on remand in prison. I wonder if he will tell the police that I tried to take out ten grand. We wander aimlessly for a while. Rosa asks if we can go into Next. She tries on a pair of trousers that she doesn't need, and because I don't have the energy to have a fight with my daughter, I buy them for her. All I can think about is how I am going to get the cash. I consider ignoring Elliott's request, but the man scares me, not just because of the power he has over Daniel, but because that chauvinistic swagger makes my blood curdle.

And then I notice a pawnshop. I suppose I have walked past it a thousand times without noticing. I slow down.

'Why are we stopping?' Joel asks. 'I want to go to the toy shop.'

I glance around. Is it safe to leave them standing on the street just for a moment whilst I pop inside?

'Rosa, I want you to be very grown-up. You are to hold Joel's hand and wait here until I come back out. Don't talk to anyone. I'll be able to see you from inside.'

She nods with a serious face and grabs Joel's hand.

I press the buzzer on the door, and it chimes loudly. A moment later, the catch releases and I push the door open. The man behind the counter peers at me as I walk towards him. He has a long straggly beard with crumbs of biscuit or other unsavoury detritus hanging from it.

'Um, I'm new to this. Please can you explain to me how it works?'

'Sure, love.' I notice a slight smirk. 'You've got a choice. Either leave us something valuable as security for a loan – jewellery, antiques and stuff – or sell it to us. If you choose the former option, we'll charge you monthly interest.'

'And how much is the interest?' If I can fudge a receipt for the bank, I won't need to borrow money for very long. This could be the ideal solution to obtain the cash today.

'Depends on the value of what you're pawning. What do you need?'

'Ten thousand pounds.'

He whistles, then picks up a laminated piece of paper. 'Four percent monthly.'

'Thank you very much,' I say and hurriedly back out of the shop. I don't know how much my jewellery is worth, but I suspect I'll be able to raise enough from pawning it. I take the children's hands.

'We're going home now.' They both whine and complain.

When we're in the car, I call Amber. We have only spoken once since Mike's murder, and that conversation was stilted. If things are awkward with my good friend, I can't imagine how horrible it will be with people I don't know so well.

'Hello, Hannah. How are you doing?'

'I've been better. I was wondering if I could ask a big favour. Any chance you could look after Rosa and Joel for a couple of hours this afternoon?'

There is a long pause. 'It's a bit difficult today. We've got rather a lot on.'

I have never known Amber to say no to helping out.

'Don't worry, I'll ask Mum,' I say, quickly ending the call. I blink away the tears as I realise how truly alone I am. Just the whiff of criminality taints.

IT IS emotional going through my jewellery. I take my pale gold silk jewellery case out of the safe and remove every item, laying them out on the bed. Other than my small ring set with a pearl and two miniature diamonds either side that belonged to my late grandmother, all my jewellery has been given to me by Daniel. I realise, as I gaze at all the pieces, how generous he has been. There are a pair of diamond earrings he wrapped up and buried in a stocking on our first Christmas together, much too valuable a gift, which I accepted reluctantly, determined to return them to him if our relationship didn't last. Then there is a row of pearls that belonged to his mother and a delicate diamond necklace that was his grandmother's. My engagement ring is a large solitaire oval-cut diamond, which was the envy of all my girlfriends, the platinum wedding band engraved with our initials, and the eternity ring set with two further diamonds to celebrate the birth of our children. I also have bracelets, necklaces and earrings in an assortment of styles, all given on my birthday, Christmas or our wedding anniversaries.

Daniel doesn't wear a wedding band. He said it would be too annoying to have to remove it prior to surgery, and he was worried about losing it. But he does have a Rolex watch, which he bought himself when he got the London consultant cardio-thoracic surgeon post. I worry when he wears it; I've heard too many stories about people being attacked for their expensive watch. I select the pieces that I reckon are the most valuable and wrap everything else up in the case and return it to the safe.

A couple of hours later, I have dropped the kids off at Mum and Dad's, and I'm in town, my handbag fully zipped up and clutched under my arm.

I ring the doorbell to the pawnshop, and the bearded man looks up with surprise when he sees me. I suppose he assumed that I, in my middle-class clothes and ignorance of pawnshops, wouldn't be back.

I take out Daniel's Rolex watch first. He got us into this mess, and if we lose the watch because of it, so be it. The bearded man takes out a magnifying glass and peers at the watch.

'I'll give you £6500 for it.'

I thought it would be worth more, but I don't know what percentage of the real value pawnshops offer. I take out some other pieces of jewellery and slowly the sums add up.

'What about that ring on your finger?' he asks, eyeing my engagement ring. I feel sick as I ease it off my fourth finger.

After much billowing of cheeks and biting of his lip, the bearded man agrees to give me ten thousand pounds for the watch and my engagement ring. I stuff the rest of the jewellery back into my jewellery pouch and hide it at the bottom of my handbag. The bearded man gets me to sign various papers and then puts my items in small paper bags that he seals.

'I'll be back in a mo,' he says. He opens a door by punching in a series of numbers and disappears. I wait nervously. What if he has run off with my jewellery? How do I know that this place is legitimate? I pace around the small shop, glancing up at the cameras in the corners of the ceiling, blinking at me. After four or five long minutes, he reappears. He hands me over ten stacks of banknotes. 'A grand in each,' he says.

I remove a plastic bag from my handbag and place them inside. I had assumed that so much money in cash would take up more space, be more conspicuous. I wonder if I should count the money to be absolutely sure, but as I hesitate, the doorbell rings and a twenty-something man in a black hoodie walks in, eyeing me suspiciously. I nod goodbye to the bearded man and hurry out of the shop.

I feel like a fugitive as I clasp the bag housing all the cash. I glance over my shoulder constantly as I hurry towards the car park.

'Hannah!' a voice says.

I jump.

20

It's Rachel Mole, possibly one of the last people I want to see.

'Dreadful thing with that man being found dead at your place,' she says, tightening the belt of her Barbour more securely around her considerable girth.

I hug the plastic bag with the money in it even more tightly to my body. For a moment, I feel a burst of hysteria threatening to erupt upwards from my belly to my throat and mouth as I imagine Rachel's look of shock if I showed her all the money stashed in my plastic bag.

'How is Daniel holding up? No one locally thinks he did it, by the way. We're all on your side.' She reaches out to pat my arm, but I take a step backwards.

'Thank you,' I mutter.

'Said on the lunchtime news that this afternoon it's the funeral of the man who was murdered. Mike Smith, was it?'

'Jones. Mike Jones.'

'Oh yes. Three p.m. this afternoon, apparently, over in Congleton. Strange that he's going to be cremated there. I'd have thought that they would have chosen somewhere further afield from home for their holiday. Did you know they came from Congleton?'

I shake my head. I don't want to be fodder for Rachel's gossip. It does seem strange, though.

'They'll be lots of folk who won't want to know you for love nor money after this, but not Jamie and me. You need anything, just shout. And if you decide to sell up, let me know. Jamie's always hankered after your place!'

I can't think fast enough to respond and stand there staring at her. So that's what she wants; that's why she's being nice to me. They want to buy our house on the cheap.

'You take care, Hannah,' she says, giving me a finger-wiggling wave. To my relief, she strides away.

But it's not Rachel I can't stop thinking about as I slip into the car, placing my precious cargo on the front passenger seat; it's the fact it's Mike's funeral this afternoon. I want to look Nadia in the eye. To know if she's really grieving, or is it all a pretence, because she is the real killer? Slender, wispy Nadia, overcome by her magic stones and obsession with fortune telling. Perhaps she was consumed by some evil spirit and couldn't restrain herself from smashing a wine bottle over Mike's head.

I am driving up the road to our house when a bird of prey swoops so low, right over the top of the car, its claws, the size of my fists, are visible just feet above the glass panel in the car's roof. Daniel would have been exhilarated by such a close sighting, but those terrifying talons, capable of decapitating a small dog, frighten me. And then I think of the missing camera and SD card. The chances are that the police removed it, but what if Nadia took it? Kayleigh knew about the hidden camera, so it's not an unreasonable assumption to think that she told her parents. I want to know if Nadia has it.

I need to go to the funeral.

I HIDE the bag of cash in the linen cupboard upstairs, stashed behind a pile of pillows that were once upon a time vacuum-packed and are now puffed up to their original size. Then I ring Mum.

'Could you keep the kids until bedtime?'

'You must be exhausted, love. Why don't Joel and Rosa stay here for a few days; give you a bit of a respite? We'll pop over later to collect their things. Dad said he'll take them to Chester Zoo tomorrow.'

'Thanks, Mum. That would be great.' I'll miss my babies, but being alone gives me some time and space to investigate.

'You need to rest, Hannah. Put your feet up and have a snooze.'

I smile wryly into the phone. I don't think stalking the funeral of the man the police have accused Daniel of killing can be deemed as restful. But that's where I need to go. I pull on a black jacket and a pair of black trousers, although as I'll be staying in the car, there is probably no point. I then plug the address of the crematorium into my phone and set off.

It's not far, just over fifteen minutes to Congleton, and if the funeral is at 3 p.m., then I'm more than half an hour early. I had hoped that the crematorium would be in the town with off-road parking, but unfortunately, it is located at the end of a quiet residential street, with a small car park for mourners. I drive through the entrance with its brick pillars and realise immediately that I will be utterly conspicuous if I park along-side the twenty or so cars that are in the car park. I turn the car around and drive slowly along the residential street, doing a three-point turn in the driveway to a house and parking alongside a tall wooden fence, with the passenger's side tyres up on the pavement. Here, I have a good view of the cars driving in, so I slide down in my seat and prepare for the wait.

I wonder if Nadia will arrive in one of those black limousines behind the hearse. She doesn't. She is driving their Mercedes with its bashed doors and an exhaust that pops as she slows down. Dark glasses obscure much of her face. Three cars follow her in quick succession, so I hop out of my car, pull on my own sunglasses, and walk, in what I hope is a nonchalant fashion, towards the gates of the crematorium. I stop next to a laurel hedge and take out my phone. I pretend to study it, but I am staring at Nadia as she gets out of the Mercedes. She looks totally different today. Gone are her voluminous dresses, and instead she is wearing a tight black miniskirt that stops mid-thigh and a black V-neck jumper that shows every curve. Kayleigh gets out of the front passenger seat. I hadn't even noticed her when they drove past. She is wearing black leggings and a pink T-shirt. Nadia grasps her daughter's hand and bends down to say something to her. My heart bleeds for the child. Nadia looks up and glances in my direction. I turn immediately and stride back towards the car. I can't accost her now. Not before the service.

I hurry back to the car. I expect more cars to arrive, but most of them are leaving; mourners from the previous funeral, no doubt. I switch on the radio to pass the time, and just as I'm closing my eyes, there is a loud rapping on my window. I jump.

It's DS Lizzie Hargreaves, dressed in a navy trouser suit. She narrows her eyes at me. I lower the window.

'What are you doing here, Mrs Pieters?'

'I wanted to see Nadia. To see if she's really grieving.'

'And why does that concern you?'

'Because Daniel didn't kill Mike, so Nadia must have done it, or a hit man she employed.'

'You must realise that not only is it totally inappropriate for you to be here, but it throws suspicion on you.'

'I don't understand why you're not investigating Nadia?'

'It is not your position to tell the police how to do their job.'

'No, I realise that. I'm sorry,' I mumble. I want to ask her about the bird camera, whether they found it, whether there is any incriminating evidence on it, but I press my lips firmly together.

'Was there anything else?' DS Hargreaves asks.

'No. Sorry. I'll go now.' I groan as I drive away.

21

I am dreading Elliott arriving. I pace around the house, trying to calm my nerves. Is he dangerous? He knows that I'm all alone here. Will he attack me or threaten me somehow? I tell myself that I'm being ridiculous. This is a transaction, and he has as much to lose as I do. I cuddle Peanut and feel a relief that the dog is here, even though he's unlikely to do much to protect me.

The white van chugs down our road on the dot of 6 p.m. and pulls up outside the front door. I wonder whether Elliott is as punctual for work. He doesn't get out immediately. I stand a couple of feet back from the window, trying to see what he's doing. The angle is wrong. After a long couple of minutes, he gets out of the van, his shoulder pressed to his jaw, a mobile phone caught in between. He catches sight of me staring at him and raises a hand in a wave, as if he's here on a social call. I stride to the kitchen patio doors to let him in. He bounds up the steps and has his right hand on the door as I open it, his mobile phone clutched in his left hand.

'Hello, pretty lady.' He grins. He leans forwards as if to give me a kiss on the cheek, and I step backwards, jamming my back into a chair. Peanut growls, but as soon as Elliott has stepped into the room, the dog drops his head back onto his bed.

Elliott stands in front of me, his hands in his jeans pockets, his legs wide apart. 'So, have you got it?' His tongue darts out of his mouth, and he runs it slowly over his bottom lip.

'Yes, but how do I know that you'll keep your side of the bargain?'

He pulls out a chair and sits down, his jeans-clad legs sprawling in front of him. He places his mobile phone on the table.

He leans towards me, his bare forearms on the table. 'Just give me the money, love.'

'How do I know you won't tell anyone?'

He shrugs his shoulders. 'Me and Daniel had an arrangement. It worked fine. So long as he's banged up, it'll be between me and you. I can throw in a few added benefits if you like, now that you're missing your man.' He leers at me.

I turn away and grab the plastic bag with the money in it. I place the bag on the table.

'A Sainsbury's bag?' He grins. 'Would have thought Harvey Nicks was more your style.' He tips the bag upside down, and the piles of cash slide out onto the table. 'Aren't you going to offer me a cuppa or a beer?'

I just want this man out of my house, but it seems he has no intention of going anywhere fast. I turn away and walk over to the kettle. As it's boiling, he lines the piles up on the table.

'How much is this?' he asks, scowling.

'It's ten thousand. I don't have any more to give you.'

He slides the chair backwards violently and stands up.

'That, Mrs Hannah Pieters, is not good enough. It's not what we agreed.'

I stand upright, my heart hammering, and hoping that I'm looking stronger than I feel. I stare him in the eyes. 'We don't have it. Ten thousand is quite sufficient.'

'I think you've forgotten who is calling the shots here.' He takes three steps towards me, then reaches out and puts a finger under my chin, tipping it upwards. I back away and he lets his arms fall to his sides. He stares at me, those green eyes narrowing, and I can feel myself trembling again.

'I need to take a piss. Where's your loo?'

I don't want Elliott walking through the house, but I'm so shocked by his casualness that I reply, 'Down the corridor, first door on your left.'

'White with two sugars, by the way. Don't look so worried, love. I won't bite. Well, I might if you don't produce the dosh!' His laugh chills my insides.

I turn to stare at the steam snaking out of the top of the kettle. Why the hell should I show any hospitality to this creep of a man? I decide not to make him a drink. I stand in the corner of the room with my arms crossed.

After a couple of minutes, Elliott walks back into the room with a swagger.

'Nice house you've got. Lots of lovely, jubbly antiques worth a fair sum. That fancy piano must have cost a penny or two. What was it, thirty thousand? Forty?' I feel sickened that he has opened the doors into our rooms and had a good look. My piano room is my sanctuary, and just by breathing the air, I feel as if he's tarnished it. He slides back into the chair.

'Where's my tea, then? Or a nice chilled beer would do.'

I glare at him and he smirks. He starts counting the money. All I can do is stare at his back and wonder what hell our family has fallen into. After a few minutes, he shoves the piles of notes back into the carrier bag and stands up.

'Fifteen grand short.' He walks towards me, but my back is up against the counter. He is standing right in front of me now as he reaches forwards and runs a finger along my jawline. 'I'll be back 6 p.m. tomorrow to collect the rest. You're lucky I'm a patient man. No funny business, okay? Remember I know where you live, and I know what your husband Daniel is capable of.'

I recoil, but he laughs in my face. And then he turns around and strides out of the kitchen, leaving the door swinging open behind him. I stay totally immobile, shaking. He starts the engine of his van, and I listen as he turns the vehicle around and then puts his foot on the accelerator. Only when the sound of the van is fading do I move across the room and watch the van disappear up the hill, clouds of dust spraying up behind the rear wheels. I close the door and bolt it, and then do the same to the back door.

I sink down onto the floor next to Peanut's bed and wrap my arms around the bemused dog. What the hell am I going to do? Should I try to sell some investments or pawn more jewellery, or should I brazen it out with Elliott?

I NEED to know exactly how much money Daniel has tied up in investments, and I must work out if there's a quick way I can raise more cash. Perhaps he took the eighty thousand out of the savings account and invested it in an investment portfolio. As Daniel has always been the main earner in our family, I've left money decisions up to him. Yes, I know it's stupid, but in all marriages there is a division of labour, isn't there? I'm responsible for all the day-to-day things: groceries, the children, the running of the house, my minimal income from teaching. Daniel pays the big bills for our household and car insurance, the mortgage; he paid for the renovations of the barn; he manages our pensions and investments. I brought nothing of any material value to the marriage, so it made sense for Daniel to carry on as he had done before I came into his life. But now, I regret it. I simply don't know how much money we have. I don't even know exactly how much he earns, around one hundred thousand, I think. A lot.

I walk down the corridor to his small study and switch the light on. His pedestal mahogany desk sits in front of the window, with a bookcase spanning the full length of the left-hand wall and a filing cabinet, made from the same wood as the desk, centred on the right hand wall. Above this hang Daniel's many certificates and a few of his favourite photographs, close-ups taken of various birds of prey.

I sit down at his desk. There are three drawers. I pull each one open, but there is nothing of interest inside: just some notebooks, pens, an old camera, a stethoscope and a pile of photographs of me and the kids. The filing cabinet houses anything relating to our household: bills, warranties, letters and the like. I haven't been into the cabinet in a few years. It is my job to pay the household bills, although most things such as the utility bills are on direct debit. I then leave paid invoices on Daniel's desk. He looks through them, normally on a Friday night after work, and files them.

The top drawer is locked. I tug at it as hard as I can, but it remains closed. I search the study for a key, even looking underneath the desk, hoping to find a secret drawer or a key taped to the underside. Eventually, I give up. It's probably on his bunch of keys, and now I'm thinking about it, I don't remember seeing them. Perhaps the police still have them. I will need to look through the inventory of items they took. I find a screwdriver in Daniel's desk, and I poke and jam it into the drawer until eventually I manage to break the lock. The drawer slides open.

Daniel is organised. Every hanging folder is named. The first one is labelled investments, and the second one is labelled bank statements. I take out the bank statements folder, which is further divided into four. Current account, savings account, business account and personal account. It's the latter that interests me. I pull out the statements. The account is in Daniel's name only, and the latest statement is dated last month. There is thirty-four thousand and seventeen pence in the account, but what interests me more are the sums going out. I flick back to September 2018. On 3 September there was one payout of eight thousand pounds in cash. That tallies with what Elliott said.

I look through all the intervening statements, right up until the one last month. On the first of every month, a regular sum of £3,000 goes out of the account to E.F. Who is E.F., and why is this person or company listed just by initials? And why is Daniel sending so much money on a regular basis? It's thirty-six grand a year going goodness knows where. Is it money that he inherited from his father? That is a possibility, but where is it going? It's not to Elliott, because his surname is Moreton.

But my biggest question of all is, why has Daniel got a bank account that he has kept hidden from me?

I sigh in frustration. I look through all the other files. He has an investment portfolio managed by a stockbroker called Geoffrey Sweetman, or is Sweetman his accountant? I can't recall. Either way, there's a lot less in the portfolio than I had anticipated. I suppose we live an expensive lifestyle, with a hefty mortgage, Daniel's golf membership, and the considerable sums we ploughed into the barn. Why didn't he put a halt to the build if it was stretching us too much financially? I wouldn't have minded. And now it strikes me that if Daniel remains in jail for any length of time, all of the financial responsibilities fall onto my shoulders. My earnings are peanuts. They won't even cover the cost of buying the kids new clothes, let alone pay the mortgage. Daniel has to be exonerated, and evidently, it's down to me to make that happen. For starters, he should stop paying out to E.F.

I put everything away, switch off the light, and pad back upstairs to bed. I switch on Daniel's iPad and scroll through all of his contacts. But I don't see any reference to E.F., or even anyone with the initials E.F. Who has he been paying three grand a month?

22

I wake up with a start, my heart thumping, breathless, sweat coating my body. I switch on the bedside light, but there are no sounds. It's the thoughts in my head that have awakened me. I dreamed that I was at the bank, locked inside a room that had bars across the window, and no visible door. I was frantically searching for the door, banging my hands on the rough brick walls until my fingers bled. And then Elliott appeared at the window, holding Rosa and Joel, his arms around their necks. Both of whom were crying, fear and pain etched on their young faces. He demanded all our money, every single thing we owned in exchange for my children's freedom, even my beloved piano. I was screaming, sobbing, begging him to let them go, telling him to take anything he wanted. I glance at my clock. It's 3.04 a.m.

I read a novel for a bit and then switch off the light. I fall back to sleep eventually because when I awake, Peanut is whimpering downstairs. It's nearly 9 a.m. No wonder the poor dog is unhappy; I should have fed him nearly two hours ago. After a strong coffee, I take him for a quick walk. How I wish I could talk to Daniel. Yes, I could call him or visit him again in prison, but we can't speak freely. Telephone calls are recorded, and there are too many potential eavesdroppers around when we meet. And then there is the unpalatable thought that Daniel may not want to tell me the truth, and if that is the case, I will need to do my own digging. As I'm pacing up the hill, my breath coming in short bursts, I decide to talk to the person who sees Daniel several times a week and who, after me, knows him the best. His long-term secretary, Coleen. We haven't spoken since Daniel was accused of murder; I know she must be distraught. I need to see her. To look her in the eyes and find out if she knows things about Daniel that I don't.

The Cheshire hospital where Daniel works is about a forty-minute drive away, and the journey gives me time to work out what I want to ask Coleen.

I park my car, stride into the building, walking straight past the reception desk, and take the lift up to the second floor. Although Coleen is based here in the private hospital, she manages Daniel's diary for both his NHS and private patients, liaising with other secretaries in London and Manchester. I walk briskly along the blue-carpeted corridor and knock on Coleen's office door.

'Hannah!' she exclaims. She jumps up, and two red blotches appear on her cheeks as she walks towards me. The other two women in the office do little to disguise their curiosity. I hate to think what the rumour mill will be like around here. 'How are you? How is Daniel?'

'Do you have time for a quick coffee?'

I wonder which consultants she's been reassigned to now that Daniel isn't working. For a moment, she appears unusually flustered, but she quickly smooths down her tweed skirt and removes her reading glasses.

'That would be lovely,' she says, bending down to pick up her handbag.

The door opens and a young nurse walks in. 'Coleen, have

you got Vikram Chandran's file to hand? He's being trans-ferred–' And then she notices me and does a double take.

'Oh, hello.' She opens and closes her mouth, obviously at a loss as to what to say. I glance at her name badge. Scarlett Brown. I don't recognise her, but she clearly knows me.

'Scarlett, have you got it?' Another nurse pops her head around the door. I do recognise her. Beth. She's on Daniel's team, and he mentions her from time to time, particularly when he's recounting a complex operation.

'I'm so sorry about Daniel,' Beth says. 'We were all really shocked and can't believe it. It must be a terrible time for you.'

'Yes, well...' I let my voice fade away. She reddens and disappears.

COLEEN and I go downstairs to the hospital coffee shop. I buy her a cup of tea and a cappuccino for myself. We sit at the table the furthest away from any other customers.

'How are you coping, Hannah? And the children?'

I shrug. 'As well as can be expected. Rosa and Joel don't know the truth at the moment.'

'Of course not. He didn't do it. Daniel wouldn't be capable of taking a man's life. Not him.' She shakes her head vehe-mently, her grey curls bouncing around her head. 'You should see the state of him when he loses a patient. Takes it so badly. It's a terrible travesty of justice, what's happening.'

'Thank you, Coleen.' I don't think I've ever seen the older woman quite so worked up. She takes a sip of tea, but her hand is shaking, and a drop slurps onto the table. 'It's not the same without Daniel around,' she says, wiping it away with a paper napkin. 'And the gossip is just dreadful.'

I smile at her. Sometimes I think that Coleen is more in love with Daniel than I am.

'Please send him my very best regards and tell him we're all waiting to celebrate when he's released and this terrible travesty is put right. Don't get me wrong, Hannah. I feel sorry for the poor man who lost his life, but for the police to think that Daniel did it is just crazy.'

'How was he in the past few weeks? Did you notice anything different?' I ask.

She shakes her head, but Coleen doesn't meet my eyes. 'Nothing out of the ordinary. He was working as hard as he always does.'

I think she is hiding something.

'Did he have any issues with patients or problems with colleagues?'

'Good heavens, no!' Coleen says. 'Everyone loves Daniel. He's the best cardiothoracic surgeon we have and one of the preeminent doctors in the country. This is all a terrible mistake, isn't it?'

I nod. 'I think so. Have the police been to speak to you?'

She flushes bright red this time. 'Yes, and I didn't like it one bit. I don't know what they expected from me, but I told them as it is. That Daniel is an excellent doctor and a fine, upstanding man, and that his temper is no worse than anyone else's. He is a man who works under constant pressure and keeps a cool head, making life-and-death decisions. It's a load of codswallop to think that Daniel would have hit that man with a wine bottle.'

I smile. I can imagine Coleen giving the police short shrift.

'Do the initials E.F. mean anything to you?'

Coleen shakes her head. 'No, should they?'

'I was just wondering if Daniel had a patient with those initials.'

'Very probably. He has hundreds of patients, but no one stands out. How is this related to Daniel's incarceration?'

'It probably isn't. I just need to work out how we can get Daniel off the hook.' I can hardly tell Coleen that my husband has been making questionable payments, one as hush money and the other regular one... I have no idea. After some more small talk, I bid Colleen goodbye and reassure her Daniel will be back saving lives as soon as possible. I wander out of the hospital and across the car park.

As I'm walking towards my car, a red sportscar drives past me and slows to a halt. There can't be many people around here who drive a red E-type Jaguar.

'Hello, Gary!' I say as he lowers the window.

Gary is Daniel's best friend. They went to medical school together and bonded over bodies. Daniel chose to make sick people better; Gary is a pathologist, and he cuts them up. If Gary had been accused of murder, that at least might have made more sense. On the other hand, I can't imagine pedantic Gary doing anything as rash as bashing someone over the head with a wine bottle.

His eyes shift away from mine, as if he's feeling awkward talking to me. 'I need to park the car.'

I nod. He drives a few metres and pulls into a space with a sign that reads 'Doctors Only'. I walk to his car. Gary unfolds his long limbs and narrows his eyes when he realises I'm standing right next to him.

'What are you doing here?' he asks.

'I came to see Colleen, Daniel's secretary.'

He nods. 'How is the legal case coming together? When's the bail hearing?' He reaches across to the passenger seat to get his briefcase.

'The date hasn't been set yet, but Daniel's solicitor has it in hand. Daniel didn't do it; he's innocent,' I say, with a conviction I'm still not sure is one hundred percent warranted.

'Of course Daniel wouldn't do something like that. It's a mess. It's a shame the autopsy wasn't done at this hospital,' Gary says.

I wonder whether the autopsy report showed that Mike had

drugs in him. Could it have shown something that might be relevant to us? 'Can you get hold of the autopsy report?'

'Probably, but why?' He puts his briefcase on the ground and lays his palms on the roof of the low-slung car. 'What's all this about?'

'Me trying to do my best to help my husband prove his innocence,' I say.

Gary seems to mellow, and a brief smile ripples across his face. 'Of course he is innocent, Hannah.'

'Could you get Mike's autopsy report for me?'

'For you, no. But I can have a read of it. I'm not prepared to implicate myself in anything, Hannah. Even for my best mate.'

'I quite understand, but if there's anything strange in the autopsy report, will you let me know?'

'I'll do whatever I can to help you and Daniel, but I'm not going to do anything that puts me or my career in jeopardy.'

'That's fair enough.'

Normally, Gary leans in for a quick peck on the cheek, but today he just nods at me and briskly walks away.

I DON'T KNOW what to do about Elliott. He said he would be coming over at 6 p.m. to collect the rest of the money, but I don't have any money to give him. What will he do to me? He can't make me produce the money. He could tell the police about Daniel, but my bet is, he won't. He obviously sees us as his cash cow, and why kill us off when he hopes he'll get more money out of us? That doesn't mean I'm not scared of him. I am.

I have two options. I can either stand up to him and be brazen, or I can be away from home. I decide to do the former. Why should I be intimidated by Elliott? I'll keep the phone with me and call the police if he does anything untoward. I check Peanut is in the kitchen and then I lock the house from the inside. I walk upstairs to our bedroom, where I have a good view of the drive and a reasonable vantage point over the front of the house. From our en-suite bathroom window, I can see the back of the house. I sit on the carpet behind the curtains and wait.

Once again, he is punctual. My heart is thudding as he gets out of the van. He is holding his phone, and even from here inside the house, I can hear it ringing. He answers it, but there appears to be a problem. Either he hasn't got enough reception, or the battery has died, because I can see the scowl on his face. He reopens the door to his van and leans in. It looks like he's plugging the phone in. He then leaves the driver's door ajar and runs up the steps to the patio doors in front of the kitchen. He knocks loudly.

Peanut barks. When I don't answer, he walks along the front of the house and rings the front doorbell. I open the bedroom window and lean out.

'Go away, Elliott.'

'Go away!' he sneers. 'I'm here for the money. Come down and give it to me.'

'I haven't got it. Just go away!'

'Nope. I'm going nowhere until you give me the cash.'

'If you don't go, I'll call the police!'

He throws back his head and laughs at me. I'm furious. He knows damn well that I won't be calling the police, not unless he does something to threaten me or our property. I slam the window shut and step back into the room. He rings the door-bell again, and Peanut is barking furiously now. Elliott turns around and walks around the other side of the house, out of view. I scuttle across the bedroom and into the bathroom, standing as far back as I can. I can't see him, but I hear the back doorbell ring. Poor Peanut.

'Open up, Hannah!'

I shiver. He bangs on a window. What if he tries to break in? Surely he wouldn't do that. I can hear the crunch of his work boots as he prowls around the side of the house. I catch a glimpse of the top of his head as he peers into the living room window.

'Open up, Hannah! Stop playing games. Give me my money, or I'll go to the police!' he hollers at the top of his voice. He stands still for a while, rocking backwards on his heels, but then he strides away. I think he's going back to his van, but he walks straight past it towards the barn. Why is he going there? Now I can't see him, and I've no idea where he is or what he's doing. I sneak along the inside of the house, keeping down low, and gently open the kitchen door. Peanut bounds up to me, his tail wagging.

'Shush, boy,' I say.

What on earth is Elliott doing?

I watch the second hand go around and around on the clock in the kitchen. Four minutes. Five minutes. Six minutes. This doesn't make sense. When twelve minutes have passed, I decide I need to find out what he's doing. I put my phone in my pocket and attach Peanut's lead to his collar. I unlock the patio door, lock it behind me, and walk down the steps. I'm just a couple of metres from Elliott's vehicle when I jump. His phone starts ringing from inside the van. I glance around, expecting Elliott to appear, but he doesn't. So I step towards the van and peer in through the driver's window. His phone is attached to a lead and lying on the driver's seat. And as it rings, I do a double take. It feels as if all the blood has rushed out of my head, and I have to hold onto the van's door to stop myself from keeling over.

There is a photo of the caller, and I would recognise that face anywhere.

Nadia.

I rush away from the van as if I have been scalded. Peanut is tugging me, propelling me forwards as he barks. I let him lead me along the path between the house and the barn, the exact place where Mike had lain, where I thought I would never be able to tread again. But I can't think of Mike right now. I need to know what Elliott is up to. Peanut tugs me as he scampers around the side of the barn and onto the patio that faces the fields and our green, expansive views.

'I assumed you'd come out of hiding sooner or later,' Elliott says languidly. He is sitting on a patio chair, his legs stretched out in front of him, smoking a cigarette. The ash has accumulated in a little pile at his feet.

'I wasn't hiding,' I say.

Elliott doesn't look at me as he speaks. 'Unlike your husband, you're not a very good liar, Hannah. Where's the money?'

'I don't have it.'

He swings his head around to face me. 'Not the right answer.'

'We don't have enough cash to give you.'

He laughs, but this time it's a hard-edged laugh, and his thin lips curl. 'Don't give me that. You're bloody loaded. Just look at this property and all the lovely things you've got inside. And what's your old man earning? A hundred, two hundred grand a year? Is his freedom worth so little to you?'

'Paying you doesn't guarantee Daniel's freedom.'

'You want me to tell the police about him?' He smirks. 'I'm happy to do that. No skin off my nose.'

'You'll be incriminating yourself.'

'Hardly. Daniel offered to pay me. Not like I've been blackmailing or anything. Last chance saloon, Hannah. You pay up or I speak out.' He stubs the cigarette out on the patio and grinds it in with his heel. I wonder if it will leave a stain. He stands up and walks towards me. I step away from him. He leers at me as he passes.

'Get the money,' he says. 'I'll be back.'

23

Over the years, I've become adept at hiding fear. It sits at the base of my sternum and I imagine it as a small lump of coal. Sometimes it gets ignited and the burning heat rises up my oesophagus and floods my head. When it's at maximum heat, I'm in danger of melting. My meltdowns. They're not true panic attacks, not like I had on the airplane all those years ago, but I do become breathless and dizzy, and my head feels so full as if it's going to burst.

I haven't had one in years. Even the sight of Mike with his brains bashed didn't propel me into one. Perhaps when you have children and people relying on you to be strong, you can't allow yourself to be anything but.

But... now, I am alone at home. My children are safe with my parents, and my husband is in jail. And Elliott has something to do with Nadia.

I am scared.

The coal is burning.

I don't think I can cope. I must breathe. I must stay calm.

Trembling from head to toe, I manage to walk back into the house, and then I collapse in a heap on the cold floor next to

Peanut's bed. I sob, my tears soaking his soft fur as he licks my hands and gazes at me with his dark, soulful eyes.

What has Elliott got to do with Nadia? Are they in this together? I try to recall the couple of times Nadia and Elliott were in the same place. The pub, that awful meal we had with them. Elliott was seated at the next table, but I don't recall any knowing glances passing between them. And then at Joel's party. Elliott was here with his son. Did they meet then? Did Elliott get in touch after Mike's death? It doesn't make sense. I don't think they acted as if they recognised each other. Surely I would have remembered.

Did Elliott kill Mike? It makes more sense than Nadia having done it. But why? Are they friends? Lovers? Relatives? In some ways, I suppose this is good news. It means it's more likely that Daniel is really innocent, and at that thought, I let out a huge sigh. Of course my husband is innocent. And he is relying on me to prove it.

'I'm going to have a drink,' I tell Peanut as I get up from the floor. I pour myself a brandy, which really does burn the back of my throat. Then I find my laptop, place it on the kitchen table, and do another search for Mike and Nadia Jones. There is more information about them now, all related to Mike's unfortunate death. I dig out the booking form that they completed before arriving at the barn and plug their home address in Sussex into Google maps: 2, Rune Lane, Horsham, West Sussex. I get no results. I search for Rune Lane, and I can't find that address anywhere in England. I suppose it shouldn't surprise me that they listed a false address. But why? And why pay the full amount for renting the barn in advance? Rune Lane. Rune readings are probably part of Nadia's arsenal of weird occult activities.

I then do a search on Elliott, who is all over the internet. He lives in Congleton, he works as a mechanic for Dirk & Co Garage, and he is a regular poster on Facebook. His profile is private, but I can still see that he is listed as single and his profile picture is of him with his young son sitting on his shoulders. Unfortunately, I can't see who his friends are. But as Nadia and Elliott obviously know each other, and Mike's funeral was held in Congleton, is it possible that Nadia and Mike actually lived locally? If so, why on earth did they choose to spend nearly one thousand pounds to rent our holiday cottage?

I TOSS and turn all night and am awake with the dawn chorus. I decide to find out more about Elliott. Once I have worked out the connection between him and Nadia, perhaps I'll have something concrete to tell the police.

It's 7.30 a.m. when I do my first drive past his house. He lives at number 11, Blakely Road, in the middle of a row of terraced houses. It is red brick with a brown framed window on the ground floor and another directly above it. His front door is painted crimson red, and his white van is parked directly in front of his house. The curtains are drawn on the top floor. I park on the other side of the road, wedged in a small spot between a black VW Golf and a blue transit van. I switch on Radio 4 and slink down in the driver's seat, pulling a baseball cap low over my head. I just hope that he doesn't recognise my dark blue Toyota Rav. Shortly after 7.45 a.m., the front door swings open, and I slide even further down the seat. Elliott opens and closes the door but doesn't lock it behind himself, so I assume there's someone still in the house. I can't hear him, but he looks as if he's whistling as he unlocks the van and climbs inside. He revs the engine, and the van emits a belch of grey smoke. Then he pulls out and drives away.

I let out a deep breath. Now I'm not sure what to do. I'd like to have a snoop around his house, but I'm concerned that if there's someone inside, they'll catch me. I decide to wait another half an hour. If there's no movement, then I'll either walk along the pavement and peer in, or I'll give up and go home.

A mere ten minutes later, the front door opens again, and I gasp as Nadia walks out holding Kayleigh's hand. Nadia turns and locks the door behind her. She is wearing a black leather jacket, a black miniskirt, bare legs that look as if they've had several layers of fake tan applied, and black ankle boots. They are walking on the other side of the road towards me, and if Nadia looks this way, she'll see…

I bend down towards the footwell of the passenger side of my car, as if I'm ferreting around for something I've lost. After what I hope is sufficient time, I resurface and glance in the side mirror. I can see Nadia's and Kayleigh's backs, and then they turn into a street on the left and disappear.

Leaning my head back in the seat, I close my eyes. Either Nadia is Elliott's sister or some relation, or he is her lover. The former seems more likely than the latter, but it still doesn't make much sense. She simply hasn't had the time to move on from Mike's death to shack up with someone else. For a moment, I wonder whether she and Mike were really married, but surely the police must know the truth about that.

Just as I start up the car to leave, my phone rings.

'Hannah, it's Gary. Sorry for the early call, but I won't get a chance to ring you later. I've had a read of Mike Jones' autopsy report.'

'Yes,' I say eagerly.

'Cause of death was being hit over the head with a bottle. He was overweight, had too much alcohol in his blood, but not enough to cause death. Other than a fatty liver, there was nothing wrong with him.'

'Oh,' I say, feeling disappointed. I'm not sure what I expected to learn, but it wasn't nothing. 'Thanks for looking.'

'There was one thing that was weird,' Gary says. I grab the steering wheel in anticipation.

'His ankle was in a cast, but there was nothing wrong with it.'

'What do you mean?'

'There were no broken bones in his leg, ankle or foot. No obvious swelling or bruising. And according to his medical records, the last time he visited his GP was eighteen months ago for a case of piles.'

I snort. But actually the ramification of what Gary has just told me is huge. It suddenly all makes sense.

'Thanks so much, Gary. That's really helpful.'

'Say hi to Daniel when you next speak to him. Tell him we're all rooting for him. Must dash now.'

I let out a whistle. So it was a set-up. Mike pretended to break his leg in order to get money out of us. What a ruse. It just goes to show that my initial apprehension about them was correct. They are con artists.

As soon as I'm home, I call DS Jason Murphy. I just hope that I'm not going to get Gary into trouble. Hopefully, I can keep his name out of the conversation.

'What can I do for you, Mrs Pieters?' he says.

'It's come to my attention that Mike Jones was faking a broken leg. I think they were trying to blackmail us, saying that we were responsible for his accident, and they were hoping to get money out of us.'

'Yes, that's right,' he says, with a level voice.

'Oh.' That wasn't the reaction I was expecting. 'Was Mike Jones a criminal?'

'He had form. He was jailed three times for extortion and burglary.'

'Has he tried to get money out of holiday cottage owners before?'

'We think yes. We have a few more leads to follow up on with the constabulary in Sussex and in Northumberland.'

'So we're the victims here?'

'May I remind you that Mike Jones is dead? Murdered.'

'But Nadia could have done it, or one of her friends or relatives.' I'm thinking of Elliott. 'Nadia's a criminal.'

'Actually, she's not. She has never been charged with anything, and there was never any proof to suggest that she was Mike's accessory in any crime.'

I think of the bruises on Nadia's wrist and the long dresses that covered all her bare flesh, such a contrast to the revealing clothes she wore at Mike's funeral and what I saw her in this morning. Did she wear those voluminous outfits to cover up the marks where Mike hit her? Or is my imagination going into overdrive?

'Did Mike Jones assault Nadia?'

'No charges have ever been brought, and there is nothing to suggest that their relationship was under strain. I realise how difficult it must be for you to accept your husband's culpability, but there were witnesses to Mike and Daniel's arguments both at your home and in your local pub. We believe that your husband found out about Mike's lies, and they got into a violent fight, which regrettably ended in Mike Jones' death. The evidence is compelling.'

How I wish I could share Elliott's name with the police. I am sure that he has something to do with Mike's death, but if I put the police onto him, then it will cause Daniel even greater problems.

'Is there anything else, Mrs Pieters?'

Once again, I want to ask if they have the bird camera, but I don't. Not until I've had another conversation with Daniel.

MY APPOINTED time to see my husband is 11 a.m. This time, I am fuelled more by anger than pity, and if anyone meets my eye, I throw them a withering look or a scowl.

'How are you, darling?' Daniel asks as we sit down.

'I need you to be honest with me.' I speak in a low whisper as I smooth out the creases in my trousers. 'Did you beat up Elliott two years ago?'

Daniel hangs his head. 'Yes.'

'Did you offer him hush money?'

He nods, scrunching his head into his shoulders. I have never seen my husband look so bashful and lacking in confidence.

'Elliott is demanding twenty-five grand. I've paid him ten.'

Daniel's head jerks upwards. 'But you need to pay him whatever he asks for!'

'We don't have twenty-five grand in cash to give him, and besides, it's extortion.'

'We've got no choice, Hannah! You need to do it.'

'Then you need to stop paying E.F.' I stare at Daniel, hoping that I appear confident. But inside, I'm a wreck, and my fingernails are digging into the palms of my hands.

'What?' he says, jerking his head upwards.

'I found the bank statements for an account in your name only. I saw that you took eighty thousand out of our savings account last year before Christmas. Why are you paying out three thousand pounds a month to E.F.?'

'You broke into my filing cabinet!' He looks indignant, and I wonder if he's playing for thinking time.

'Who is E.F.?'

'It's for the business. When my accountant told me I needed to set up a limited company rather than being a sole trader... It's to do with a pension plan and investment scheme, and it's totally irrelevant to what's going on now. You need to make sure that Elliott doesn't open his mouth to the police. Sell some shares. My Rolex watch. Anything.'

I don't mention that his watch is already at the pawnbrokers. There is a lengthy pause in our conversation, during which Daniel won't meet my eyes. He gave me too much blustering information. I'm sure he's lying.

Eventually, I speak.

'If I give Elliott twenty-five grand, what's to stop him from coming back and demanding more and more?'

'Hopefully, I'll be out on bail by then, and I can deal with him.'

'What, beat him up again?'

'For God's sake, Hannah!' Daniel snaps.

The guard's head swings around, and he stares at us. Daniel holds his hands up in a gesture of apology.

'And if you don't get released on bail, how worried should I be about Elliott?'

Daniel shrugs. 'He's just a geezer. Don't think you've any reason to be worried.'

'Other than he knows Nadia,' I say, leaning back in my chair.

'What?'

'Nadia's name came up on his phone.'

Daniel gawps at me. 'Have you asked him about Nadia?' His shoulders are bunched up by his ears, and his eyes are red with little burst blood vessels.

'No, and I'm not going to. I thought I might mention it to the police.'

'No!' Daniel says much too vociferously. The guard steps over to us.

'Any more raised voices and this visit will be over. Understood?'

Daniel nods, but his face is pallid, and I can tell he is furious. People don't instruct my husband what to do.

'Look me in the eye,' I say. Daniel does as instructed. 'Tell me the truth. Did you kill Mike?'

He stares at me, unblinking. 'No, Hannah. I did not.'

24

When I get back into the car in the prison car park, I take my phone from my handbag to plug in our home postcode on Google maps. I've received a text message from a number I don't recognise.

If you don't give me the money, I'll get it off your parents.

I drop the phone.

I jab my parents' number into my phone and listen to the ringing tone. *Pick up! Pick up!* I will them. But the answer machine kicks in. I hang up without leaving a message. I try Mum's mobile number, but it goes to voicemail immediately. That's not surprising; she only ever switches the phone on if she wants to make a call. Dad doesn't even have a mobile. And then another text message pings in.

If you go to the police, they will find out everything that Daniel did. I have photographs. Every day you don't pay up, the amount will increase. Yesterday it was £15k. Today I want £20k. Tomorrow it'll be £25k. The sooner you pay up, the sooner I go away. I have all the proof that the police need to show that Daniel killed Mike. PS this is a burner phone. No point in replying. See you soon.

What does he mean by saying he has proof that Daniel

killed Mike? Is he referring to the SD card in the wildlife camera? My thoughts are in turmoil, but I can't worry about paying Elliott or wondering what evidence he has. I need to make sure that Elliott hasn't contacted Mum and Dad.

I drive much too fast, overtaking when there is barely enough visibility, my knuckles white and my fingers aching from gripping the steering wheel too tightly. A lorry hoots at me, flashing its lights as it approaches. I'm in its lane, swerving back in front of the car I've overtaken just in time, my breath ragged. I slow down a little, but even so, my fingers are tapping on the steering wheel, my breathing much too fast, and that ball of dread unravelling in my gut. I swing into Mum and Dad's cul-de-sac and swerve into their driveway, the car screeching as I come to a full stop.

Their front door is wide open.

I hurtle out of the car, sprinting up the steps, desperate to be reassured that Elliott hasn't dropped in on my parents.

Joel races out of the house and flings his arms around my legs.

'Mummy! Mummy's here!' I have never been so relieved to see him. I hug him so tightly he squeals.

'Hello, love. We weren't expecting you.' Mum appears in the doorway, coats and a blanket over her arm. She leans forwards to give me a kiss.

'Is everything all right?' I ask, my eyes darting from their car across the front of the house.

'Absolutely fine,' she says, frowning. 'We've had a lovely afternoon in the park, haven't we, Joel? We literally just got back home.' She turns around and shouts up through the house, 'Rosa love, Mummy is here.'

'Mum!' Rosa has a big smile on her face and a plaster on her knee. She hugs me as Joel lets me go.

'What happened?' I point at her knee.

'It's fine. It didn't hurt too much, and anyway I had to be brave because Kayleigh was there.'

I freeze. 'Kayleigh?'

Rosa rolls her eyes at me as if I'm an idiot. 'Kayleigh who was staying in the barn. It was such fun. Granny and Grandpa took us to the park, and we had a picnic, and then Kayleigh and her friend Abigail were there, and we all played together. I've missed Kayleigh so much, but she told me she's living nearby, so we can meet up loads.'

I am stumped for words.

'What's the matter?' Rosa asks, knitting her brows together. Joel has disappeared inside the house.

'Nothing, love. Was her mum there?'

Rosa shakes her head. 'I don't know who she was with. But it's such a coincidence, isn't it, running into her like that?'

'Yes,' I say, thinking that I don't believe in coincidences. 'Let's go inside so I can talk to Granny and Grandpa.'

ELLIOTT AND NADIA are undoubtedly in cahoots, and one or the other of them must have followed Mum and Dad to the park, probably to scare me into paying up. I am in a quandary. I can't tell my parents what is really going on, and I certainly don't wish to worry them unnecessarily. Will the children be safer with me at home or staying here at Mum and Dad's? On balance, it's probably better if they stay here. My parents have a burglar alarm, one of those fancy ones that links into the police station, and a panic button attached to their bedroom wall. The system came with the house, and as Mum had it in her head that it would be much more dangerous living up north than down south (a totally erroneous assumption, of course), Dad agreed to keep it. On top of that, my parents have neighbours all around, and if anyone shouts, someone hears. Mum is forever complaining that everyone knows everyone else's business on their cul-de-sac.

In contrast, the only living things that would hear me if I shouted at home are the sheep. Daniel mooted putting in an alarm a couple of years ago, but for one reason and another, we never got around to installing it. Or am I overreacting here? Would Elliott really contact my parents?

'You look like you have the weight of the world on your shoulders, love,' Mum says as she hands me a cup of tea. 'Daniel will be out of there in no time, mark my words.'

I smile weakly.

'Do you put the alarm on at night?'

'Oh, love, with everything that's gone on with Daniel and that man, you've got nervous, haven't you?'

'Will you promise me you'll put the alarm on when you go to bed?'

'Of course we will, dear. Would you like to stay here too? You must be rattling around all by yourself up on the hill.'

'I'm fine. I think it's better that I go home. If you could keep the kids for another couple of days, that would be great, and please don't let them out of your sight, even for a moment.'

Mum squeezes my hand. 'We managed to bring up you all right, didn't we? We may not be as agile as we used to be, but I think we know what we're doing,' she says. 'You concentrate on getting justice for Daniel.'

I AM convinced I'm being followed. A silver Kia is keeping pace with me, consistently one or two cars behind, all the way through Macclesfield and out the other side, and it's still there when I turn left to take the shortcut through the hills to home. I can't see clearly enough to make out the driver's features, but I think it's a woman. Could it be Nadia? I see her everywhere. In my dreams, when I glance over at the barn from the kitchen, I catch a glimpse of her billowing dress; in town, she's walking in or out of shops. Of course, when I look properly, she's just a plastic bag billowing in the wind, or a woman with a blonde bob who looks nothing like Nadia when she turns around.

At the next T-junction, I turn left without indicating and put my foot down hard on the accelerator. Home is to the right. But when I look in my rear mirror, I see the silver car turning right, the opposite direction to me. Cursing, I find a track where I can do a three-point-turn, and drive, more slowly this time, towards home.

After feeding Peanut and giving him a short walk, I go back into Daniel's study. There must be something in here that will give me more information on who or what E.F. is. If Daniel was telling the truth, then I need to speak to his investment advisor, Geoffrey Sweetman. I've only met him a couple of times and got the impression that he doesn't like me. When I asked a question, rather than addressing me, he peered over his substantial nose and directed his answers to Daniel.

'You're being ridiculous and overly sensitive. He is good at his job and very professional,' Daniel said. 'Besides, why would Geoffrey Sweetman have an opinion on you?'

I sit down on my husband's chair and dial Sweetman's office. Eventually, I'm put through to him.

'Good afternoon, Mrs Pieters. How may I help you?'

'I assume you know that Daniel is being held on remand, accused of a murder he most certainly did not commit.'

Sweetman clears his throat. 'Indeed.'

'I need access to my husband's accounts and investments. We need to stop some regular outgoings and liquidate some investments.'

My words are met with silence.

'Are you still there?' I ask.

He clears his throat. 'Yes. Which investments were you thinking of?'

'Well, firstly, I would like to know who E.F. is. Regular payments of three thousand pounds are being made to E.F. from Daniel's sole account. I understand that this is something to do with Daniel's pension and investments.'

'I'm sorry, but I can't comment.'

'You don't know, or you can't comment?'

'I have no authority to comment on matters that are in Mr Pieters' name only.'

'I'm his wife!'

'I'm fully aware of that. Mr Pieters is my client, and unfortunately it is only he who can issue me with instructions. And those need to be written instructions. Without an official power of attorney, I cannot release any information. If there is anything else I can help you with, regarding your joint affairs, perhaps...'

'What investments do we have in our joint names?'

He clears his throat, and I hear him rustle some papers on his desk. 'I'm not aware that there are any in your joint names. Perhaps your husband has set up accounts with another establishment.'

'Thank you for your help,' I say hurriedly, and hang up on him. I curse under my breath.

Next, I call the bank, and I'm not in the slightest bit surprised to be fobbed off. I speak to a woman this time, and in an apologetic tone, she explains that unless I have a power of attorney, I cannot get access to Daniel's accounts.

I chuck a pencil across the room.

It seems that the only way I will be able to raise money quickly is by returning to the pawnshop with the rest of my jewellery. I could sell Daniel's car, but that won't happen overnight. Or perhaps I could take out a loan? I discount that idea. If the bank won't let me take out cash that is sitting in our account without proof and a valid reason for doing so, they certainly won't give me a loan.

Elliott is going to have to wait another day. And he can go to hell if he demands more money.

My phone rings. It's a withheld number. This time I don't answer it and wait for the notification telling me I have a message. I click listen.

'Have you got what you owe me?' Elliott asks, without giving his name. 'I'll be up this evening to collect it.'

'Shit,' I mutter under my breath.

I CAN'T EAT. I can't sit still. I can't even think clearly. I could give Elliott the keys to the Range Rover or some of my jewellery, but then I get angry and think, *Why the hell should I give him anything?* I pace around the house like a caged animal, Peanut eyeing me warily. I try to watch television, but I keep the sound off so that I can hear the crunch of tyres or the slamming of a vehicle door.

The hours pass. I speak to the kids, wishing them good-night. 9 p.m. 10 p.m. 11 p.m. I'm tired and want to go to bed, but I daren't. Just before midnight, when I can barely keep my eyes open, I walk around the house, double-checking for the third time that all the doors are locked and bolted, and the windows are firmly closed. I can't even take a shower or run a bath in case he turns up and I don't hear him, so I have a cursory wash and climb into bed.

Something wakes me just as I'm drifting off to sleep. I sit bolt upright in bed. My mouth feels dry and my breath is ragged. I listen carefully, but all I hear is my heartbeat thud-ding in my ears. I tiptoe out of bed, clutching my mobile phone, and stumble across the room to the window. I've kept the bedroom curtains open, and outside it is surprisingly light, a high moon in the sky. Something is moving along the edge of the patio, a shadow. Is it a person or an animal? I swallow, but it's as if my larynx has got stuck in my throat. And then I hear another noise. It sounds like someone kicked something metallic.

'Who's there?' I shout, my hand on the window latch. Silence again. I open the window, just a few centimetres. And now I see the silhouette of a person. Clearly.

'Who's there? I'm calling the police!'

'Oh, Hannah, dear little Hannah. I wouldn't do that if I were you.' Elliott's voice gets louder as he walks along the patio until he's standing directly underneath my window. I don't know why the floodlights at the front of the house haven't come on, but I can see him clearly enough thanks to the almost full moon.

'Sorry I'm a bit late. I got held up, but anyway, I'm here now. Where's the money?'

'I haven't got it, and you need to leave.'

He laughs, that phony, cackling laugh that sends tremors through my bones. 'It's after midnight, so we're up to twenty-five grand.'

'Go away, Elliott,' I say, but my words sound weak.

'I've got a bright idea,' he says. He grins at me and his teeth catch the moonlight. He bends down and holds something up. It's large and rectangular.

'See this?' he asks.

I peer. He switches a torch on and lights up a large bright red jerry can. 'It's full of petrol.' He puts it down on the ground next to him, and then he flicks on his cigarette lighter, a large flame flickering. 'If you haven't got enough cash, I thought you could have a bit of an accident. A fire in the house or over there in the barn. It would be a nice little insurance claim and free up more than enough dosh, enough to keep both you and me happy. What do you reckon?'

'I'm calling the police!' My voice quivers.

'Bad idea, Hannah. By the way, your tits look great in that nightie!' He roars with laughter as I step back, away from the window. I don't know what to do now. Surely he wouldn't pour petrol and set it alight? It would be obvious to any investigator that it was done on purpose. Although Elliott comes across as lecherous, I don't think he's stupid. In fact, I'm sure he's not. I reckon everything he does is calculated.

I pull on my fleece dressing gown and switch the lights on in the bedroom, rushing through the house, illuminating every room. I type in 999 on my phone and keep my finger hovering over the call button, ready to ring the emergency services if I need to. As I hurry into the kitchen, I hear an engine splutter to life, and then rear brake lights flicker red, headlights come on, illuminating the road, and the vehicle drives away.

I wait, watching it disappear up and over the hill, lights bouncing until darkness once again falls and there is silence. I try to calm my pounding heart and my trembling hands.

'Peanut, you're meant to be protecting me,' I say. The dog opens one eye, lifts his head, and then flops back onto his bed. I switch on all of the outside lights, and slipping on a pair of boat shoes, I step outside. I need to be sure that Elliott hasn't started a fire or done anything else around the house or the barn. I lean back into the kitchen.

'Peanut, walkies.' The dog lifts his head again, and I can sense his confusion. Since when do we go for a walk in the middle of the night? After a little more cajoling, he scrambles out of his bed and trots alongside me as we go outside. Elliott has left the jerry can with a cheap, blue plastic lighter balanced on top of it on the front doorstep. As I'm looking at it in horror, a text pings through on my phone.

Do the right thing, Hannah.

25

I try to keep awake all night, but I suppose I drift off as the sky is lightening to an insipid grey. The dawn chorus reminds me of the relentless cycles of nature that never cease despite the horrors in our individual lives. I wake up with a start, adrenaline coursing through my veins. But in the bright light of day, I feel a shift in myself. To hell with Elliott and Nadia.

Daniel and I have been cast into the role of victims, but I have never been a victim, and I don't intend to become one now. I'm going to fight back. Elliott won't get another penny from me, and I will, come hell or high water, prove that Daniel is innocent, not because I love my husband, because I'm not even sure if I do, but for the children. To make sure that Rosa and Joel live a normal life, not as the offspring of a murderer. I don a pair of plastic gloves and put the heavy jerry can in the shed behind the house. My fingerprints will be on it because I brought it inside last night, but I want to preserve Elliott's if at all possible.

This morning, it's Mike that I'm thinking about. His actions have given me inspiration. Mike changed the lock on the barn's door, so I am going to use the same modus operandi to find out about Elliott and Nadia. The thought of breaking and entering someone's home has never crossed my mind until now, but despite the risks and the unlikeliness of ordinary, middle-class me breaking and entering, it's something I need to pluck up the courage to do. Getting into Elliott's home to find out about his relationship with Nadia and, most importantly, to see if I can find the wildlife camera and SD card and any footage recorded onto it, is the only way that I can think of to prove Daniel's innocence and potentially get Elliott off my back.

It's just before five in the morning, but I'm too wired to sleep. I take my driving licence and go into Daniel's study. I switch on his printer, connect my laptop, and then I scan my driving licence. My skills in Photoshop aren't great, so it takes me a while to replace our address with Elliott's address in Congleton on the picture side of my driving licence. Anyone looking carefully would be able to see that it's botched, but it will have to do. I then print it out on a shiny card and put it through the laminating machine. I've had the laminator for years, using it to print out sheets of music to give to members of the choir; just as well I never got around to giving it away. And now I cut very carefully around the edge. If someone picks it up, they'll know straight away that it's a forgery, but if I can hold it and show it briefly, then I might just get away with it.

The next stage of my plan involves stalking Elliott's house once again. I'm later than I was before, and as I cruise past his house, I don't see his white van. I scan the two adjacent streets to be sure that his vehicle is gone, and then park up alongside a deserted warehouse. Using my phone, I search for a locksmith in Congleton and select one at random.

'Good morning. I'm in a total flap and was wondering if you'd be able to help me? I've left my house keys in my part-ner's car, and he's gone off abroad on a business trip, and now

I'm locked out of our house. He's going to be so angry with me. I'm really stupid. It's the second time I've done it this year.'

'Okay, love. What's the address?'

'11 Blakely Road, Congleton. Can you come soon? I'm going to be so late for work, and I'm terrified they'll fire me.'

'I can be there in an hour. It'll be extra for the quick call out, and I'll need some ID.'

'Yes, that's no problem. I've got my driving licence on me. Thank you so much. You're a lifesaver!'

That was surprisingly easy to do. I wonder if I have missed my calling as an actress or a con woman. Now for the next stage of my plan.

I type out a text to send to Nadia.

Nadia, I know that you're with Elliott, who has taken money from Daniel. If you don't agree to meet me, I'm going to tell the police about your relationship with him and how you killed Mike. I have evidence. Meet me at 11.30 a.m. in the winter conservatory of the Pavilion Gardens in Buxton.

I take a deep breath and then press send.

If there's no traffic, it will take her about thirty-five minutes to drive to Buxton. She'll then need to park and hang around to meet me. I wonder how long she'll wait for me to turn up? Even if she only waits ten minutes, she'll then have to drive home. I reckon I have well over an hour to get access to the house and search it before she returns. Besides, she'll have no reason to suspect that I will be in Elliott's house. I just have to hope that Elliott doesn't come home mid-morning for any unforeseen reason. Having sent the text, I pull a baseball cap onto my head, shoving my hair up underneath it. I put on a pair of cheap, oversized dark glasses and look at myself in the car mirror. It will have to do. I would rather not be driving my navy Rav, in case Elliott or Nadia recognise it, but it's still less conspicuous than driving Daniel's black Range Rover, which would stand out a mile. I start the car and drive back to Elliott's street, passing Nadia's parked silver Mercedes. I find a space that gives me a view of Elliott's front door and Nadia's car from my rear mirror. Then I settle down to wait.

It's about twenty minutes before Nadia emerges from the house. I wonder where Kayleigh is and hope that Nadia hasn't left her at home alone. Nadia turns and locks the door to the house. She then paces quickly to the Mercedes, a stony expression on her face. A couple of minutes later, the car pulls away, belching fumes, and I let out a breath.

I am pacing the pavement, waiting for the locksmith, my fingers clutched around the SD card reader attachment for my phone. He is late. I am just about to call him, when a van pulls up and a man wearing blue overalls climbs out.

'Sorry, love. The last job took longer than I thought. Right, let's sort things out for you.'

'Thanks,' I say. 'Do you want to see my ID?' I produce the false driving licence and hold it out in front of me, trying to stop my hand from shaking. He's still a metre or so away and leaning into his van to collect his toolbox. He throws a cursory glance. I shove the card back into my pocket and start gabbling.

'I'm so stupid. Can't believe I've done it again. My partner will be so angry with me. I'm always losing things.'

He straightens up, slams the van's doors closed and walks towards me.

'This is the door,' I say, pointing to the crimson red door of number II. Standing close to it, I can see that the paint is flaking off, and the window adjacent to the door is filthy. The locksmith peers at the door.

'It's a five-lever mortice deadlock. You got a back door? Might be easier to get in that way.'

I have no idea if there is a back door, but surely all houses have more than one door, especially these terraced houses with alleyways running between them. He raises a bushy eyebrow as he waits for my answer.

'Yes, sorry. I'm so flustered this morning. Good idea.' What's the worst that can happen? If I lead him around to the back of the house, and there isn't another door, he'll realise I'm up to no good, and then I'll have to run away. But that won't work, as he has my phone number. But I've got no choice. I feel sick as I push open the rusty gate and walk around the side of the house. There's a small paved patio that leads onto a garden barely two metres square. Fortunately, there is a back door, and he is right – it looks less sturdy than the front door. The other advantage will be no nosey neighbours spotting the locksmith at the front of the house. The downside is I won't be able to see when Nadia returns home. Assuming she does. Assuming this is where she is living.

The locksmith places his box of tools on the ground and starts fiddling with the lock. I cannot stop myself from glancing at my watch every minute or so. I pace backwards and forwards, but the space is small. Why is he taking so long? I assumed it would take the locksmith five minutes or so.

'Have you rung your boss to explain why you're late for work?' he asks.

I frown, and then I remember the story I told him. 'Yes, sorry. It's just we've got an important meeting this morning.'

'Going the fastest I can,' he tuts. 'What do you do, anyway?'

'I work in a bank,' I say, unsure why that is the first thing that comes into my head. I glance at my watch again. It's been thirty-five minutes since Nadia left. She's most likely at the Pavilion gardens now, waiting for me.

The locksmith stands up, his knees creaking. He turns the door handle and the door opens. 'All done,' he says.

'Thank you so much,' I gush. 'How much do I owe you?'

'That'll be eighty-five pounds. And luckily for you, I didn't break the lock.'

It had never crossed my mind that he might have had to break it. That would have been disastrous. I imagine Elliott returning home to find a broken door lock, calling the police, checking for fingerprints, and then they might have... I can't let my thoughts go there.

I rifle in my pocket and take out my wallet. I have ninety pounds in cash, just enough to pay him.

'Got the receipt book in the van. I'll just go back and get it.'

'It's fine. I don't need a receipt.'

But he ignores me and walks away. I want to scream out loud, to tell him to hurry up, that I'm running out of time. I step into the small kitchen. 'Hello!' I shout, my heart pounding. Other than the humming of the fridge, there is silence.

I glance around the kitchen. It is small, and the appliances look relatively new. An array of cereal boxes are lined up on a shelf next to the fridge, and underneath the shelf are multi-coloured mugs hanging off hooks. There are three dirty cereal bowls in the sink, a clean frying pan and a half-drunk cup of coffee on the drainer. A cat slinks around my ankles and makes me yelp. It then jumps up onto the countertop and stares at me, its amber eyes unblinking. I wonder where Snoopy has gone, as there is no evidence of a dog in here.

I walk three paces through the kitchen and into the living room. It smells of stale cigarette smoke mixed with Nadia's pungent perfume. It catches the back of my throat, and I have to swallow a cough. There is a large black sofa with its back against the wall adjoining the kitchen. A television, much too big for the room, dominates the opposite wall and partially blocks the window to the street. The walls are white, with no pictures, and the fireplace lacks a grate. An open staircase rises from the corner of the room. I expect to see some of Kayleigh's belongings, but there is no evidence that a child lives here.

'Hello!'

I jump.

It's the locksmith, who is standing at the back door, holding out a handwritten receipt. I take it from him.

'Thank you very much,' I say.

'Ta.' He nods at me and leaves.

I turn and look around the room. Am I being ridiculous to think that Nadia might have stored the camera and SD card here? And if so, where could it be? The downstairs of the house is surprisingly empty. Adjacent to the vast television is a box full of DVDs. I quickly rifle through it; they're mainly crime series, American and English, along with a few X-rated movies. I slip off my shoes and run upstairs. Here there are two bedrooms, either side of the staircase, and a bathroom in the centre with its door facing the stairs. I glance in the bedroom on the left-hand side. There is a single bed with a blue duvet cover and a small wardrobe. The walls are bare. A man's eau de cologne stands on the bedside table, along with an alarm clock. I open the wardrobe. It's filled with men's clothes; Elliott's, I presume.

I step out of the room, into the small corridor, and push open the door to the larger bedroom. There are two more single beds, and it's obvious that both Kayleigh and Nadia are staying here. Kayleigh's clothes are scattered all over the pink duvet on the far bed and on the floor. There is a big photograph of Peanut stuck to the wall, and underneath it, a smaller photograph of Kayleigh with her arm around Rosa. I gulp, overwhelmed by a sense of sadness and guilt for intruding.

Nadia's presence is everywhere. There is makeup on a dressing table, along with a salt lamp that is glowing pinky orange, and an array of crystals and stones in a rainbow of colours. A black, lacey bra lies discarded on the tan-coloured carpet. On the bedside table is a scent diffuser and a crystal ball. So I was wrong. I assumed that Elliott and Nadia were lovers, but from this set-up, it looks extremely unlikely.

I pull open the wardrobe. There is a large tattered suitcase that I recognise from the barn. I pull it out and have a rifle through. The voluminous dresses that Nadia wore whilst staying with us are inside, along with a pair of sneakers. Nothing else. She has a handbag hanging up in the wardrobe, and I peer inside it, finding tissues, more crystals and a lipstick. If she's hidden the SD card here, she's done a good job.

I run back downstairs, glancing at my watch and slipping back into my shoes. She's been gone for an hour. My time is running out.

There is a corner cupboard next to the sofa. The doors open with a squeak. It's filled with bottles of booze and glasses. I stand in the middle of the room and run my fingers through my hair, letting out a groan. What have I proven by coming here? Just that Nadia and Kayleigh are living with Elliott, and I already surmised that. And then I spot it. The edge of a laptop jutting out from under the sofa. I grab it and open the lid. The laptop is on, but when I jab the keys, it asks me for a password. Hopeless. I jam the lid back down but notice that an SD card reader, similar to the one I have in my pocket, is hanging from the side of the laptop. I pull it out of the slot and have a look, but there is no SD card in the reader.

Wherever the SD card is, it's well hidden. I think about where I hide things. The kitchen. I pull open the cupboards, but there isn't much inside them. I jiggle a can of baked beans and a tin of tomato soup. I open the cupboard under the sink, and a swing bin slides forwards. It's a long shot, but I decide to rifle through the rubbish. I find a pair of rubber gloves and pull them over my hands, grabbing the rubbish. I place the bag in the middle of the kitchen. It stinks and my stomach heaves.

'Hellooo!'

I jump, and it takes me a long moment to realise that the woman with short blue hair and biker boots isn't Nadia.

'Oh, hello. Who are you?' the stranger asks, framing the doorway.

'I'm a friend of Elliott's and Nadia's,' I reply, blinking rapidly.

'I've brought Kayleigh back a bit early because Arthur's got an upset tum. Is that all right?'

Kayleigh pushes past the woman, and her face lights up when she sees me.

'Hannah!' She claps her hands. 'Is Rosa here?'

'Um, no. Sorry.' I am tongue-tied. This was not part of my plan, and I've no idea what to do now. Kayleigh's face falls.

'I'll be off, then. See you soon, Kayleigh, and tell your mum that I'll give her a call tomorrow.'

'Okay,' Kayleigh says.

The woman disappears. Didn't she think it strange that I am standing in the middle of someone else's kitchen, rifling through a rubbish bag? Does she think I'm the cleaning lady perhaps? And is it normal to leave a child with a stranger? But, of course, I'm not a stranger to Kayleigh.

Kayleigh and I stand there staring at each other for long seconds.

'What *are* you doing here?' Kayleigh asks, her hands on her hips.

'Do you remember the bird camera that was on the side of our house? You and Rosa watched the video of the chicks hatching.'

Kayleigh's cheeks light up like burning beacons. 'I'm sorry,' she says, her bottom lip trembling.

'What are you sorry for?' I ask gently.

'Rosa said that she was going to give me one for my birthday. A couple of days after Dad died, that policeman came here to Uncle Elliott's house and told Mum that your house was no longer a crime scene, so me and Mum went back to the barn to get our stuff. Mum was in the barn packing up, and there was no one there except that police lady who was helping Mum pack. I went outside, climbed on top of the bins, and took the camera.' She hangs her head.

'Where is it?' I ask softly.

'Under my bed. Do you want it back?' Kayleigh's lower lip trembles.

'I just want the card that's inside it. You can keep the camera.'

She nods and turns around.

'Kayleigh!' I say.

'Yeah.'

'Is Uncle Elliott your real uncle?'

Kayleigh wrinkles her forehead. 'Yeah. He's Mum's brother.'

She turns again, and I listen to her heavy footsteps thudding upstairs. A couple of moments later, she's back in the kitchen, holding out the camera.

'Does your mum know you took this?'

She shakes her head.

'Will you tell her?' Kayleigh asks. She looks at me with big eyes.

'No.' With shaking hands, I peel off the rubber gloves and drop them into the sink; then I slide the navy and red SD card out of the camera. I place the camera on the drainer, remove my phone from my pocket, plug the SD card reader in, and slide the SD card into the reader.

'Oh my God!' I whisper to myself. I watch the footage. There is Nadia at 2.14 a.m., her head held high, walking around the side of our house. She pulls on a pair of black rubber gloves and then rifles in our recycling bin. She takes out an empty wine bottle. The screen blackens, and it's the end of the video. I double-check the date and time. It all fits. Nadia calmly walked to our recycling bin, took one of Daniel's bottles that would have had his fingerprints all over it, and then walked away. She obviously used that bottle to wallop Mike over the head and left the smashed bottle next to him. I am reeling. Would Nadia have had the strength to do that? She was so much shorter than Mike, so delicate compared to his oaf-like bulk. Or were Elliott and Nadia in this together, two siblings working together to kill Mike? And if so, why?

Kayleigh lets out a little cry and grabs the camera from the drainer, holding it behind her back. I turn, startled.

'What the hell are you doing here?' Nadia stands at the back door, her hands on her hips, her eyes narrowed.

26

'Get upstairs now!' Nadia hisses at Kayleigh. The child runs out of the room.

Nadia's eyes fall to the ground and the pile of rubbish at my feet. I try to jam my phone into my jacket pocket, but the SD card reader falls out. We both lunge for it, but I'm nearest and I grab it, stuffing it into my pocket. I need to get out, to dart past her.

Her pale blue eyes are glistening with fury, and now I know that she took the wine bottle from the recycling bin, it is patently obvious that either she alone, or she and Elliott, killed Mike. And if she was capable of felling such a large man, she is certainly capable of killing me. My breath is coming in short gasps, and I can feel sweat slipping down my back.

'What the hell are you doing here?' She glowers at me.

'I've seen what you did. I know you killed Mike.'

She shakes her head. 'You know nothing!' She takes a step towards me, and even though she's shorter than me, and so slender, I bite my lip, the metallic taste of blood on my tongue.

'How did you get in?'

The cat slinks past Nadia and out through the open door into the small yard at the back of the house.

I see little point in lying. 'I got a locksmith to unlock the door. I took a leaf out of your and Mike's book.'

She laughs then. 'Oh, Hannah. You in your little safe world, with no worries and so much money.'

'You killed Mike. I've got the evidence now.' I try to dart out of the room, pushing her to one side, but she's quicker than me. She extends both an arm and a foot, and as I push her arm out of the way, I trip over her boot and stumble to the ground. She slams the door shut. As I pull myself up from the floor, she leans her back against the door.

'I know you killed Mike and you set up Daniel,' I say, fear pulsating through my veins and constricting my throat.

'You don't know anything, Hannah.'

'I've seen the video footage of you collecting the wine bottle from our recycling bin. I know you did it.'

'What footage?' She takes a step towards me, her eyes flashing.

'From the wildlife camera by the bins.'

'You have a wildlife camera?'

'Did have. But Kayleigh took it, and I've just seen the footage. I know it was you.'

'And the police?'

'Don't know anything about it. But they will when I give it to them.'

Her shoulders sag, and I realise now that Nadia had absolutely no idea that she had been caught on camera. She runs her fingers through her hair, tugging as a strand gets caught on one of her many rings.

'You don't know what my life was like. Mike was a terrible man. He hit me; he had violent rages. I know you saw the bruises on my legs and arms. What choice did I have? All I was doing was protecting my daughter. How else could I have stopped him from ruining her life in the way that he ruined mine? I'm not like you, Hannah. I don't have any money or qualifications or a posh doctor as a husband. I've got no one to help me. It's me and Kayleigh against the world.'

'But why didn't you just get a divorce like normal people do?'

'Because I would have lost Kayleigh.'

'That's nonsense. Nine times out of ten a mother gets custody of her children.'

'You know nothing! I'm not her real mother, Hannah. Her birth mother is dead. I've been Kayleigh's mum since she was eighteen months old, but there is no paperwork to prove it. We don't even share the same surname. We weren't married, Mike and me, although we pretended we were.'

'So who are you?'

'Kayleigh's mum.' For a moment, her gaze softens as if she's recalling a pleasant memory. 'I met Mike when Kayleigh was just over a year old. I was in the queue at Aldi, and Mike was there, all flustered with an inconsolable, howling baby. He looked exhausted, at his wit's end. I sang a little lullaby to Kayleigh and stroked her forehead, and she calmed down instantly. Mike looked at me as if I were a magician, but all I did was tap into the little one's aura. Baby Kayleigh was simply adorable, all squidgy cheeks and big eyes with little tufts of hair on the top of her head. Mike asked me out for a coffee there and then. Kayleigh's mum had died a couple of months earlier; she'd taken her own life, poor woman. Anyway, Mike was grieving and really not managing with little Kayleigh. One thing led to another, and before we knew it, I'd moved into their house and Kayleigh became my baby too. Whatever Mike threw at me over the years, I had to take it, for Kayleigh's sake. She doesn't deserve a father like him. And imagine what it would do to her, losing two mothers. Mike knew how much I love Kayleigh, so he had a hold over me. He knew I'd never leave her with him, to get beaten and abused. Kayleigh's life would have been ruined if she had to live all alone with that bully of a man.'

'Couldn't you have gone to social services? They would have helped you and Kayleigh.'

'You're so naïve, Hannah. You think social services are going to listen to someone like me?'

'Does Kayleigh know you're not her real mother?'

Nadia nods.

'But surely any court of law would see that you have been her mother all of this time, and you'd be able to formally adopt her.'

She shakes her head. 'Mike told me that if I left him, I would never see Kayleigh again. And I believed him. Mike has contacts. Here and in Spain. He knows people. How could I risk that? My job is to look after Kayleigh and protect her. I needed a way out, and believe me, I thought of everything. This was my only option.'

'To kill Mike and set my husband up as the murderer?' I ask, my voice laden with sarcasm.

A faint smile tugs at the edges of her lips. 'It's worked though, hasn't it?'

'I don't see why you couldn't have gone to the authorities and got protection against Mike.'

Nadia laughs bitterly. 'Maybe you'll understand one day. The only person who can look after you is you. And the only person who could look after Kayleigh was me. I can't have children, Hannah. Do you know what it's like to be told that you're infertile? It's like a dagger through a woman's heart, as if all your hopes and dreams have been smashed to smithereens. Kayleigh is the only child I'm ever going to have, and I'd give up my life for her. You're a mother. Surely you understand?'

It makes sense now, why Kayleigh is so big boned, with

none of Nadia's delicate features. 'But why us? Why target Daniel?'

'He was the perfect fall guy. When Elliott told me and Mike how your Daniel had paid him to keep quiet, Mike latched onto that. He knew that Daniel was a soft touch and quick to anger. All we had to do was provoke Daniel a bit, get your Daniel to rough Mike up, get some witnesses. We got all of that in the pub and at the kid's party. Then Mike was going to force Daniel to pay cash in return for keeping quiet about everything. His broken ankle from the trip hazard on your patio, beating Mike up, whatever else he could pull off.'

I shake my head. This all seems so ridiculous and naïve. I remember DS Murphy telling me that Mike has form. That he has done time for extortion in the past, so I assume other people have succumbed to his bullying.

'Mike's ankle wasn't even broken, was it?'

Nadia sighs. 'You found out about that?'

'It was in Mike's autopsy report.'

'We wouldn't have let you go to your insurers, because they would have demanded a medical report. No, Mike had it all planned out. He was going to threaten to tell the press how Daniel beat him up, how you were running an unsafe holiday home, and he was going to go to the police and show them the injuries he sustained when Daniel beat him up. We knew your husband would pay out to keep us quiet. We would have got loads of money, enough to sail off into the sunset. Mike was talking about going to Spain.'

'But Daniel didn't hurt Mike! What are you talking about?'

Nadia rolls her eyes. She takes a step towards the kitchen counter. My breath comes in short, shallow bursts as I imagine her grabbing a knife and plunging it into me.

'Mike's plan was for me to beat him up and make it look like Daniel did it. When Daniel and Mike got into that shouting match and Daniel was totally pissed, it was the perfect night to make it happen.'

'You killed Mike!' I say, my voice quivering.

'Don't you see? It was the perfect plan within the plan. Mike told me to slash his arm with the wine bottle, make it look like him and Daniel got into a brawl. But I had it all worked out. I told him to crouch on the ground so I could reach him. He'd had a load to drink too, wanted to use the alcohol to take the edge off the self-inflicted pain. He strutted around like he was the big, butch man, but in reality, he was weak and pathetic.'

I feel like nodding in agreement, but I am too wary of Nadia to even twitch a muscle, my eyes darting from her face to her hands.

'Mike used his strength to beat me black and blue and I took it. I took it meekly so as to protect Kayleigh, because I knew he'd start on her next. So there he was, crouching on the ground like a fool. I stood behind him and swung the bottle with all my weight, walloping him on the head, again and again. He never saw it coming. And you know what, Hannah?' She takes another step towards me. 'It felt great!'

My back is up against the kitchen cupboards. There is nowhere for me to go. I put my right hand behind my back and try to feel for a drawer handle.

'You can't think you'll get away with it,' I say. 'You killed your husband and set up mine.'

'But I am getting away with it. It's Daniel who is banged up in jail, not me.'

'And when I tell the police what's on this SD card...'

'You won't,' Nadia says. She takes a step towards me. 'You can't turn me in, Hannah. If you do that, Kayleigh will go into care, and all of this will be for nothing.' She jabs a finger at me. 'You're a mother. You know how much a child needs her mother.'

'But Daniel doesn't deserve to take the blame for a murder he didn't commit? How can that be justice?'

'Daniel might be a doctor, but it doesn't make him a good man. Look at what he did to Elliott. He thinks that if you chuck money at a problem, it'll go away. He doesn't deserve you or the cosy life he's living.'

Nadia may be right about Daniel, but it doesn't mean that he should be punished for a crime he didn't commit.

'Have you and Mike done cons like this before?'

She smiles wryly. 'Mike may have been many things, but he wasn't an idiot. He was a builder back in the day and a lock-smith. Being so practical was helpful. He only introduced me to his sideline businesses when we'd been together for a year or so, and by then I couldn't extricate myself. I didn't want to, because of Kayleigh.'

At least the changing of the locks makes sense now.

'And Elliott? What about Elliott?'

'Yeah. What about me?'

Nadia spins around and I gasp. Elliott is standing in the doorway, his legs planted wide apart, his arms across his chest.

'What are you doing here?' Nadia asks.

'It's my home, Nads, in case you'd forgotten. I left my sand-wiches in the fridge.' He turns to look at me. 'Brought me the dosh, have you?'

'You need to leave, Elliott,' Nadia says, glaring at him. I swivel around and make a dash through the doorway, into the living room towards the front door.

'Stop her!' Nadia yells.

Heavy footsteps thunder after me, and an arm snakes around my neck, yanking me backwards.

'If my sister tells me to do something, I'll do it,' Elliott says, his breath moist and hot against my cheek. I recoil.

'So what's going on here, then?' Elliott asks, releasing his grip. He steps away from me.

'Don't let her go!' Nadia has moved around us and is blocking the front door now.

'Please don't kill me!' I say.

'Kill you?' Elliott laughs. 'The only killer I know is your lovely husband, Daniel.'

'Daniel didn't kill Mike. Nadia did!'

'Shut the hell up!' Nadia yells. She strikes me on the side of my head with the television remote control. I gasp from the pain and see bright sparks. I grab the stair post to stop myself from falling down.

'What's going on, Nadia?' Elliott asks.

My hand goes up to the side of my head and comes away sticky with blood.

'You can't always be the big brother, you know!' Nadia snarls. 'My protector, looking out for his little sister. You didn't protect me against Mike, did you?'

'What?' Elliott frowns.

'She killed Mike,' I say as the room stops spinning. My head throbs. 'She admitted it. Besides, the evidence is on the SD card.'

'No, not our Nadia.' Elliott glances from Nadia to me and back again, his face lined with confusion. 'Our Nadia is no killer. Don't talk a load of bullshit!' Unless he is the most extraordinary liar, I am convinced he knew nothing about Nadia's plan. 'We talked about getting money out of Daniel, and I thought the scam had just gone horribly wrong. That Daniel took the wine bottle to Mike's head. That's what you told me, Nadia!'

'Nadia killed Mike,' I repeat. 'Admit it!' I snarl at her.

She narrows her eyes at me.

'You can't go around making accusations like that!' Elliott shouts at me. 'Nadia's a good person. Tell her you didn't do it, Nadia.'

Nadia crosses her arms in front of her chest and stares

at me.

'I'll show you the footage of her collecting the wine bottle from our recycling bin in the early hours of the morning Mike died,' I say to Elliott. But before I can reach into my pocket to take out my phone, Nadia screams, 'No! Get the card reader out of her pocket, Elliott! Now!'

But Elliott just stands there staring at his sister, his jaw slack. And then Nadia rushes towards me, her fingernails scratching my cheek, her ankle boots kicking my legs and grabbing my cotton jacket so that it rips. She lunges for my pocket, and the SD card reader flies out. We both dive towards it as it slides under the sofa.

'Help me, Elliott!' Nadia yells.

I can't look to see what Elliott is doing. I just need to get the card reader. I'm on the floor fumbling for it, but Nadia is there too, pulling at my hair, striking me, arms and legs flailing. But I'm quicker. I grab it just as she throws her weight on top of me, her fist with all of those sharp-edged rings coming straight for my face. In that millisecond, I realise she is about to gouge out my eye. I swing my head away, steeling myself for the pain.

It doesn't come.

Nadia lets out a shriek. 'Get off me!"

I glance up and see that Elliott has her in a neck hold, pulling her away from me. It's then that I have my chance. I leap up, run towards the front door, tug it open, and race out onto the street, running at full pelt until I get to my car. I grab the keys from my pocket with trembling fingers and open the doors. I'm in the car, starting the engine, pulling out without looking if anything is coming, and I go.

27

I am trembling all over, and it's a miracle I'm able to keep my foot on the accelerator. My head throbs from where Nadia hit me, and I know I have cuts and bruises all over. But it's as if my brain has frozen, for it's a good couple of minutes before I realise I should call the police. I don't want to stop the car in case Nadia and Elliott are chasing me, but fortunately the phone is automatically connected to the Rav via Bluetooth. With my left hand, I jab 999 on the centre console.

'Emergency. Which service?'

'Police.'

'Hold the line, please.'

'You are through to Cheshire police. What is the emergency?'

'Someone has committed a murder, and she's going to get away!'

'Is the victim unresponsive?'

'No, no. Sorry. The murder happened a few weeks ago. It's just someone has admitted to the killing, and my husband is in jail for it, and he didn't do it,' I say breathlessly.

'Are you in danger?'

'No. I escaped.'

'What is the address?'

'11 Blakely Road, Congleton. It's the home of Elliott Moreton and his sister Nadia Jones. She's the killer.'

'And what is your name?'

'Hannah Pieters. Look, I need to speak to the policeman investigating the murder, but you need to send a car around to Elliott's house to apprehend Nadia before she runs away.'

'Just to clarify–'

'I'm going to call DS Murphy.'

I hang up on the woman. There is no point in explaining everything to some remote operator in a control room. I need to speak to the team on the case, tell them that I've got the SD card and all the evidence they need to arrest Nadia and release Daniel. I suppose I'm in perilous danger now. Nadia will undoubtedly come after me. She will be desperate to get hold of the SD card, and if she kills me, then all the evidence will be destroyed. My thoughts are swirling manically around my head. I mustn't go home; that's the first place she'll come looking for me. I do a U-turn in a residential road and head for the dual carriageway. I'm going to go to the prison and let Daniel know that he's going to be freed.

When I'm at a set of traffic lights, I search for DS Murphy's phone number and dial it. I get his voicemail.

'It's Hannah Pieters. Please call me back urgently.' I debate calling again and leaving another message on his voicemail, recounting everything I know, but I don't suppose he will believe me if I tell him he needs to go and arrest Nadia. When I'm sure there are no cars following me, I pull over onto the side of the road to call DC Miles Buchanon, but I get his voicemail, too. I don't leave a message and decide to try him again in half an hour if I don't hear back from DS Murphy.

I am terrified and skittish, constantly looking in my rear-view mirror, keeping a watch out for the silver Mercedes or

Elliott's white van. The irony isn't lost on me, but at least if I go to the prison, I'll be safe. I don't have a slot booked to visit Daniel, but surely, they'll let me in. I imagine his face when I tell him that Nadia has admitted to killing Mike and that he will be a free man. We will have a chance to be happy, to put our relationship back on track; perhaps he might work shorter hours, spend more time with us. That should make our relationship more equal. I hold the key to his freedom, and how can he be anything but grateful to me for the rest of his life?

I can't stop smiling, imagining how Daniel will throw his arms around me and shed tears of joy. The newspaper headlines will scream, *Heart surgeon freed in massive travesty of justice!* The police will issue a formal apology, and then a nationwide hunt will be launched for Nadia. I just hope that Kayleigh is safe. And then I think of Rosa and Joel and my parents. Will Nadia go after them? Are they safe?

I jab in my parents' phone number and sigh in relief when Mum answers.

'What's the matter, love?'

'There's stuff happening. Please can you stay at home today; stay indoors and don't answer the door to anyone except the police.'

'What's going on, Hannah? Are you all right?'

'I'm proving that Daniel is innocent, and I'm fine.' I don't tell her that I have a gouge in my head, my hair is matted with blood, and I have a stonking headache. 'Just stay at home, Mum, and call the police if there's anything you're unsure about. Tell the kids that I love them.'

I hang up before she can question me any further. I don't want to worry my parents unnecessarily, but now I know that Nadia is a murderer, I need to ensure they're safe.

As I pull off the dual carriageway, I see a white van approaching from behind. My heart quickens and my mouth feels dry. It's driving quickly. I put my foot down on the accelerator and only just make it through a set of traffic lights that are turning red. A lorry sounds its horn at me. I glance in the mirror. The van has stopped at the lights. I am safe.

I park the car a few metres down from the entrance to the prison, knowing that I won't be let into the car park without a formal time slot. I try calling both the policemen again, but still get their voicemails, so I don't leave any further messages. I get out of the car and glance down at my jacket. It's ripped, the seam flapping open and fraying at the bottom. I don't care. I put my hand into my pocket, and my fingers curl around the SD card reader.

I won't be able to show it to Daniel, but that doesn't matter. I have the evidence for the police. I lock the car and slowly walk towards the prison gates, wondering how I will be able to persuade the guard to allow me in to visit Daniel. And then I see a young woman walking out, her head down, her shoulders shaking as she cries. There is something familiar about her. The way she walks, the cascade of mahogany brown hair. Where do I know her from? As we pass, I see the NHS lanyard around her neck.

'Hello,' I say.

She stops and stares at me. Is it because I look terrible, my hair matted with blood, my face scratched?

'Hannah.'

I frown, surprised she knows my name. 'Are you all right?' she asks as she wipes her blood-shot eyes with the back of her hand and stares at me.

I recognise her from the hospital. She's a nurse, but I can't recall what she's called. 'You work with my husband, don't you?' I ask.

She nods. 'Yes. I'm Beth.'

'What are you doing here?' I ask.

'I came to see Daniel. I wanted to know how he is. It's terrible what has happened to him.' She sniffs.

'Did they let you in?'

'Yes.'

'How come? They only allow people on his visitors' list to see him.'

She hesitates for a moment. 'I'm on it.'

'You? Why?'

Her cheeks redden. My eyes fall to her name badge, and that's when I realise. Elizabeth French. They call her Beth, but her initials are E.F.

'He's been paying you.' I spit out the words like venom.

She just stares at me with big hazelnut eyes and plump, bee-stung lips. How old is she? Mid-twenties, late twenties, at a push.

'He didn't want to hurt you,' she says. 'But he was going to leave you. When Phoebe starts nursery school. We want her to have his last name.' She glances away. 'I'm sorry.'

I take a step backwards. It's as if someone has speared my heart. Phoebe was Daniel's mother's name. 'How long?' I ask in a whisper.

'Two and a half years. I'm sorry, Hannah, but he loves me. He loves us.'

We stare at each other for long, painful seconds, and then she mutters, 'I've got to go.' I watch her as she hurries along the pavement and climbs into a little white sports car, much too expensive for a nurse's salary. After she starts the engine, she puts on a pair of dark glasses; then she reverses the car out of the space and drives away.

I don't know how long I stand there. Seconds. Minutes. And then I turn too and walk slowly back towards my car. Once again, I'm driving, but barely registering the road and my surroundings. All I'm thinking about is Rosa and Joel and how they deserve better than this. When I have everything sorted, I will go and get them. Together we will decide where we want to live. Mum and Dad can come with us, too. I find myself driving up the hill towards home, unsure of how I actually got here. The phone rings. A surprise, as I don't normally get reception on this hill.

I jab the answer button.

'Hannah, it's DS Jason Murphy returning your call. What is it that you wanted to tell me? You said it was something urgent, I assume about your husband's case.'

I am silent for a few moments.

'Mrs Pieters?'

'Sorry.' I slow the car down to a crawl. 'It turns out I was mistaken. I don't have anything to tell you. I'm sorry I wasted your time.'

28

We arrive early so we can get good seats with a clear view of the stage. These days, parents aren't allowed to video events, but I hope that the school will produce an official version so that Mum and Dad can see the performance. I let Joel settle into the aisle seat, and we study the programme, which is headed *Year 6 proudly present "Fame, The Musical!"*

'Look, Mum, her name is first on the list!'

And so it is. *Kayleigh Jones-Pieters – Carmen.*

'Where's Rosa's name?'

He finds it three lines beneath Kayleigh's.

I smile with pride. My girls both have leading roles.

'You've got to remember not to sing along, Joel? Just because we know all the songs inside out and back to front doesn't mean that we can sing them, too.'

'I know,' Joel says, rolling his eyes. He's copied that one from the girls.

'Hey, Hannah, how are things?' Amber asks as she slides in next to us.

'Busy as normal. The excitement levels in our house are through the sky. Just glad that the kids' Year 6 musical doesn't clash with the musical at my school.'

I tried very hard to get a teaching job at the same school as my children, but there were no vacancies. It doesn't make for an easy life, dropping them off early and rushing to teach at another school across town.

As the lights lower, I wonder if Daniel is here with the third Mrs Pieters. I doubt it. When I see him these days, I feel absolutely nothing. Actually, that's not totally true. I feel a lightness and a relief that I no longer have to put up with his bullying. I relish my freedom. And I feel sadness that my children haven't got the father I had hoped they would.

Joel shuffles in his seat excitedly.

'There she is!' he whispers, pointing at Kayleigh, who is dressed in a red leotard over black leggings. She bursts into song, and I feel such pride.

I THINK BACK to the day of my fight with Nadia. I thought both Daniel's and Nadia's destinies lay in my hands, that it would be my decision whether or not to show the critical evidence to the police. After meeting Beth outside the prison, I decided Daniel should pay for cheating on the children and me. He deserved to fester in jail and have some time to repent. But it turns out that we don't have the right to play Russian roulette with anyone's lives, not even our own.

An hour after arriving home, DS Murphy and DC Buchanon turned up. Jason Murphy explained that my call to the emergency services had triggered a swoop on Elliott's house. The uniformed officers found a bewildered, incoherent Elliott muttering about me, Nadia and Mike. Nadia was nowhere to be found.

'You told the emergency services that Nadia Jones is the killer. Why did you break into Elliott Moreton's home, and why did you make that accusation?' DC Buchanon asked, peering at me closely.

In that moment, I had a choice. Hand them the SD card with the footage of Nadia rifling in our rubbish bins or destroy the evidence for ever.

I came to an instant decision. I opened the palm of my hand and let the SD card tumble onto the kitchen table.

They launched a massive hunt for Nadia, but I don't think anyone believed she would be gone for too long, not without Kayleigh. She loved that girl too much. Just three hours later, Nadia returned to Elliott's house and handed herself in to the police, begging them to give Elliott custody of Kayleigh. By all accounts, Elliott was horrified by the proposition. Combining the forensics, the video and Nadia's own admission, Daniel was released from prison with great media fanfare. It wasn't me who was there to rejoice in his freedom, but his lover, Beth French, and Phoebe, their baby.

Nadia was sentenced to life imprisonment for the premeditated murder of her common-law partner, Mike Jones. Her legal team have announced that she's going to appeal soon, that her sentence was too long in light of Mike's years of coercive behaviour. My bet is that she won't be out of prison any time soon.

I received a letter from Nadia just a few weeks after she was remanded in custody. I keep it in a box that I will give to Kayleigh when she's older.

Dear Hannah,

I am sorry for everything I did. Not for killing Mike, but for doing it at your home and for causing you so much upset. I'm not sorry for what happened to Daniel either. He's a bastard. I did it for Kayleigh, and my greatest fears have come to fruition. I can't bear the thought of her being in the care system, sent from one foster home to another. She loves you and particularly Rosa. I know things must be harder for you now, but would you consider adopting her? Please say yes. It would make everything worthwhile. All I want is for her to have a safe, secure and happy life.

Yours,

Nadia

IT TOOK MONTHS OF BUREAUCRACY, but I am, at long last, Kayleigh's official mother. I had to jump through numerous legal loopholes – not least Daniel's protestations, but it was eventually allowed. And I've grown fond of the girl. With Mike as her role model, it was hardly surprising she used to swear and be rude. She still drops the odd clanger, but she always apologises.

It has been hard for Kayleigh. She misses Nadia enormously, and even though she has known from a young age that Nadia wasn't her birth mother, Nadia was for all intents and purposes her loving mum. We've made it quite clear that she has three mothers: her deceased birth mother; Nadia, whom she visits in prison from time to time; and me, her day-to-day mother. I've told her that she's extra special to have so many mums. Considering everything she has been through, she really is a remarkable child.

My divorce to Daniel came through six months ago. I would have been quite happy to give up the Pieters name. I'm no longer Daniel's wife and would rather return to my maiden name, but I couldn't ask Rosa and Joel to relinquish their identities. Kayleigh, too, has absorbed our family name into hers. Rosa is thrilled with her new sister. They're inseparable, those two girls, and I just hope they'll be kept in the same class when they move up to senior school next year. Daniel offered for me and the kids to stay in the house, for me to carry on with the holiday cottage. I declined. Perhaps I will run a holiday cottage again one day in the future, but for now, home is a modern three-bedroom house in a new development on the outskirts of Macclesfield, with a small, low-maintenance garden. I miss the views – of course I do – but I like the sense of community here. The school bus from the local secondary school stops at the bottom of the road, which will be perfect when the girls move schools next September. Peanut is the only real loser. He's had to forego his freedom and outdoor space. Daniel made a half-hearted attempt to get custody of Rosa and Joel, which gave me a few weeks of sleepless nights. Fortunately, he changed his mind, but then he threatened to fight for Peanut. Luckily for us all, the third Mrs Pieters isn't very keen on dogs.

I often wonder how many Mrs Pieters there will be. I very much doubt that Beth will be the last of Daniel's wives.

As for Elliott, I see him around school from time to time. He's probably here tonight, sitting in the audience. Nothing was ever mentioned about the money both Daniel and I paid him, and these days, I'm eager to avoid him as much as he's eager to avoid me. He's a nasty piece of work and an opportunist, and I wish he had got his comeuppance, but some things are best left alone.

As my girls leave the stage, my mind wanders, as it frequently does. Would I really have sat back and watched Daniel be sent away for a murder he didn't commit? Would I have watched Beth struggle all alone with Daniel's third child? Would I have got used to being shunned as the ex-wife of a killer?

Probably not.

The audience is applauding. I catch a colleague's eye. She sent me an email earlier saying she wanted to talk to me after the show, but I can't recall what it was about. I am having to juggle so much these days. There is nothing about my current life as a single, working parent that is easy. Not that I mind. I've come to realise that an easy life doesn't necessarily equate with a happy one.

I smile and luxuriate in my newly found contentment.

A LETTER FROM MIRANDA

Thank you for reading *The Visitors*. Of all my psychological thrillers, this is the one most rooted in reality because Best View Barn actually existed. Twenty years ago, we bought a derelict wreck in The Peak District. After completing the house renovation, building control announced we either had to convert the adjacent barn or board it up. Thanks to a couple of local craftsmen, during the next seven years, we renovated the barn. When it was completed, I turned it into a holiday cottage. We welcomed amazing guests from all over the world and you'll be relieved to learn that none of our visitors were anything like Nadia and Mike, and my husband and I bear no similarities to Hannah and Daniel!

In August 2015, I was diagnosed with Ewing's Sarcoma (a rare bone cancer), got on a train to London and never returned home. Over the year of my treatment, we sold our property and the new owners decided not to continue with the holiday cottage. Although we had planned to move south to be nearer to family at some point, I found the loss of our home very difficult. Five years on, the time has come to lay it to rest, and this book is my strange homage to a beautiful property.

Sarcoma is called the loneliest cancer because most people have never heard of it, and as it accounts for only 1.3% of cancer diagnoses in the UK, many doctors have little knowledge of it. In support of Sarcoma UK, earlier this year I ran a fundraising initiative, offering people the chance to name one of the characters in this book. Stacey, the winner, chose the name Daniel. There are limited treatment options for Sarcoma (the chemotherapy is particularly brutal) and funds are desperately needed for research. I will continue raising money for Sarcoma UK. Should you wish to contribute, details are here: https://www.justgiving.com/fundraising/mirandarijksauthor

I'm blessed to have wonderful friends and family who I call upon to seek their expert advice. In particular, I would like to thank Paul Docking, Toni Russell, Nicki Murphy and Becca Macauley. I'm so grateful for your help and of course all mistakes are mine. Also special thanks to my sister, Juliette Scott, who is one of my greatest supporters both in life and in my writing journey.

This book, and my previous novels, wouldn't exist without Brian Lynch, Garret Ryan and the team at Inkubator Books. I am so lucky to be published by such a forward thinking and supportive publisher. I can't thank them enough.

Lastly but most importantly, thank *you* for reading my books. Without you and the reviews left on Amazon and GoodReads, I wouldn't be living my dream life as a full-time author. Reviews help other people discover my novels, so if you could spend a moment writing an honest review on Amazon, no matter how short it is, I would be massively grateful.

My warmest wishes,

Miranda

www.mirandarijks.com

ALSO BY MIRANDA RIJKS

THE VISITORS

(A Psychological Thriller)

I WANT YOU GONE

(A Psychological Thriller)

DESERVE TO DIE

(A Psychological Thriller)

YOU ARE MINE

(A Psychological Thriller)

ROSES ARE RED

(A Psychological Thriller)

THE ARRANGEMENT

(A Psychological Thriller)

THE INFLUENCER

(A Psychological Thriller)

WHAT SHE KNEW

(A Psychological Thriller)

THE ONLY CHILD

(A Psychological Thriller)

THE NEW NEIGHBOUR

(A Psychological Thriller)

FATAL FORTUNE

(Book I in the Dr Pippa Durrant Mystery Series)

FATAL FLOWERS

Published by Inkubator Books
www.inkubatorbooks.com

.

Printed in Great Britain
by Amazon